Y0-DGY-349

Shadow of innocence

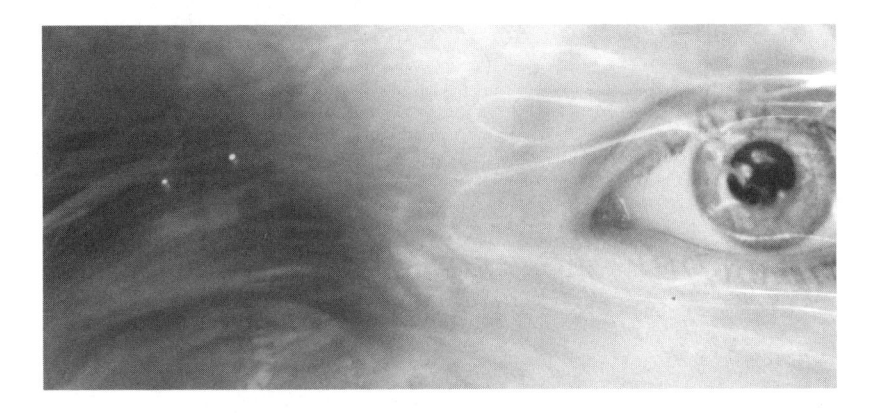

"Here's a recipe for a page-turner."

"*Take a moment of high American drama—the tumultuous year of 1968. Add some cool New England locations—Harvard Square and the Newport Jazz festival. Throw in a wisecracking Boston detective. No, wait ... make that a whole family of Boston detectives. Let Ric Wasley cook it all up for you. Then sit down and enjoy. You'll be glad you did.*"

■ William Martin, *New York Times* best-selling author of *Back Bay*, *Harvard Yard*, and *The Lost Constitution*.

Shadow of innocence

A NOVEL

Ric Wasley

KÜNATI

East Baton Rouge Parish Library
Baton Rouge, Louisiana

SHADOW OF INNOCENCE

Copyright © 2007 by Ric Wasley.

All Rights Reserved. Published and printed in the United States of America by Kunati Inc. (USA) and simultaneously printed and published in Canada by Kunati Inc. (Canada)
No part of this book may be reproduced, copied or used in any form
or manner whatsoever without written permission,
except in the case of brief quotations in reviews and critical articles.

For information, contact Kunati Inc., Book Publishers in both USA and Canada.
In USA: 6901 Bryan Dairy Road, Suite 150, Largo, FL 33777 USA
In Canada: 2600 Skymark Avenue, Building 12, Suite 103, Mississauga, Canada L4W 5B2,
or email to *info@kunati.com*.

FIRST EDITION

Designed by Kam Wai Yu
Persona Corp. | www.personaprinciple.com

ISBN 978-1-60164-006-2   LCCN 2006930187
EAN 9781601640062   FIC022000 FICTION/Mystery & Detective/General
Published by Kunati Inc. (USA) and Kunati Inc. (Canada). Provocative. Bold. Controversial.™

http://www.kunati.com

TM—Kunati and Kunati Trailer are trademarks
owned by Kunati Inc. Persona is a trademark owned by Persona Corp.
All other trademarks are the property of their respective owners.

Disclaimer: This is a work of fiction. All events described herein are imaginary, including settings and characters. Any similarity to real persons, entities, or companies is purely coincidental and not intended to represent real places or living persons. Real brand names, company names, names of public personalities or real people may be employed for credibility because they are part of our culture and everyday lives. Regardless of context, their use is meant neither as endorsement nor criticism: such names are used fictitiously without intent to describe their actual conduct or value. All other names, products or brands are inventions of the author's imagination. Kunati Inc. and its directors, employees, distributors, retailers, wholesalers and assigns disclaims any liability or responsibility for the author's statements, words, ideas, criticisms or observations. Kunati assumes no responsibility for errors, inaccuracies, or omissions.

Shadow of Innocence

A McCarthy Family Mystery

———————

Is dedicated to all of my family and friends,

and especially my wife, for all of their support,

help and encouragement.

Acknowledgements

Special thanks to my editor James,
Derek my publisher, Kam for his great cover art
and graphics magic, and all of the other talented folks at
Kunati for their support and enthusiasm.

Summer, 1968, Newport, Rhode Island

The summer cottage of Margaret and Jonathan Vanderwall is modest by Newport standards, with only ten bedrooms and six baths. But they're proud of their world, and their acknowledged place in it.

As a matter of fact, though it's been nearly three-quarters of a century since the robber barons drove their gilded carriages through the ornate gates of their massive marble palaces, life along Bellevue Avenue still whispers sweetly to those, like the Vanderwalls, who 'have.'

And they do have. Cars, yachts, summer houses in Newport, winter houses in Manhattan, winter/summer houses in Palm Beach, and great looking tans.

Yes, life in America's summer 'have' capital is indeed idyllic for the idle rich.

Except…

For the past few years, during the height of the summer season, when the prevailing wind from the ocean side of their 'cottages' drops, they seem to hear the sound of music.

Not the delightful warble of Julie Andrews dancing through the Austrian Alps, or the soothing strains of a Schubert sonata or a Mozart concerto, but the raucous sounds of guitars and banjos playing crass folk and blues tunes.

It seems that the 'have-nots' have found a way to insert themselves and their unwashed music into one of the last bastions where everyone knows their place. Or used to!

And nowhere are the summer rain clouds of musical disturbance known as the Newport Folk and Blues Festival dreaded more than in the first house on the seaside end of Bellevue Avenue, that of the Vanderwalls.

But not by their oldest daughter, Blair Prentiss Vanderwall.

Blair has made some distressing connections with the 'great unwashed' down by the harbor. Not only does she like their music, she has become one of them. A hippie, or so it seems.

It's quite obvious to all concerned that things can't go on like this.

Something must be done about Blair.

Chapter 1

Falmouth, Massachusetts | Cape Cod | Father's Jazz and Folk Club

July 25, 1968 | 10:13 p.m.

The smoke from hundreds of smoldering cigarettes and joints swirled around the sweating black singer rasping out a hard version of 'Cocaine Blues.' His dark, craggy features had a Mephistophelian look, Blair Prentiss Vanderwall mused, and the thought gave her a delightfully wicked little shiver.

"What are you smirking about?" asked her friend Valerie from across the tiny, wine-wet table.

Blair took a deep, languid drag from the innocuous looking Salem cigarette dangling between her left index and forefinger. She held the smoke in her lungs for a moment and let the mellow Acapulco Gold, with which they had replaced the tobacco, free her mind to drift a few planes closer to her own personal nirvana.

The third girl at the table, Jackie Trainor, watched Blair watching the stage and giggled to Valerie, "She's wondering what it would be like to make love to a... *black man.*"

The whispered words only heightened Blair's amusement and excitement. She loved the smoke and the smell of pot, the noise, the wine, but there was something Blair Vanderwall loved more than anything else.

Dangerous boys.

She shifted her gaze to the long bar at the right of the stage. A pair of reckless, dangerous eyes stared back at her.

She drew another deep drag and let the smoke slide out through her nostrils, where it hung around her honey-blond hair like a wavering halo crowning one of hell's cutest little angels.

The tall, lanky guy at the bar pushed his sweat-stained leather cowboy hat back onto his forehead and smiled at her.

Blair took the Salem out of her mouth, and with the innocent-erotic look she had perfected, slowly licked the rim of her upper lip.

She watched with the satisfaction of impending conquest as the guy in the denim shirt and faded jeans pushed his elbows off the bar, picked up his beer, and walked toward their table.

Looking into his smoky blue eyes as he closed the distance to her table, Blair allowed herself a small smile.

Those eyes held the promise of new thrills. Maybe even of danger!

The rangy 'cowboy' strode over, pushed his leather-tooled hat back on his head and grinned.

"Evenin', little lady. Cody Ewing. Mind if I sit down?"

Blair pushed a chair out from the table with her foot and nodded.

"What kind of name is Cody?" she asked, twirling her long blond hair around her right forefinger.

"Well, hell, little lady," he drawled, "what kind of name do ya want it to be?"

"Ummm, I don't know, something interesting," Blair mused, pretending to look up at the ceiling so that she could arch her long, graceful neck and stretch her arms, artfully allowing the scoop neck of the peasant blouse to fall open and provide a tantalizing glimpse of firm, round breasts.

The view was not lost on Cody. He grinned again and said, "Well, if you like wild, good ol' boys and bad-ass outlaws, then yeah, I guess you could say it's sort of interesting."

"Tell me," Blair whispered, "and make it exciting."

Cody's grin widened, and he moved his chair closer.

"All right, then. Well it goes back to my granddaddy, Cyrus. It seems that when he was just a kid, one day he was down in Louisville with his pa, sellin' tobacco, when this Wild West show came to town."

Blair raised her white-blond eyelashes and looked up over the rim of her glass. "Go on."

"Well, Miss—what was your name again, darlin'?"

"Blair."

"Blair. Now that's a beautiful name fer a beautiful lady."

"I said go on," she smiled. "You already have my attention."

"Well, like I was saying, my granddaddy saw this here big feller, riding out in front of the Wild West show. Sittin' way up high on a big white palomino horse, two pearl-handle 'Peacemaker' revolvers on his hips, that he commenced to shootin' off as the parade wound down the main street.

"And, ma'am," the boy drawled as he slipped an arm around Blair's shoulders, "he was so taken by that feller that he just up and runned off and joined up with that show. He got a job taking care of the horses and the other livestock, and so's his daddy wouldn't know where to find him if he came a-lookin', he changed his name. He changed his first name in honor of that feller on the big, white horse. Buffalo Bill. And I wound up gettin' part of that name that Granddaddy took."

The cowboy put his lips next to her perfect pink ear and whispered, "Cody."

Blair moved her head a fraction of an inch closer to those lips and whispered back, "Tell me more."

Cody drew in a breath and started to speak, but Blair put her fingers to his lips and said, "Not here. On the dance floor."

The club's jukebox played between the live music sets. Blair smiled, intertwined her fingers with Cody's and pulled him up from the table.

"Dance with me. I like this song. It's slow. You know how to dance slow, cowboy?"

"Jest try me, darlin,'" he grinned.

Chapter 2

Newport Neck Tennis and Beach Club

July 26, 1968 | 9:06 a.m.

"Come on, Davy," four-year-old Timmy Perkins whined at his older brother. "Let me see."

"No," David answered with a scowl. "Go back to the sand castle. I'll be there in a minute."

As the big brother, David's mom had drilled into him, he was expected to take charge, set an example, and above all, keep Timmy out of trouble.

As Davy stared at the big pile of seaweed, Timmy inched closer and reached out with his right hand to pull aside the long strands of green and brown.

"Damn it, Timmy!" Davy yelled. "I told you to go back to the sand castle. Now get out of here!"

Timmy looked at his older brother for a moment then his face crumpled and he let out a wail. "Mom! Mom!" he yelled, running to her.

Freshly lathered with Johnson's Baby Oil, she glanced up just long enough to assure herself that her youngest wasn't drowning then let her eyes drop back to her Harold Robbins novel.

After the third eardrum-splitting "mom-my!" she reluctantly inserted a finger between the pages of her paperback and looked up.

"What is it now, Timmy?" she sighed.

"Davy's not being fair!" Timmy gasped, stamping his foot. "He said we should go look for seashells for the sand castle. And I did, but I didn't find any." Timmy stopped long enough to draw a breath and went on in a rush, "And Davie found a whole, giant, humongous, super-big pile of shells and all this seaweed, and then when I came over to get some he told me to get away and go back to the sand castles and… and…" Timmy paused once more and then added triumphantly "…and he swore!"

Shielding her eyes from the glare of the morning sun, she looked at her oldest boy, poking a pile of seaweed with a stick.

Timmy followed his mother's gaze and said, "See, he's got a whole big pile of shells and stuff, and he's hogging them all for himself."

Timmy's mother looked at him again, wondering if she was really going to have to leave her comfortable chair and Harold Robbins to deal with the situation. She looked down and sighed. *It was just getting interesting, too. That guy had just gone into that girl's apartment in Hollywood and found her sprawled on the bed and she was dea…*

Timmy added the coup de grâce. "Mom, he's not sharing."

That did it.

It always happens, she thought. *No sooner do I get a chance to sit down and read when one of them has a problem.*

With the long-suffering sigh of beleaguered mothers everywhere, Mrs. Donald Perkins got up from her chair, and, still clutching the paperback, walked over to the harmony-shattering pile of seaweed.

"Really, David," she said, "I don't see why you can't let Timmy play with the silly seaweed, too!"

Right away Timmy ran to it and gleefully pulled shells out of the seaweed pile.

"Hey, Davy," Timmy asked, his hurt appeased with the achievement of his goal. "What's this?"

"I told you," his brother answered with a frown. "Leave it alone!"

Timmy ran to his mother.

Davy looked up at her, his eyes filled with seven-year-old seriousness. "Mom, I think there's something bad here."

His mother took two steps closer, bent down and picked up the stick that Davy had been using. Hesitantly she pushed two long strands of seaweed back from something white.

"Oh, no," she murmured. Was it a dead seagull? No, too big. A seal? No, too white. Good heavens, she shivered, you don't suppose it's a shark?

"No," she mumbled, peeling back a few more strands of seaweed. It was too thin to be a shark, thin and pale and wrapped in dozens of strands of thick black fishing line. She moved the stick a little higher and pushed away another clump of seaweed. She froze. Harold Robbins dropped unnoticed from her fingers as life chose once again to imitate art.

She clapped her hand, sticky with Johnson's Baby Oil and sand, over her mouth, but it couldn't stifle the scream. The thin, slender white thing wrapped in black fishing line was attached to—a slim white neck!

A bone-white face, framed by a tangle of blond hair and seaweed, and a pair of cold blue eyes stared back at her.

Chapter 3

Cambridge, Massachusetts | Inman Square

July 26, 1968 | 3:56 p.m.

Michael "Mick" Prescott McCarthy pulled the big BSA motorcycle back onto its kickstand with a grunt, swung his right foot over the handlebar and sat back on the long leather seat. He bent his head backwards and looked up at the top floor of the three-story apartment building, to make sure that Bridget, the love of his life, best friend, and a God-Almighty nagging mama, wasn't looking down from the small third-floor porch.

She wasn't.

He slipped a slim, zigzag-wrapped stick of 'Cambodian Red' out of the top pocket of his denim jacket and, taking the big old Army Zippo lighter out of the left pocket of his jeans, dragged the tiny wheel across his dungaree leg and lit the joint's twisted tip.

He drew the acrid smoke deep into his lungs and held it there then let the numbing smoke out in a slow exhale.

Christ, he thought as he sucked in the next toke, *I promised Bridge I wouldn't do this shit anymore. I guess my friggin' nerves are shot from all the damn nightmares I've been having.*

He paused with the joint halfway to his lips and looked at it. He lifted it toward his mouth again and slowly shook his head.

"Screw it," he said. "A Goddamn promise is a promise," and he flicked the glowing joint into the street.

A pair of soft lips touched the back of his neck.

"Thank you, darlin'," the familiar voice breathed in his ear.

Mick tilted his head backward until Bridget's delectable upside down image filled his field of vision.

"Hey, babe," he said.

"Hey, yourself," Bridget said, kissing him on the cheek.

"You saw," Mick said.

"That I did."

"But I tossed it," Mick said, still looking at her upside-down image.

"That you did," Bridget acknowledged, "which is the only reason why I'm not gonna beat you like a redheaded stepchild."

"Damn fucking kind of you."

Bridget hit him on the top of his head with her index and middle fingers.

"Ow-w-w. Jesus." Mick rubbed the top of his head. "That hurts!"

"It's supposed to, McCarthy," Bridget answered with a satisfied smile, "so kindly watch your damn language!"

"Hell, yes, Mother Superior." Mick laughed, sliding off the bike as Bridget reached out to whack him again and missed.

"Or maybe I should just say 'Sister Bridget,'" he teased as he ducked under her well-aimed left hook and caught her around the waist.

"Stop it, McCarthy," she hissed. "Fer pity's sake, we're right out here in the middle of the street practically, where everyone can see!"

"Then let's give 'em something to look at." Mick lifted her off her feet and pressed her against his chest.

"Oh, darlin'," she murmured, "you turn me bones to water."

"That's the idea," he whispered in her ear.

From the open window on the third floor porch, the ring of a telephone broke into their love play. Bridget pulled toward the front door.

"Uh uh," Mick said, holding her tight.

"Mick, the phone."

"I hear it," Mick said, his arms still tightly wound around her.

"It may be something important," she said weakly.

"Could be," he nodded.

For a moment, she seemed to capitulate, and laid her head back down on his chest.

"Mickey," she said, raising her head from his chest, "I think you better answer it."

"Why, babe?" Mick sighed.

"Because it may be the same person who called before."

"Who was it?" Mick asked, wondering if he really wanted to know.

Bridget took a deep breath. "He said he was from your old squad in Vietnam."

Mick's eyes grew cold and distant.

"Go on," he said.

"His name was Smitty and he said he needed your help."

Chapter 4

Cambridge, Massachusetts | Harvard Square

July 26, 1968 | 5:35 p.m.

Mick paused for half a second in front of the pebble-glass door that read *McCarthy & Son – Private Investigations*.

He smiled with equal parts pride and trepidation as he thought of the scarred old ex-cop on the other side of the door, and of what he was probably going to say, probably in very loud and profane terms, when Mick told him what he intended to do as the *very* junior partner of McCarthy & Son.

Mick yelled, "Hey, Pop, are you busy?" as he pushed the door open and walked in.

The former Boston beat cop didn't look up from the form he was laboriously filling out. He just pointed to the hard-backed wooden chair in front of his cracked old roll-top desk and grunted, "Sit."

Mick sat.

He stared out the dusty, semi-opaque window behind his father and let his mind wander to the scratch, scratch, scratch of his father's n o. 2 pencil. He thought about the first twenty-two years of his life, about his older brother, Frankie, his sister, Bronwyn, and his parents and their unlikely union: his Boston Brahmin mother, the former Miss Felicity Parker Prescott and his father, the beat-up old beat cop from Southie.

He let his mind drift three months back, when his father had shattered a dozen generations of McCarthy 'lone wolf' tradition by asking his son to partner with him in his post-cop incarnation, as a private detective.

Mick had been drifting ever since 'Nam. And even before that.

A prep school misfit despite his mother's connections and what she'd always said was his 'birthright.' Kicked out of Harvard in his freshman year for fighting. A gung-ho PFC and reluctant sergeant in Vietnam.

And now?

Now partner and hopefully a good son to the guy from D Street in Southie sitting behind the old roll-top desk in front of him.

He was trying like hell to get his life back on track.

Partially through his mother's Ivy League connections but mostly due to Bridget's well-meaning nagging, he was back at Harvard, majoring in Pre-Law as 'Miss Felicity' liked to tell her friends. In truth he was majoring in history, because the past seemed so much safer than the future, with a philosophy minor. No one could figure that one out and Mick didn't feel like talking about it. Not even to Bridget.

But probably his buddies in the old squad would have understood. When you've stared into the barrel of an AK-47, a cat's whisker away from having your brains blown all over some steaming jungle trail, you needed something to wrap your mind around and give it all meaning.

Bridget said Mick would get all the philosophy he needed if he came to Mass with her and sometimes he wished it were that easy. A few times he'd even tried it. But like everything else in his life, his religious upbringing had been a confused oil-and-water mix of back-to-back Sunday services with 'Big Mike' at the Catholic Church in Southie, and the First Congregational Church in Cambridge with his mother.

He had to smile when he thought about singing in the boys' choir next to his cousins Danny and Kevin, as they tried to look angelic while Father Kennedy stared at their latest black eyes and scarred knuckles, acquired in pursuit of their favorite pastime: fighting.

And from that atmosphere of ceremony, incense and fun-loving family brawls, he would be driven from South Boston to the austere but elegant white clapboard church on Brattle Street in Cambridge. His stoic-faced father deposited him on the steps of the First Congregational Church where his mother would be waiting in her Bonwitt Teller navy blue dress and plain but expensive Tiffany pearl choker. She would nod to her ex-husband, take Mick's hand and walk with him to the Prescott family pew from where three hundred years of Prescotts had stood watch over the 'correctness' of things on Brattle Street.

Mick had always felt like an impostor sitting in the hard, puritan pew next to his mother, his brother Frank, and sister Bronwyn. Frank had made it clear to his father that he had no desire to do anything in Southie and for some reason Mike had never asked to have his daughter accompany him to Mass. Only Mick.

Some would have said that he received a 'rich and diverse' religious training. Mick just thought it was screwed up. And the net result for him now was a rational mind filled with philosophy, but a subconscious populated by demons and angels. During the day he kept them well locked up behind the bars of Kant and Kierkegaard. But at night—especially in the dark hours just before dawn—they all came out to play in his dreams. That's when he saw the village and the shapes and the…

"What the hell are you looking at?" Mike asked.

"Nothing, Pop," Mick answered, still staring out the window onto the square.

"Well, if it's nothing, then I thank you very much for the visit, give my best to Bridget, and goodbye. I've got a whole lot of work to do."

"Actually Pop, it's business—sort of."

"What do you mean? Are you cutting classes? 'Cause if you are I'm gonna' kick your butt all the way back to Inman Square. Or maybe I'll just call Bridget and let her do it for me. Or could it be that you had some free time between classes, decided to take your junior partner role in this business seriously and stopped by to help your old man with some of this damn paperwork?"

Mick shrugged. "None of the above, I'm afraid."

"Well then?"

Mick took a deep breath.

"Dad, I think I've got a case, but you're not gonna like it."

By the time Mick had finished telling Big Mike about the phone call from Smitty and his plan to go to Newport to help out the cousin of an old friend, Mick could definitely tell that his father wasn't on board with the project.

"First of all," Mike said with a bulldog scowl, "what the hell makes you think you can get your buddy's cousin out of jail if he's been charged with murder?"

"Because," Mick answered, jiggling his right cowboy-booted foot, dangling over the chair's arm, "the Newport police picked him up as a 'material witness,' but they haven't charged him with anything yet."

Mike snorted, unimpressed. "So what's your plan?"

Mick looked down at his hyperactive jiggling foot, and with a final application of willpower, stopped it.

"I dunno, Pop," he finally answered, shaking his head.

Michael McCarthy Senior put down the stubby no. 2 pencil and pushed the long, half-completed form to the other side of the desk. He focused a long hard look on his youngest son. It was the kind of look that had caused many a mugger or dope dealer to start confessing, whether they'd done anything or not.

Mick's foot began to jiggle again.

Finally Mike growled in an ominous undertone. "We don't walk out of this office with an action plan that consists of 'I dunno.'"

Mick's foot jiggled faster and he fidgeted in the hard-backed wooden chair. "Well, I was gonna fire up the BSA and take a run down to Newport and kinda look around." He looked at his father hopefully. Nope, not impressed. In fact 'not impressed' was being way too optimistic. His old man was looking like he'd just been given a flat beer down at Clancy's. Not good.

"Aw, I'll come up with something, Pop. You know I always do."

Mike continued to stare at him and growled, "That's one hell of a plan, Mickey. And what is McCarthy and Son's fee for taking on this case?"

That was the question Mick had been dreading.

He looked directly into his father's eyes, drew a deep breath and answered, "Not one red cent. But I need to do this, Pop. It's for Smitty. He saved my ass in 'Nam."

Mike looked back at his youngest son and smiled.

"Okay, boy-o, I can understand that."

He pulled open the small top left-hand drawer and reached inside.

"Here," he continued, pushing a roll of $20 bills across the desk to Mick. "Take this."

"Dad, I—"

"Expenses. Take it."

Mick's hand hovered over the wad of twenties. Before he could make up his mind, his father reached into the roll-top again and brought out a .38 snub-nosed Smith and Wesson Police Special.

Mick looked at it for a moment then shook his head. "Christ, I dunno, Pop, I haven't even held a gun since 'Nam."

Mike looked across the desk at and responded in a cold voice, "Then I think it's time you started again. There's a lot more bad guys outside of the jungle than in it."

Cambridge, Massachusetts | Inman Square
July 26, 1968 | 7:56 p.m.

"So, then, what did your mother have to say?" Bridget asked as soon as Mick had hung up the phone. Mick could tell she was trying to keep her voice casual and nonchalant.

"Well, she wanted to see how I was," he answered carefully then added hastily, "and you too, of course."

Bridget snorted.

Mick smiled. "You're the only person I know who could make a snort sound ladylike."

Bridget shook her head, smiled, and flopped down on the tired old double bed with the broken spring.

"Oh, you're bloody impossible, McCarthy!" She propped herself up on her elbows. "Now really, what did your mum have to say?"

"She's been talking to Pop. It's amazing. Here's a guy who's been taking down bad guys for the last thirty years, tough as nails, but put him on the phone with Miss Felicity Parker Prescott—" his Boston Brahmin mother's impressive full maiden name, "—and he crumples like a cheap suit."

"Why were they talking?"

"She called Pop looking for me, and he told her I was going to Newport to help out Smitty with his cousin, and… oh, yeah, I guess I forgot to mention that. Bridge, I—"

"And just when were you planning on telling me about this, McCarthy? Two minutes before you climbed on your damn bike and rode away from me?"

"Well, no, I was… I mean, I wasn't… Oh, Christ, Bridge, I just didn't want you worrying."

Bridget studied him carefully. "So, this is another one of those things that you've gotta do?" She sighed. "Like always."

"Yeah, babe," Mick answered. "I owe Smitty."

"And like everything else you've ever done, it's gonna be dangerous, right?"

"Oh, no," Mick said, shaking his head. "Not at all. It'll be a walk in the park. A day at the friggin' beach. So don't worry at all."

"Oh I won't, Mickey, darlin'," Bridget smiled.

"You won't?"

"Not one little bit, luv," Bridget answered, her smile growing brighter and her eyes twinkling mischievously. "Because I'm coming with you!"

Chapter 5

Newport, Rhode Island | Newport Police Department

July 27, 1968 | 10:22 a.m.

"Where's all the mansions and coaches and the gents in top hats?" Bridget asked as Mick edged the front wheel of the BSA in between a VW Beetle and an old Buick in front of the Newport Police Department.

"Skip forward about seventy-five years," Mick answered over his shoulder. "This is 1968, not 1897."

"Yeah? Well, for your information, McCarthy, "Bridget said, unwrapping her arms from around his waist and sliding off the back of the bike, "it just so happens that I know a whole lot more about what goes on behind closed doors in this town than you do."

"Oh, do you?" Mick pulled the BSA up onto its kickstand. "And where does all of this intimate inside knowledge come from, my dear delectable Miss Connolly?"

"Well," she answered, bending down to smooth her feathery soft black hair in the reflection of the big motorcycle's handlebar-mounted mirror, "it just so happens that my great auntie, Bridget McMahon, as who I'm named after, was the upstairs parlor maid for none other than the Astors up in one of them big marble piles on Bellevue Avenue."

"Is that so?" Mick smiled. "And what did your 'great auntie' see peeping through the keyholes of America's aristocracy?"

"Enough to know that they're too much like the drooling idiot landed gentry that have plagued Ireland for the past three hundred years!" Bridget snapped.

Mick leaned forward and kissed her on the forehead. "Enough, my

Wild Irish Rose. We're not here on behalf of Sinn Fein, we're here to help Smitty's cousin."

Bridget took a deep breath and sighed. "You're right. I'll be good, I promise. And Mickey?"

"Yeah, babe?"

"Thank you, luv, for bringing me."

"It is my distinct and undying pleasure, my dear," Mick said, bowing low and letting his long, curly brown hair fall forward over his eyes.

"You are too, too kind, Mr. McCarthy." Bridget drew herself to her full five-feet, two-inch height and used her best Radcliffe accent while she held out her tiny white hand to be kissed.

Which it promptly was.

Mick put his arm around Bridget and they walked up the granite steps to the old red brick Newport Police Station. *What a combination of contradictions she is*, he thought. *The only daughter of an IRA gunman and hit squad member and, amazingly, on full academic scholarship to one of America's most prestigious and exclusive women's colleges, Radcliffe College in Cambridge, Mass!*

"What?" she asked, looking up at him as he pushed the big old wooden doors open.

"You turn me bones to water, darlin'," Mick grinned as they stepped inside the musty-smelling front entrance hall.

At the front desk Mick pushed a short note written by his father across the faded old booking desk to the duty sergeant.

"Good morning, Sergeant," Mick said, in what he hoped was his most reasonable and professional voice. "We're here to see Cody Ewing, a banjo player from Gravel Switch, Kentucky. You're holding him as a material witness and on suspicion of murder."

"MISS," SAID THE assistant desk sergeant with the salt-and-pepper hair, looking over his shoulder at Bridget. "You may want to wait out here." He gestured to the long, scarred oak bench in the dingy Day Room, painted in a flaking shade of greenish yellow, and located just outside the corridor leading back to the holding cells.

Bridget looked up at the officer for a moment before she asked, with a quizzical look, "What was your name again?"

The assistant desk officer, who had been dragooned into taking Mick and Bridget into the depths of the holding cells, looked like he was going to laugh at the little elf with the big mouth but thought better of it and answered with a sigh. "It's Fahey, Jonathan Fahey."

"Well, Johnny lad," Bridget said as the outer door to the holding block clicked open. "You may or may not have heard of Sinn Fein and them darlin' lads of the IRA, but just in case you haven't, and don't know what's expected, or have, and don't know the measure of an IRA Major's daughter, then let me tell you, boy-o, I'd spent more time conversing through prison bars by the time I was ten than you've probably spent in your whole time working in Cinderella's castle here."

Bridget stood in the entrance hallway to the holding cells, her arms folded across her small, firm breasts. Her right foot tapped dangerously.

The assistant desk sergeant paused, opened his mouth, looked from Mick to the pugnacious pixie, and thought better of saying anything.

Mick said, "Come here," to their guide, putting a companionable arm around his shoulder. "Johnny, old pal, you really don't want to get our Miss Connolly pissed. So, I'll tell you what." He motioned to Bridget with his eyes. "Why don't you just lead us back to Mr. Cody Ewing's cell, and then go get a cup of coffee on me and Little Miss Spitfire there."

Mick grinned at Bridget and she stuck her tongue out at him.

"Which one is it again?" the jailer asked when they reached the sub-basement.

"Cody Ewing."

"In here," the turnkey said flatly. He swung open the big barred double-doors to the first of three large cells running the length of the building.

"Which one of you big-shots is Cody Ewing?"

No one spoke. Hell, no one even moved. Finally, an old guy sleeping it off in a corner of the dirty, overcrowded cell raised up his turtle-like head with a dry, coughing cackle and said, "Hey, banjo boy, you got company."

As Mick walked into the cell, he turned back to the profusely perspiring station house cop and said quietly, in what he hoped was his best Andover/Harvard voice, "You've been a great help, Assistant Desk Sergeant Fahey, so now, if you could give us a few moments alone."

"Yeah?" Fahey said. "How do I know that the minute my back is turned, you and Little Bo-Peep over there won't be trying to break this cracker out of here?"

Mick took a deep breath and smiled back. "Well, for starters, you've got my personal word on it, unless maybe you think my word isn't worth anything."

The jailer opened his mouth, but he looked in Mick's eyes and closed it again just as quickly.

Mick continued, "Or if you like, perhaps you'd care to put the question to 'Miss Bo-Peep' personally."

The Assistant Desk Sergeant looked from Bridget to Mick one last time before he silently dropped the huge key ring into Mick's hand, politely nodded to Bridget and disappeared up the back stairs.

Mick gripped the cold, clammy iron bars of the cell door with his left hand as his right hand inserted the key into the rusty old lock.

"Cody?" he called softly to the silent figure huddled in the darkness of the cell's shadows.

The seconds stretched on, interrupted only by Mick's unconscious tapping of his right-hand fingers on the bars, Bridget's shallow breathing behind him, and the intermittent snore of the drunk sleeping it off, three cells down.

"Cody Ewing?" Mick called again. Someone shuffled in the dark corner of the cell and finally, a weary voice answered in the Harlan County accent Mick remembered so well from his corporal and best friend in 'Nam.

"Who wants ta know?"

"A friend," Mick answered quietly. "A friend of your cousin Smitty. And yours, if you want."

"She-e-it, man," the voice from the shadows laughed bitterly. "Come on in. Hell, I sure could use one."

Chapter 6

Newport, Rhode Island | Newport Harbor

July 27, 1968 | 12:06 p.m.

After talking with Cody for more than an hour, Mick had an uneasy feeling between his shoulder blades. That same tingling, paranoid feeling he used to get walking down steamy jungle trails when all the jungle sounds would suddenly stop and he'd sense something dangerous watching him, waiting for him to make a mistake. And he knew that whether in the jungle or the marble mansions of Newport, one mistake was enough to get you sent home in a body bag or a brass-handled coffin.

Cody was puzzled, confused, and for a guy who didn't look like he ever worried about tomorrow or even today, damn scared. And he should be, Mick thought. His jumbled, half-remembered account of beer, drugs and lust on the night he'd met the honey-blond fox, Blair Vanderwall, wouldn't hold up for a minute under cross examination by the most bumbling, last-in-the-class assistant prosecutor from Suffolk Law School. Mick had smiled back at Cody with a confidence he didn't feel and said "hang in there man, we'll figure something out." Cody had rubbed his hand across his unshaven jaw and tried to smile back. But his attempt had fallen flat in the cold damp air of the holding cells and came across as just forlorn.

"I sure hope so."

As they rode down from the police station to the narrow, tree-lined cobblestones of the old harbor district, Mick tried to shake off his jungle instinct of impending ambush, but a little Cassandra voice in the back of his head wouldn't shut up.

'Who do you think that grey-haired dude in the grey pinstriped suit was?' the little voice asked. 'And why do you think he got out of that long black Bonneville with the dark tinted windows and went into the police station?'

The man had smiled at Mick and touched the brim of his pearl grey fedora to Bridget as he climbed the steps at the station. That smile stuck with Mick. It was perfect, wide and confident, showing pearly white teeth. Like a shark.

"Slow down, Mickey," Bridget yelled over the roar of the BSA's twin exhaust pipes. "I think this is the street coming up on the left."

Mick pumped the foot brake and brought the big 650 cc machine to a stop at the corner. He pulled a crumpled piece of paper out of the top pocket of his denim jacket and pushed his dark, aviator-style sunglasses up onto his forehead.

After talking with Cody, they realized they had to spend some time in Newport. The desk sergeant sent them to his sister, a "free spirit" who had a couple of rooms to rent. He said she knew a lot of the people who hung out at the Folk Festival. Mick hoped she'd be able to help him clear Cody.

He coasted the bike to a stop in front of a narrow old red brick building with a canary yellow door.

"This is it," she said. "22 B Nickerson Way."

"Man, that door stands out like a whore in a convent." Mick laughed.

He took Bridget's hand and they walked up the three worn brick steps. "Shall we meet the 'free spirit'?"

"Lead on, McCarthy, I'm right behind you." With a stage whisper, she added, "Just in case she decides to welcome us with a broom handle."

Mick picked up the worn old brass doorknocker. Before he could let it drop back onto its striker plate, music floated out of the second-floor window right above them. It sounded like—yep, Joni Mitchell. Someone was singing a pretty fair duet with Joni. He took a step back from the door.

The high, pleasant voice sang about the "Big Yellow Taxi" right along with Joni, perfectly duplicating her, right down to the last *"Please!"* The last high note climbed with a theatrical trill, and Bridget caught Mick's eye and stifled a giggle.

Whoever was playing guitar along with the record gave a loud double strum on the final two chords. Mick winked at Bridget and applauded loudly, throwing in a few between-the-teeth whistles for good measure.

A beaming red face, framed by frizzy brown curls, appeared at the window and called down excitedly, "Did you like it? Really?"

"Absolutely," Mick yelled back.

"Then come on up," the woman laughed. "Door's open."

Mick swung the door inward and ushered Bridget in with a sweeping bow.

"I think, my dear," he murmured as she stepped into the hallway, "we've just found a place to stay."

"OH, NO, MISS O'DONNELL," Bridget smiled up weakly from her third cup of pungent herbal tea, "I'm fine, thank you."

"Me too," Mick added hastily, putting his left hand over his cup to forestall the obviously sweet, but definitely spacey, sister of the Newport Police Department's desk sergeant from filling his half-full cup with more tea.

Bridget looked back at him and shook her head with a 'hang in there' look.

Putting her mug of tea down on the pottery-and incense-laden coffee table, she said, "Well, Miss O'Donnell, your brother said as how you might have a room to rent, and well, we're certainly lookin' for a place to stay. That is, if it's not too dear."

"Oh, I just love the way you talk! Bridget, is it? You sound like a cross between the Beatles, the Stones and Donovan!"

Bridget smiled weakly.

"Hey, you two, lighten up! What's with the 'Miss O'Donnell?'" She bubbled. "It sounds like I'm my mother. You know what they call me down at the clubs on Bowen's Wharf?"

Mick and Bridget shook their heads in unison.

The desk sergeant's 'free spirit' sister laughed. "Sparrow."

"Excuse me?" Mick said as politely as he could, with a half-filled, hand-made pottery mug of herbal tea cooling in his right hand.

"Sparrow," she laughed again and jumped up, twirling around and letting her long colorful skirt sweep the floor as she dropped into a curtsy. "Because I'm their little songbird."

"Ah-ha," Mick responded. "That's cool." He took a sip of the pungent, tepid tea. *I'm not sure if 'songbird' is the word I'd choose. Cuckoo might be closer to the mark.* Mick raised the hand-painted mug to take another sip but before it touched his lips, Sparrow shouted, "Wait!" and dropped to her knees in front of him. Mick slammed the mug down on the table sloshing most of the remaining contents onto his knee. *What now? Is this stuff poison?*

"Your palm—I saw it when you reached for the mug. Here, let me look."

She took his hand, wet with spilled tea, and turned it over, palm up. Mick gave Bridget a desperate look out of the corner of his eye. She shook her head with a look that said, "Hey, don't ask me."

But that look turned to intense interest when Sparrow traced a fingernail roughened by pottery making and sculpting, down the length of his palm. "It's your fate line," she breathed. "I've never seen one like this."

Bridget leaned forward eagerly. "You read palms, then?"

Sparrow nodded. "Yes. Tarot cards too."

Bridget who had grown up in her native Ireland with a firm belief in fortunetellers, gypsies and good luck charms, laughed delightedly. "That's wonderful. Then you've just got to do me fortune!"

Mick, whose hand Sparrow was still holding, gave a half-hearted laugh and said, "Okay, crystal-ball lady. What's my fortune? Rock star? Big time folk singer maybe, with a dozen cherry bikes in my garage and a dynamite looking little black-haired chick sitting next to me?" But the laugh died away as Sparrow continued looking at his hand.

"I'm not sure." She said slowly. "I've never seen anything quite like this. Look." She turned Mick's palm toward Bridget. "It's so strange. The fate line just sort of fades into this dark spot on your palm. Like a—shadow."

"Is that good or bad?" Bridget asked.

"I don't know." She curled the fingers of his hand up and pushed it back to him.

"Like a shadow," she said again, staring into her mug of tea.

The room fell silent.

Suddenly, the thirty-something hippie laughed with a bright, sweet, free-flowing laugh. "You both think I'm totally nuts, don't you?"

"Oh no, Miss O'Donnell, I mean, Miss Sparrow."

And then Bridget looked at Mick and they both looked at the open-faced woman in the yellow, long-sleeved, paisley print dress, and all three burst out laughing.

"Yeah, Sparrow," Mick said, shaking his head and wiping his eyes. "You got that right."

"IT SEEMS OUR Miss Sparrow is quite the Renaissance woman." Mick said, unpacking his spare pair of jeans in their tiny room under the eaves.

"That's right!" Bridget agreed, folding a periwinkle blue blouse and laying it neatly in the top drawer. "And I want her to do me fortune."

"Oh, come on," Mick laughed, moving behind her and brushing his lips across the feathery soft hairs on the back of her neck. "You don't believe in that crap, do you?"

"There's a lot more of what you don't know than what you think you do, McCarthy," she answered, smoothing the woolen Fair Isle sweater and closing the drawer.

"Well, then, why don't you teach me all those things that I don't know?" he grinned, slowly turning her around and pulling her down onto the narrow bed beside him.

"Stop it now," she protested halfheartedly, "we're not even moved in proper, and she's right down the stairs, and…"

"And I want you right now," Mick said, pressing her shoulders toward his.

"And yes, me too, McCarthy," Bridget breathed as Mick began licking the tip of her left earlobe, "but…"

"But what, Miss Connolly?" he whispered, unbuttoning the top button of her blouse.

"But, in case you've forgotten, you promised that poor Cody lad that we were gonna come back to bail him out." She moved Mick's hand away then re-buttoned her blouse.

"Ah-h-h," Mick sighed, flopping his head down on the hard, lumpy pillow. "So you're going to shame me with duty?"

"Lord knows," Bridget said with a wry smile, "I need to find something to shame you with, before I become as wicked as you and shame the both of us!"

BACK AT THE POLICE STATION, the afternoon sun cast long, smoky shadows through the Venetian blinds, like horizontal prison bars slanting across the booking room floor.

"Hey, Sarge," Mick called as his boots clattered across the faded linoleum tiles in front of the booking desk. "Thanks for the tip. We've got a room at your sister's."

Sgt. O'Donnell looked up with a small smile. "Yep, she's a character, isn't she?"

He bent his head back down to the papers in front of him and said without looking up, "So what brings you back here?"

"We want to talk to Cody Ewing again. My mother's wiring me some money from Boston."

"So what?" O'Donnell said, writing.

"So," Mick said, knowing that he'd probably live to regret it, "we're here to bail him out."

Sergeant O'Donnell slowly put down his pencil and looked at Mick.

"Well, you can't," he said with an unreadable expression.

"Why not?"

"Because somebody else did, over an hour ago."

"Who?" Mick's eyebrows shot up.

The Sergeant's expression remained inscrutable. He shook his head. "That information is confidential."

"Can't you at least tell me if it was the guys in his band, or relatives?"

But already Mick knew that either of those scenarios was highly unlikely.

The sergeant shrugged.

Suddenly Mick had a thought.

"As we were leaving here this afternoon, a grey-haired guy in an expensive suit that screamed 'high-priced lawyer' was walking in. Did he bail Cody out?"

"Sorry," the sergeant said again. "Can't help you. Now if you'll excuse me, I've got to finish up the daily reports."

The sergeant bent his head down, picked up his pencil, and returned to the reports on his desk.

Bridget whispered, "come on, Luv," took his hand and pulled him towards the door.

THE SERGEANT WATCHED them walk back across the scuffed black and white linoleum and open the heavy station-house door. For a moment they were outlined on the threshold by the late afternoon sun. Two silhouettes of uncertainty. Probably two nice kids. Too bad.

Sergeant O'Donnell picked up the phone and dialed a number.

"Parmenter? Yeah, it's O'Donnell."

MICK AND BRIDGET sat on the rapidly cooling granite steps in front of the station. The summer sun sank below the rooftops, turning the sky from a dark blue to pink, and finally to a deep fiery red, confirming the promise of another clear, hot day tomorrow. Mick stretched his legs down the three worn steps and closed his eyes, letting the last few rays of the sunlight wash over his upturned face and reproached himself for his probably empty skull.

"How could I have been so frigging dumb?" he muttered.

"What's that, darlin'?"

"Cody told us how important Blair's family is, how many 'big shot' connections her father has. Christ, I should have known someone would be coming for him." Mick shook his head, his eyes closed. "I'm sure that guy who tipped his hat to you on the way out is the one."

"Why? Cody doesn't know anyone around here, except for his band and some of the kids at that club up in Falmouth where he met Blair. It doesn't sound like any of them could afford a lawyer like that."

Mick gazed at her for a moment with a look that said he'd already been down this road, and it led to a dead end. But often when Mick had been chewing over a problem like a dog with a gristle-tough bone, he liked to get Bridget's take on it, even if it led to the same nowhere conclusion he'd already come to. Because sometimes, her path took an unexpected turn—straight to the truth. So he looked at her and said, "Go on."

"However," she said, leaning forward and holding up her right index finger, "the Vanderwall girl's rich family surely could."

Bridget's eyes narrowed. "But why on earth would Blair's parents want to bail out their daughter's suspected murderer?"

"I gotta admit, I don't have that part nailed down yet," Mick said. "One thing's for sure, though. I need to talk to the Vanderwalls and Blair's rich friends."

"But," Bridget went on, "Cody remembers meeting only two other girls at Blair's table, and after he danced with Blair he never saw them again."

"Yeah," Mick said. "Blair must have been something to look at. Cody said her two friends were cute but next to her they looked like a couple of crows."

Mick leaned back on the steps and looked up at the slowly darkening sky. He sighed. "The sad truth is that all Cody remembers is having a whole lot of beer and drugs and dancing with the gorgeous little fox named Blair. Then Miss Foxy Lady whispered that she knew a real nice private little beach where they could talk and look at the stars, and…" Mick propped himself up on one elbow and grinned, "and get to know one another better."

"McCarthy," Bridget sighed, "you men have all got one-track minds."

"Guilty as charged, m'lady." Mick ran one hand up the soft denim of her bell-bottomed leg, "but at least mine is always on the right track."

"Keep yer mind on yer work, lad," Bridget said, prim and businesslike. She removed his hand from her leg and folded both of hers. Her brow furrowed. "So then, they leave the club in Falmouth and drive down to a secluded beach in Newport. The next thing he remembers is coming to at the Folk Festival grounds the next morning, and a bunch of really big guys in blue uniforms rousting him out of his sleeping bag."

"And holding him on 'suspicion' of murder."

"But we both know he couldn't have done it, given the fact that he was sleeping it off outside the performers' tent at the back of the festival field."

Mick watched her out of the corner of his eye. She was getting that look, the one she reserved for things in trouble: animals, kids, and especially big dumb things like him. He'd seen that look often enough after she'd patched him up and bawled him out after some particularly stupid and dangerous escapade.

"You think he's innocent, don't you?"

She nodded. "I know his type. He's wild and reckless, and when he gets a belly full of whiskey and a scent of some pretty little thing in his nostrils, he'll lose what little sense he has. But in that, he's not so unlike some other lads I know, is he, darlin'?"

"Can't think of who you mean. Good thing you keep me away from those 'bad boys.'"

He closed his eyes to small slits against the slanting rays of the red setting sun.

"So, what's your plan to help clear the misunderstood man from Kentucky?" Mick asked.

She chewed the inside of her lower lip for a moment. "Well, all we need to do is find those mates of his who can swear they tucked him in after he had a pint too many. Then we tell that officer that Cody Ewing is innocent, and he can tell that posh lawyer to pass the word on to the poor lad. Yer friend Smitty's cousin is cleared, and the case is closed!" she finished triumphantly.

Mick paused for a moment before shattering her insufficiently skeptical conclusion.

"Yeah," he said, his voice low as he let his eyelids absorb the last few rays of sunlight. "Except, Cody can't remember the names of anyone he met that night and even if he did, they'd only corroborate that he left the club with Blair. He was the last one seen with her. In other words," Mick sighed, "his half-assed alibi is worse than none at all. We need to find someone who saw Blair *after* she and Cody parted company—if they actually did."

"You don't think he's guilty do you?"

Mick was silent for a moment. "No, I can't picture a cousin of Smitty's being a stone-cold killer."

His eyes grew cold and distant again. "But I've been wrong before, dead wrong, and it cost the lives of…" His jaw tightened. "So let's just say that the cousin of my best friend is innocent until proven guilty. And I'm gonna try my friggin' best to help him."

Mick wiped his palms on his jeans, as if wiping away all the little germs of doubt that had kept him second guessing since that morning in 1966 when he'd chosen the wrong jungle trail and had led his squad into a V.C. ambush. No, damn it! He was going to do this right.

He looked into Bridget's eyes and said with a certainty that he wasn't entirely sure he felt. "We're gonna track down everyone that Cody was with that night, find out if anyone saw Blair after she left the club, but more important, find out if anyone who knew, loved, lusted after or loathed Blair Vanderwall left the club *after* she left with Cody."

"Someone who followed them from the club and…"

"Exactly. Right now anything is possible. Ever read Sherlock Holmes?"

"A silly English make-believe detective." She gave a contemptuous shake of her head. "I spent my time with real writers with important things to say, like James Joyce and William Butler Yeats."

"Well not to put too fine a literary point on it, my gorgeous Hibernian, but we are engaged in the process of gathering clues, not sonnets or impassioned prose. And so my lovely 'Miss Watson' we're going to take a page from that silly English detective who might have been make-believe but his ideas were pretty friggin' right on the money."

"Which were?"

"Once you've eliminated everything that's impossible, whatever is left, no matter how improbable, must be the truth… or pretty damn close to it."

Bridget sighed. "So where do we start?"

"With the guys who knew Cody best. His band."

Chapter 7

Newport | Rhode Island | Festival Grounds
July 27, 1968 | 7:32 p.m.

A warm wind blew into Mick's face as he leaned the BSA around the last turn into the nearly empty field where the set-up for the Newport Folk & Blues Festival had just begun. Mick downshifted from second to first gear and felt the big bike's rear tire fishtail as it caught the soft wet grass and spit it out below the twin tailpipes.

He looked around, expecting to see Bridget's eyes staring back at him from the rear seat with disapproval.

But she wasn't there.

She was following up on her intention to have the Desk Sergeant's Tarot card–reading sister 'do her fortune' and had stayed back on Nickerson Way, with the slightly spacey, always interesting, Sparrow.

Sparrow—there was a head case all right. Hell, the old farts who said that doing too much dope would burn out your brain cells could use her as a poster child.

And her freaking Tarot cards. How the hell could somebody as smart as Bridget fall for that crap?

"Oh, Bridget, it's the House Struck By Lightning followed by a Cups and Wands. That could mean that you're on a dangerous road to some terrible truth."

Yeah, right. As far a he was concerned, Sparrow could take her Tarot cards and palm readings and stuff them...

Yet the words stuck in his mind. "...a dangerous road to some terrible truth." Did she really see that in the cards? Nah. More likely the Bowen Wharf songbird had other, more prosaic sources. Maybe a good old-fashioned telephone call from her brother—the Newport P.D. Desk Sergeant. Yeah, maybe that was it.

And yet—the way she'd looked at his palm and then at him… It gave him the frigging creeps. What was it she said about his fate line ending in a shadow? He looked at the palm of his hand. Hell, that "shadow" was probably just a mark from some burning jungle hooch or a roach-end in some dingy Saigon bar.

His eyes narrowed as he scanned the field filled with vans, old day-glow painted school buses and a makeshift tent city.

He shook his head.

He was here to find Cody's band, or better, someone who had some idea what the cousin of a Kentucky coal miner's son, to whom he owed his life, did when he left that club on the Cape with a cute little blond. That is, if anyone would talk to him at all.

The hard twang of a banjo and the strumming of a guitar came from the far side of the field. Mick killed the engine. The music bounced off the old granite walls. Someone was singing.

"*Ten years ago, on a cold dark night, someone was killed in the town out-right.*"

Yeah, he knew the song, an old tune from the hills that Cody came from. He'd heard it for the first time in 1963, when he and Wesley, his geeky but sweet roommate at Andover, had gone to Club 47 in Harvard Square to see Joan Baez. They'd both fallen in love with the thin, intense brunette, and with folk music, on that night.

The song ended. "*Nobody knows, nobody sees, nobody knows but me…*"

The last notes drifted away on the salt harbor air. Mick took an auditory fix on his position and kicked the BSA's 650 cc engine back to life. He feathered the throttle lightly with his right hand and steered the bike toward the lit tents peeking out from behind the big dark stage at the end of the field.

He glided up to the first tent. Four or five musicians sat in folding aluminum lawn chairs in a semicircle around the amber-red dying campfire. He killed the engine and pulled the bike up onto its kickstand. Swinging one foot over the handlebars, he pulled a half-crumpled pack of Old Gold cigarettes out of the top pocket of his denim jacket. He scraped a wooden kitchen match across the heel of his boot and lit one.

He drew the smoke deep into his lungs. The bluegrass/folk group launched into a jam from the last chords of 'Long Black Veil.' The banjo, a mandolin and a couple of guitars reached a free-flowing crescendo and died away on the summer night.

Mick brought his hands together in applause.

The fire-lit figures looked up. A big guy in a flannel shirt walked around the fire to Mick.

"Kin ah hep ya, fren'?"

Mick smiled. The same eastern Kentucky accent he'd heard so often from his 'Nam corporal and best friend, Smitty. *Can I help you, friend?*

"Yeah," Mick nodded, pushing his butt off the bike. "I hope so."

"An' who the hell are you again?" a thin, rawboned banjo player asked, as if he didn't really want an answer.

"A friend of Cody's. And his cousin."

"And just who is that?" the banjo player asked.

Mick took a last drag of his cigarette before he flicked the butt into the fire and answered, "Harland Beaufort Smith. Smitty."

The bearded giant tuning the tiny ten-string mandolin paused with one enormous thumb and forefinger enveloping the 'E' string tuning peg.

He looked up at Mick. "Where you from, boy?"

"Boston."

"An' jest how does Smitty know someone from Boss-toon

Massatusetts." That was just how Smitty had always said it.

Mick shrugged.

"We were only in Boston for three days, in the South Boston Army Induction and Embarkation Center. We spent the next fourteen months together—in Vietnam."

"You know Smitty from Vietnam?"

"He was my corporal. I was his sergeant."

The big man's face creased into a gigantic bear smile.

"So, you're Smitty's sergeant from 'Nam? Hot damn, son, why the hell didn't you say that in the first place! Hell, Smitty told me all about you. I'm Dale Warwick, his second cousin on my mama's side, from Versailles, Kentucky."

The giant got up and grasped Mick's right hand in one meaty paw and said, "Now, I know that some big old po-lice men came and dragged Cody outta' his sleeping bag and hauled him off on suspicion of murder or some such thing. But when we went to see 'em, they wouldn't let us talk to him. So why don't you jest set yerself down here and tell us all about what kinda mess old Cody has gone and got his-self into now."

FIFTEEN MINUTES LATER, Mick finished with, "But when we went to bail him out two hours ago, he was gone. Someone bailed him out. I don't know who that someone is, but I've got a pretty good idea of *what* that someone is."

"Okay fren', I'll bite," Dale nodded throwing a few more twigs on the dying fire. "Jest *what* is this feller' who's taken such an interest in ol' Cody?"

Mick kicked at the glowing coals with the toe of his boot.

"He's rich, really friggin' rich."

Mick looked at their faces in the dimming firelight. "And I gotta tell you guys, I've known a whole lot of rich people, probably way too many. But there's one thing I can tell you about them. Despite what they may say for the society pages or the Garden Club, when they spend money, it's never just to do something 'nice.' They expect to get something for it."

The eyes around the campfire watched Mick expectantly.

"And I got a real bad feeling of what that 'something' may mean for Cody."

Chapter 8

Hyannis | Massachusetts | Cape Cod
July 28, 1968 | 1:22 p.m.

Mick throttled up to the red light on Sea Street and put both feet out as he braked to a complete stop.

"I thought we were going to Falmouth," Bridget said, lifting her cheek from the back of his jacket.

Mick put the bike back into first gear and slowly motored up the old elm tree–lined street. Halfway up the block he nudged the front tire into the curb in front of a one-story, white clapboard building. A brightly painted sign hung over the door: Cape Cod Music Company. Guitars bought and sold.

He turned the bike off and eased it up onto the kickstand.

Pulling off his sunglasses, he swung around and said, "We are. But first we need a little camouflage so nobody gets suspicious. Just like a 'Special Ops' in the jungle. I'll be right back."

Five minutes later Mick emerged with a four-year-old Guild F-50 Dreadnought acoustic guitar in his hands.

"Okay, McCarthy," Bridget sighed, eyeing the guitar, "I know I'm probably not gonna like it, but what's the plan?"

"Simple," Mick answered, standing next to the bike. "We show up at Father's with this baby, and as far as anybody knows, we're a couple of performers looking for a gig. A guy and a girl. Pretty standard, right?"

"Sure," Bridget shot back. "And suppose they ask us to *prove* we're performers by actually performin'?"

"Hey, I can play, sort of. You forget that I belong to Club 47, merely the premier folk music club in the Northeast. I'll drop a few names, play a couple of chords on the Guild. It'll be a piece of cake."

"Right, McCarthy," Bridget snorted, "You can 'sort of' play and I can 'sort of' sing. What does that make us?"

"It makes us," Mick said, tickling her under her ribs as she unbuttoned her suede leather jacket, 'the 'Sort of-Almost Trio.'"

"Trio means three, McCarthy." She swatted his hand away, trying unsuccessfully not to smile.

"Sure it does: you, me and Miss Guild, here."

"Ahh, fer the love of God."

"C'mon, babe, don't you understand? We've gotta do this. Everyone who was with Cody and Blair was there, and they're all part of the music scene. This is the quickest way for us to get into that world and find out who wanted Blair Vanderwall dead. Once we know that, we'll know who the hell bailed Cody, and why. Maybe they just wanted to shut him up."

"All right, you win. You're bloody impossible, McCarthy!"

As Mick slung the guitar over his shoulder, she added quietly, "And God willin', may you always stay that way."

"DAMN IT, MICKEY," Bridget yelled as they roared up Route 28 toward Falmouth, "either this bleedin' guitar goes, or I do."

"Think of it as a new friend." Mick shouted over his shoulder.

"A new friend that's gonna wind up splintered all over the pavement in about two minutes if you don't get the damn thing out of my face," Bridget grumbled into the back of Mick's denim jacket.

The light up ahead turned yellow, and rather than try to run it, Mick downshifted to first gear and coasted to a stop. He looked over his left shoulder at Bridget and her new friend. He fingered the canvas case and sighed. It was a helluva lot more guitar than he could play, or even afford. But Christ, it was a damn beautiful instrument!

"Michael Prescott McCarthy," Bridget said in her quietest, most dangerous, voice, "if that stringed piece of wood was a woman, I'm beginning to think I'd scratch her eyes out. And then maybe I'd start in on you."

"Babe," Mick called back to her, "if I ever get to the point where I want to have a piece of stringed wood warm my bed at night, then you're welcome to scratch both of our eyes out!"

He clicked the left toe of his cowboy boot down into first gear, slowly let the clutch out with his left hand, and he, Bridget, and the newest member of the family, Miss Guild, drove up Route 28 to the last place that Cody Ewing could remember. And the last place where Blair Prentiss Vanderwall was seen alive.

"SWEET SUFFERING JESUS," Bridget hissed from between clenched teeth while trying to maintain her pasted-on smile, "why do I let you talk me into these things?"

"What?" Mick asked innocently, looking around the rapidly filling club as he tuned the high E string on the big Guild F-50.

"We are *not* professional musicians." Bridget never dropped the plastic, polite grin despite the fact that she probably felt like her insides were turning to water.

"It's okay," Mick soothed. "We've done this a million times at home, and at parties."

"Yes, Michael," Bridget breathed out Mick's full name, a clear sign of how nervous she really was, "but never in front of a room full of people who've paid good money to hear professional musicians. God help us all, they're about to get something called 'Mickey and Bridget!'"

"We're gonna be great," Mick said absently, tuning the guitar. His distracted frown metamorphosed into a relieved grin as the top E string finally rang out true and sweet.

"We're all set to go." He gave her a thumbs-up sign.

"Maybe you are, McCarthy," she displayed her grim-as-death grin, her milk-white Irish complexion turning a "whiter shade of pale," as the Moody Blues would have put it.

"Oh, God, Mickey," she gasped, "I think I'm gonna be sick."

"No time." Mick pointed toward the center of the small stage. "Look."

A fat, perspiring, bald guy in a ratty old sweater and baggy khaki pants moved to center stage and adjusted the stand of the big acoustic microphone.

"Hey, guys, chicks. How's everyone doing tonight?" He frowned when the microphone hissed and popped from feedback. The room erupted into applause and whistles. He motioned to the sound man, and the feedback gradually receded.

The club owner gave a relieved smile and turned back to the crowd, which had by now filled every available chair and table for the 9:00 p.m. show.

"So, where's everybody from?" he shouted.

"U Mass," a drunk frat boy bellowed three tables up from the stage's left-hand side.

"U Conn!" two tables of giggling freshman girls screamed from the other side of the room. And so it went around the room: college kids working their way through the first pitcher of beer, getting primed for a night of music and *whatever*.

Mick looked out at the crowd from the wings of the makeshift stage. Small groups of more 'hardcore' hippies, too-cool-for-college types, surreptitiously took hits off well-concealed joints and smirked at the beer-guzzling college crowd.

There was a whole bunch of people Mick wanted to talk to and according to Cody, they all hung out here. More importantly, this was the last known hangout of Blair Prentiss Vanderwall.

His musing was broken off when Bridget grabbed his wrist so tightly that he felt every one of her fingernails. Her normally soft, cool hands felt different than they ever had before. They felt clammy.

Her eyes looked panicked as the club owner announced, "We've got a really fantastic lineup for you tonight. Just in from San Francisco, Richard and Mimi Farina, the blues guitar of Taj Mahal, and Boston's own native son, who will also be appearing at the Festival in Newport this weekend, Tom Rush!"

More applause and whistles.

The club owner smiled and held up his hands. "And to start us off tonight, a new folk duo from Cambridge, debuting right here on our stage. People, let's hear it for Mickey and Bridget."

Bridget pinched her death-white cheeks into two red spots and crossed herself. Mick slung the Guild over his shoulder and grabbed Bridget's hand.

She whispered, "If we get out of this alive, remind me to kill ya, McCarthy."

Mick gave her hand a gentle tug, and they stepped onto the stage.

Mick smiled at the crowd as the applause died away, and, stepping up to the microphone, adjusted it until it was about four inches from Bridget's mouth. She sat on a three-legged stool, tucking one wavy lock of short black hair behind her ear.

I don't think I've ever loved her more than I do this minute, Mick thought as he unslung the guitar and pushed the capo up to Bridget's best octave.

I know she'd like to run off this stage like the devil was chasing her, but she's gonna stay and give her all.

He took the tortoiseshell pick out of the strings and winked at her.

She took a deep breath, squared her shoulders, and smiled back at him.

"Thank you," Mick said to the crowded room. "We'd like to do a song that was made popular by Ian and Sylvia. And I guess it sort of sums up how we feel about one another."

He looked at Bridget.

"Ready, babe?"

"You bet, luv."

Mick struck the opening chord of "You Were On My Mind," and the sound of the big Guild filled the crowded, smoke-filled room. Their harmony swelled together and the crowd of college kids and peripheral hippies, recognizing the words to the song and the special meaning that it obviously had for the two singers, began to applaud.

It was going to be all right.

Chapter 9

Falmouth, Massachusetts   Cape Cod
July 28, 1968   10:09 p.m.

"Hey, man," the skinny kid with long, dirty blond hair and scraggly Fu-Manchu mustache called to Mick and Bridget as they stepped down off the stage. "You guys were boss."

"Yeah," said the girl with long straight brown hair and blue tinted sunglasses sitting next to him. "Like, really far out."

Mick gave Bridget a quick look out of the corner of his eye. This was what they'd been hoping for, and he answered in his 'coolest' tone.

"Hey, man, thanks. Like, right on."

"Sit down, man," the blond guy said, indicating two empty chairs at the large table where eight or ten beaded, peace-medaled hippies already slouched. "Your chick, too." Mick heard the barely audible word "chick" muttered under Bridget's breath as he steered her into one of the two empty chairs.

"It's Mickey and Bridget, right?" the self-appointed table host asked.

"Yeah, man," Mick said.

"Oh, wow," said his brunette girlfriend, "I really dug your arrangement of Dylan's 'Girl from the North Country.' I've never heard it done as a duet. Really far out."

"Hey, thanks," Mick said, brushing his hair back out of his eyes.

"Are you guys playing down in Newport this weekend?" a heavyset red-haired girl in a long-sleeved paisley dress asked.

"Yeah," Mick said, "we're doing a couple of sets with the Rounders, Cody Ewing's band." He looked around the table for a reaction.

The blond guy and the brunette in the blue-tinted shades exchanged a quick look.

Mick smiled at the two. "Like, hey, I must be spacing out tonight. I can't remember your names."

He could tell they were trying to remember if they'd given them.

The skinny blond kid said, "It's Paul. PJ. And this is Marcy." She gave Mick and Bridget a quick, cool smile.

"So, did you guys hear Cody play here the night before last?" Bridget asked innocently. She gave the table her most disingenuous smile and continued, "Me and Mickey were so bummed that we missed him. But I heard he was great."

"Oh yeah," the red-haired girl bubbled from the far side of the table. "He was fantastic! Remember, PJ? He did a set with those friends of yours who were doing all that old Buffalo Springfield stuff."

"Ah, yeah, Janet," PJ smiled weakly, "that's right."

"Shit, man," Mick sighed, shaking his head. "I wanted to jam with him before we played Newport this weekend, but I guess I won't see him till then. The guys in his band said he took off with some new chick, and you know what Cody is like when he gets a new chick. Right, Bridge?"

Bridget rolled her eyes and shook her head. "Oh, ya got that right, luv."

"Jesus, what was her name?" Mick turned back to PJ while slowly tapping one finger on the table.

"Shit, man," PJ said, shaking his head, "I don't think I…"

"You know who it was, PJ," the chubby red-haired girl broke in. "Hey, man, you ought to know her. I mean, after all, she was your girlfriend's sister's best—"

"Janet," the unsmiling brunette said slowly, her voice even. "We've got to—"

"It was Blair," Janet said, turning to Mick and slapping one pudgy hand down on the table. "And she was just like she always is. Sitting at the table right up close to the stage with her two stuck-up friends, acting like they're just too cool for everything. Don't you remember, Marcy, I said, 'oh wow, that Cody is so cool, but just you wait and see, Blair will get him. She always does.' Remember?"

"Yes, Janet," Marcy breathed in a low, exasperated voice, "I remember."

"So, what do you think, Bridge?" Mick said. "Maybe Cody is shacked up with this Blair chick." He swung his head back to Janet, but watched Marcy out of the corner of his eye.

He asked casually, "Do you know where they went that night?"

But before his carefully set up scene could play out, a hand dropped onto his shoulder and a deep voice said, "Hey, kid."

Mick spun around, the old 'Nam reflexes taking over.

"Hey, you guys were pretty good."

It was Manny, the heavyset owner of the club, the same guy that had auditioned Mick and Bridget a few hours ago. Mick thought he was a sleaze-ball then and he hadn't seen anything to change his mind. As a matter of fact, he'd seen him stooping over a table in front of the stage, no doubt putting the make on the two cute chicks sitting there. One of them looked a little like the girl with the blue shades sitting across the table.

Manny looked at him with hard eyes. "You want to do another set?"

Mick paused, but Bridget gave him a look that said he better not push his luck if he didn't want to start leading a celibate life.

"Hey, thanks, man, but we've got a big gig coming up this weekend. Don't want to overdo it."

The owner shrugged. "Suit yourself." He motioned to one of the waitresses and said, "Hey, Bev, bring these kids a couple of pitchers on the house."

"Thanks," Mick smiled as the waitress put down two pitchers of beer. Just then the girl he thought looked a little like Marcy came over and handed her a note.

"Here, I'll pour," said Marcy, with the first smile she'd shown since Mick and Bridget had sat down. She half-rose out of her chair and grabbed a pitcher with her right hand. Leaning forward, with her long brown hair almost touching the tabletop, she poured the pale golden lager into two frosted mugs. She tucked her hair back behind one ear and pushed the two mugs across the table to Mick and Bridget.

"Here's to making far-out music when you find good old Cody… and Blair." She smiled again as she raised her mug in their direction.

Alarm bells went off in Mick's head. This wasn't a chick who smiled easily, or often.

He took a small sip of the beer and stopped, his mouth still on the rim of the mug. There, just visible through the frost and foam on Bridget's mug, was something small and dark at the bottom of her glass!

She was already drinking.

He saw the muscles in her slim white throat move.

Mick leaned back in his chair and raised his mug back at Marcy.

"And here's to new friends who really know where good music is at!" Mick swung the frosted beer glass from left to right in a sweeping toast and knocked Bridget's mug out of her hand.

"Oh damn, Mickey!" she cried, beer spilling down her blouse, soaking her through to the skin.

"Aw, crap," Mick said, reaching for a handful of napkins. "Jesus, I'm sorry!"

"Fer pity's sake, I'm wet clear through!"

She stood up, holding a handful of wet napkins.

"Here, I'll help you," Mick said, standing up quickly.

"That's all right, you don't need to."

"Oh yeah, I do. I feel like a real jerk. Hey, I'll check backstage and see if they have something you can change into."

"I don't think—"

"*Don't* think. And don't talk!" Mick hissed in her ear as he took her elbow and steered her toward the stage. "We're gonna slip out the back door."

"Why?"

"Because there was something in your beer, and in mine, too. And if it's what I think, we've gotta get out of here, fast!"

Bridget grabbed Mick's arm as he continued to propel her toward the back door.

"What do you mean 'something in my beer'? Then you knocked it out of my hand—?"

"On purpose—right. Come on, move it. We don't have much time."

"Oh Lord, are you sayin' we've been poisoned?"

Mick shook his head and put his hand on the heavy metal fire-door that lead to the delivery lot at the back of the club.

Bridget pulled her arm out of his grip and stopped.

"Michael Prescott McCarthy, you're going to answer my bloody question before I take another step!"

Mick paused, hand still on the door.

"Look, we've been drugged, you more than me, 'cause you drank two full swallows before I saw the stuff at the bottom of your glass."

"Stuff? What sort of stuff?"

"Come on Bridge, we haven't got time for twenty questions."

"I need to know. Am I in danger?"

Mick drew a breath. "No, and yes. I'm afraid we both are."

He opened the back door a crack. There was no movement in the lot and he could see the bike in the light of the red and blue beer sign over the back door. So far so good. He took her arm again and pulled her toward the door.

"I'm sorry. I was too slow on the uptake. My eyes took it in but my brain didn't put it all together. The girl who walked over and handed something to Marcy—it just looked like a small piece of paper. It wasn't. It was a nice little sheet of acid tabs. Obviously somebody doesn't want us asking questions about Blair Vanderwall."

Bridget's hand went to her mouth. "Oh my God, are you sayin' that I've drunk LSD?"

Mick nodded.

"Holy Mother, what is it gonna do to me?"

"I'm not sure, but it's gonna start affecting you—and soon. I've got to get you some place quiet, as far from this dump as possible. Now come on."

"But why should those girls want to hurt us? They don't even know us?"

Mick opened the back door and stepped out into the lot. He took Bridget's hand and pulled her quickly toward the bike.

"Those kids weren't trying to stop us. They just wanted to slow us down for someone else who would."

Chapter 10

Falmouth, Massachusetts | Cape Cod
July 28, 1968 | 11:02 p.m.

"Mick," Bridget said as she climbed to the back of the BSA, "you forgot your guitar."

"No, I didn't," Mick said as he quickly primed the bike's carbs and stamped on the recoil starter. "We've got to travel fast, and light. See that guy over there? I got a strong hunch he's not coming this way to get our autographs."

A man in a black suit and white turtleneck jersey stepped through the club's back door and looked at them.

It was not a friendly look.

The BSA's engine caught, Mick squeezed the hand clutch, popped the bike into first gear and headed for the curb cutting between the club's back entrance and the street.

A big black Pontiac Bonneville convertible blocked it from curb to curb. Mick stopped for a moment. That car—the same one he'd seen at the police station. And now it blocked their only way out of this alley.

But a Pontiac was just a big old piece of Detroit steel. Mick had a 650 cc bike.

He opened the throttle all the way.

"Hold tight!" he shouted over the roar of the engine.

Bridget ducked her head, gripped Mick's waist tighter, and buried her right cheek in the back of his coarse denim jacket. She murmured an old prayer. "Holy Mary, Mother of God, pray for us sinners now and at the hour of our—"

She screamed as Mick wound the big machine all the way into first gear until the front wheel left the pavement.

The Bonneville's driver, seeing the motorcycle careening straight toward him, jammed the car into reverse and tried to back up. The car had barely moved when Mick leaned left and slung the big machine over on one wheel. He headed straight for the only chance they had to escape, a stack of wooden pallets between the club wall and the curb.

The back wheel of the BSA chewed its way up the stack of pallets, skidded down the top of the Bonneville's hood, and out into the busy traffic of Route 28 where a station wagon with a pair of horrified parents and a back seat of screaming kids screeched to a stop in front of them. Mick regained control of the bike, kicked into second gear, and headed north up Route 28.

When he'd put at least ten miles between him and the Bonneville, he pulled off the highway, downshifted into third gear, then second, and coasted the bike to a stop under a streetlight, swiveling his head to Bridget. She had a dreamy smile on her face, and the pupils of her normally emerald-green eyes had shrunk to pinpricks.

Oh, shit!

That first swallow had done it. She was tripping. And from what he knew about this stuff, which only the hardest of hard-core, out-of-control grunts had used in 'Nam—and some of them after—it was very, very bad shit.

As a matter of fact, he felt a little woozy himself, and he'd barely touched his lips to the glass.

Someone was gonna pay for this.

But first, he had to get Bridget to somewhere quiet and safe before she started tripping. And it wasn't gonna be here, because the rearview mirror lit up as a pair of headlights came over the hill.

Yeah, the Pontiac was still on their tail.

"Damn, I thought I lost them."

Mick revved the bike and looked around quickly. The road they were on crossed under the Mid-Cape Highway then wandered down to the 6A Shore Road. As the headlights drew closer, he spotted what he'd been looking for. A small black and white sign that read, Beach–1 mile.

The headlights were closing fast. Mick stepped down into first gear and skidded the tires off the sandy road then roared flat out for the beach.

"WHERE THE HELL did I think we were gonna go?" Mick muttered as he coasted to a stop at the end of the beach parking lot. He felt Bridget slide off the back of the bike as he sat there, feet planted on either side of the motorcycle, watching the small waves retreat with the outgoing tide.

Damn. Looks like the only option is to take the bike onto the beach. Maybe he could make it.

But could the Bonneville do it, too?

"Hey, baby. Whoa, momma! Bring some of that over here, sugar!"

Mick looked across the parking lot. Half a dozen cars formed a rough semicircle. Fifteen or twenty guys sat on car hoods or leaned against their fenders. Even if Mick hadn't seen the piles of empties strewn around, it was evident from the sound of their voices that they were all more than a few sheets to the wind.

What the hell were they hooting about?

Then he turned around.

Bridget. In the middle of the parking lot. Dancing. Stark naked.

"Oh, Jesus!" Mick muttered.

Her beautiful white body moved with fluid grace as she sang some ancient song in Gaelic.

She turned her face to the moon and pirouetted on one dainty toe.

It was beautiful, almost spiritual, though it was obvious that the 'drink-till-you-puke' crowd on the other side of the parking lot entertained no such 'spiritual' thoughts.

Three of the group sauntered over, laughing, nudging one another.

Mick pulled the bike onto the kickstand and quickly gathered up Bridget's discarded clothing.

"Hey, little chick," leered a fat-gutted kid with long, scraggly sideburns, "come over here and do that dance on my face."

His two buddies guffawed and poked one another. The fat kid made a grab for Bridget's swaying body. The next thing he knew, he was flat on his back.

"I don't like handing out sucker punches, pal," Mick growled, "but I'm just about out of time and patience tonight, so you and your buddies back off."

"Kenny, Brad," the fat guy shouted, struggling to get up. "Jump 'em. C'mon, guys!" he called to the rest of the group across the parking lot.

Mick had been in enough firefights to know when he was outnumbered, and he sure as hell was now. He pushed Bridget behind him and she put her arms around his waist, still humming the strange Celtic chant.

Mick tensed for what was coming.

Suddenly he remembered one of his father, Big Mike's, favorite sayings, "It's an ill wind, boy-o, that don't blow no good for someone."

Because that ill wind screeched into the parking lot and skidded to a stop twenty feet away. The doors of the black Bonneville opened, and two men in dark suits and narrow ties climbed out.

"Piss off, you little bastards," the shorter of the two growled to the crowd of half-in-the-bag kids.

The kid with the scraggly sideburns was good and ready for a fight. "Fuck you, shorty!"

The short, brutally compact one backhanded the fat kid and walked toward Mick and Bridget, pulling a blue-steel automatic as he walked.

Mick froze.

The guy with the gun drew a bead on Bridget. Mick tried to push her behind him. The man smiled as if rearrangement of his targets suited him just fine. He raised the gun and—

"What the fuck?" A 'Tall-Boy' Budweiser can smacked into the back of his head. His finger jerked down on the trigger and the bullet burrowed into the sand.

The second gunman drew his automatic and leveled it at the crowd of drunken teenagers, who lobbed half-filled beer cans and bottles at them.

Mick had only seconds. The shooting was about to start. He pulled Bridget to the bike, stuffed her clothes into the saddlebags, and sat her on the rear seat. He pushed the motorcycle down off the kickstand, clicked the clutch into neutral and let the bike coast noiselessly onto the beach. The tires sank in the soft sand, but he held off starting the bike until he heard voices yelling louder. One of the dark suits stepped around his partner, turned to the jeering crowd and aimed.

A BOTTLE SMASHED in front of the gunman. He raised the barrel and barked out, "Here's one for you, kid."

Before he could shoot, his partner, still rubbing the back of his head, pulled the hand holding the pistol down. "Not them, Vinnie. Mr. C. don't want nobody else popped—at least for now. Just them two on the bike."

"What about those little pricks throwing the cans and bottles?"

"If they get too close I'll put a few slugs close to their feet, that'll sober 'em up."

Vinnie turned to the beach and drew a bead on Mick's head. He had him sighted perfectly. He couldn't miss. The bare-assed broad on the back of the cycle was gonna get splattered with her boyfriend's brains in about two seconds and then it would be her turn. He drew in a breath and slowly squeezed the trigger.

"Mr C. said don't whack 'em—yet. Just put a few holes in 'em that'll put their asses in a hospital bed."

Vinnie frowned. They were moving away. He was losing his shot.

He re-sighted the gun, this time aiming for Mick's leg. He pulled the trigger.

"CRAP!" MICK SCREAMED as the bullet took a chip out of the left heel of his boot.

"Time to go!" he yelled, stamping down on the recoil starter. He steadied the bike with both feet as it fishtailed through the sand.

One, two, three more shots rang out.

The bike zigzagged through the soft sand. The next shot was close. Too close. They'd have to abandon the bike and run for it if this kept up.

Finally they made it to the hard packed sand of the tidal flats and the knobby tires bit down. The moon peeked out from behind a cloud revealing miles of flat, firm, silvery sands stretching out in front of them.

"Yes! We're home free!"

His left rearview mirror exploded in a shower of glass, followed half a second later by the loud bang of a pistol shot.

Mick jammed the foot-gear lever into second and leaned forward, accelerating onto the hard, wet sand. He'd shifted into fourth gear, and the speedometer needle nudged sixty miles an hour before he risked a look in his remaining rearview mirror. His heart sank. The headlights of the big black car raced across the sand after him.

Shit! The wind flattened his long hair back. *Can I outrun the bastards?*

Something whizzed past his head, and he heard the almost instantaneous pistol report again. The next one might go right through his poor naked lady behind him.

A ribbon of silver shimmered up ahead.

He set his jaw and shouted, "Hold on really, really tight! And do another one of those Hail Marys, or Celtic chants, or whatever you think is up to looking out for fools and idiots." He headed the BSA straight toward the shallow tidal stream that crossed the silvery beach.

Throttle wide open, the big bike hit the rushing water at over seventy miles an hour. Mick almost bit clear through the bottom of his lower lip.

Not more than five feet into the stream of outgoing tide, both of the bike's big knobby tires hydroplaned and there was no way to steer, or slow. Or stop.

He put his head down, fought to balance it and hoped his whacked-out lady would keep her hands fastened around his waist.

The BSA hit the hard, packed sand across the stream at a hydroplaning eighty-two miles an hour. The back wheel dug in, throwing up seashells, sand and water. Mick gritted his teeth until they felt like they'd splinter right out of his head as he fought to keep the big machine from sloughing out of control and spilling them onto the beach at a bone-crushing eighty miles an hour.

He held on for almost another quarter mile, screaming at the top of his lungs and praying to the capricious gods of motorcycles and fools.

A quarter of a mile from the stream, he braked to a stop.

The kickstand wouldn't hold in the wet sand, so he slid down onto one knee, holding onto the dripping metallic blue frame, and vomited into the seaweed-speckled sand.

"That was too frigging close," he mumbled, wiping his mouth with the back of his hand. He spat out the last of his too-distant dinner then reached down with one shaking hand and scooped up a handful of sea water from a tidal puddle. He sucked the bitter, fishy liquid and swirled it around in his mouth.

"Damn," he coughed as he spat it back into the sand. Nausea came over him again. It had to be that drug, and he'd tasted just a little bit, not one-tenth of what poor Bridge had—

Bridge!

She was gone from the bike's back seat, but she couldn't have gotten far. She must be…

There. Walking into the retreating sea, a hundred feet away. Her arms outstretched, palms and face turned to the silver-sliced moon, she was still singing that haunting Celtic chant.

"Oh, Christ," Mick murmured. He let the bike drop and started unsteadily after her.

The outgoing tide, now up to his knees, slowed him. "Bridget!" he called, just before a 9 mm slug cut a shallow crease through the dungaree denim of his right thigh.

He looked over his left shoulder. The black Bonneville was just the other side of the tidal stream. In the light of the moon, a gunman knelt on the hood.

"Bridget!" he screamed and covered the last few yards that separated them. She turned toward him, an eerie, lost, Celtic Princess smile pasted on her face, and he charged through the surf and tackled her.

They rolled into the outgoing waves. A second slug from the sniper's rifle hissed through the water, inches from where Bridget's pale bare skin had been only seconds before.

They came up sputtering and coughing.

"Come on!" Mick cried, pulling her wet, slippery hand. "We've gotta move—fast!"

A part of her mind seemed to come back for a moment, and she nodded. Mick kept hold of her hand as they ran back to the bike. He pulled it upright and fired it up as he felt Bridget's wet, fish-cold body slide up behind him.

A third slug kicked up the wet sand three feet from the front tire while Mick punched into first gear and wound the bike down the beach. The echo of a fourth shot caught up with them, but they must be out of range, because he couldn't see the slug hit.

He went a few hundred yards further and turned back in a partial semicircle.

The tiny figure of the gunman climbed down off the hood of the Pontiac and got inside. The black car reversed for about a hundred feet then came forward at top speed, straight for the tidal stream that separated them.

Mick sat astride the bike, breathing heavily, foot poised over the gear shift pedal. The big black Bonneville hit the stream at around fifty miles an hour, throwing up a huge spray of water, seaweed, sand, and crushed razor clams.

It stalled. Right in the middle of the frigging stream!

Mick let out his breath. "Yes! Now let's get the hell out of here."

MICK SLOWLY CRAWLED to the top of the windswept sand dune

using the soft sand and tough sea grass to make the belly-crawling moves he'd taught his 'cherry' PFCs back in 'Nam. He parted the salt-encrusted sea grass on the dune's crest.

So far, so good. No sign of the black Bonneville. He sighed and slid down over the dune's tiny, knife-like blades of sea grass.

Unbelievably, they were alive.

Bridget was sitting where he'd left her, staring at the moon, tears running down her cheeks. In the light of the near-dawn moon, the tears looked silver.

"Oh, my frigging word," Mick said.

He dropped down onto his knees in front of Bridget and took her naked, wet body in his arms. He pulled off his damp jacket and wrapped it around her. Then he pulled her clothes out of the bike's saddlebags and laid them out in the shallow depression of the sand dunes' most protected spot.

She shivered. She was coming out of it.

So he wrapped her in the clothes and in his arms, and as the silver-tears moon sank behind the western dunes, rocked her to sleep.

Chapter 11

Cambridge, Massachusetts Brattle Street
July 29, 1968 12:22 a.m.

The sound of the two-hundred-year-old grandfather clock filled the small spaces and cubbyholes in the parlor of the eighteenth century Brattle Street house.

But it was the only sound, outside of an occasional creak or pop, as several centuries of patrician living passed their hand lightly over the ancient seat of traditional power that the Prescotts had wielded over the Bay State.

But not any more. That line of steadily escalating strategic alliances had come to a screeching halt when Felicity Parker Prescott had married a young Irish cop, one Michael Francis McCarthy.

It hadn't been a good idea, and it hadn't lasted. But it had, Mrs. Felicity Parker Prescott-McCarthy reflected, produced three lovely and exceptional children. Francis, Michael and Bronwyn.

Francis, her firstborn, was the youngest partner at the venerable Boston corporate law firm of Hayward, Elliott and Delbert.

I wonder if he's still seeing Charlton Elliott's daughter? Felicity mused.

She had likewise tried her best to 'direct' her middle child, Michael Junior—Mickey, as his father insisted on calling him—into what would have been a marvelous alliance of two wonderful and important families. But it hadn't worked out. Not at all.

She loved Michael Jr. dearly, as only a mother could, but she had to admit a certain degree of disappointment and reluctant acceptance of the fact that her secretly favorite son had, well, a decidedly common streak.

He had, against all common sense, propriety, and three hundred years of Puritan heritage, fallen madly in love with a little Irish waitress!

The fact that Bridget Connolly was also the recipient of numerous awards for academic excellence, and was on full academic scholarship to Radcliffe, the Alma Mater of both Felicity and her daughter Bronwyn, was an inconvenient reality.

But, she reflected, she did try to be broad-minded. The Irish could certainly be charming, amusing and physically attractive. Hadn't she married one?

And my goodness, talk about passionate!

She allowed herself to bask in the delicious, warm memory of the big, burly South Boston cop picking her up in his arms as if she weighed no more than a feather. He'd rescued her from an assault (or worse), quite literally swept her off her feet and escorted her home to her father's house on Beacon Hill.

Daddy had been so mad when she married him. She giggled.

"Miss Felicity?"

Felicity twisted around in the pale gold brocade chair.

"Oh, Rosa," she said. "You startled me."

"I'm sorry, ma'am. Will you be needing me any more tonight?"

There was a part of Felicity that wanted to say "Yes," but she shook her head and said, "No, Rosa, thank you very much."

Then she added, "Are you going somewhere for the weekend?"

"Yes, ma'am," the housekeeper replied proudly. "I'm going up to Revere to stay with my son. He lives just two blocks from the beach, and we're gonna have a picnic on Saturday." She turned to leave the room. She stopped and turned back to the thin, pale woman in the cream-colored silk dress, sitting all alone in the center of the two-hundred-year-old parlor, an empty wine glass in her hand.

"Miss Felicity, I hope, well, you have a nice weekend too."

"Thank you, Rosa," Felicity Parker Prescott-McCarthy said to the empty hall two minutes later.

POOR MICHAEL. Felicity giggled out loud as she poured another glass of chardonnay from the bottle on the sideboard. *You would have thought he was hearing a ghost when I called him.* She bit her lip, and a tiny tear started at the corner of her eye as she thought about her ex-husband living in the squalid little apartment off Lechmere Square.

Oh, I wish we could have made it work, she sighed.

But they hadn't. They really never could have.

She'd put it out of her mind. Just like Scarlett O'Hara, she'd think about that tomorrow.

Right now? Well, right now she was making plans for the weekend. She was going to spend it with her children! She reached for the phone and dialed. It was picked up on the third ring, and a sleepy voice said,

"Hello?"

"Bronwyn, dear!"

"Mom?"

"Darling, how are you?"

"Mom, it's one o'clock in the morning. I'm in bed!"

"What? No date on a Friday night?"

A sigh on the other end of the line. "No, afraid not, Mom."

"Well, me neither, dear. So, I tell you what: you and I are going to have a wonderful getaway weekend. Do you remember my dear friend, Bunny Bradstreet?"

"No, Mom," Bronwyn Prescott-McCarthy yawned.

"She was my roommate, senior year at Radcliffe. Oh, what fun we had. Bunny and I and Margaret Cabot, we were inseparable. Well, I was thinking about them tonight, so I called Bunny and she said, by all means, come down for the weekend. So we're going, dear. You and I. A girls' getaway."

"Going where, Mom?"

"Why, Newport of course, silly. Bunny has a lovely house down there. And so does Margaret, she's now Margaret Vanderwall. Oh, we're going to have the best time. Who knows who we may see down there? As a matter of fact," she smiled into the phone, "I found out from a gruff old Irish bulldog someone else that we might find. Your brother Michael!"

BRONWYN HUNG UP the phone after hearing the latest of her mother's typically whimsical plans. *She must have been sampling the Chardonnay*, she thought, wide awake now. Going down to Newport with mom to spend the weekend, listening to the two ex-roommates play endless games of, "Do you remember…?" would not have been her first choice for a fun getaway.

"Bo-o-o-ring!" she sighed, clasping her hands behind her head and staring up at the dark ceiling.

On the other hand, if Mick were there, and—oh, yes! This was the weekend of the Newport Folk Festival! As a matter of fact, one of her friends, Laney Hewitt, had said that she and her boyfriend were going down. Hey, if she could ditch Mom and the "Tennis, anyone?" crowd, she just might have some fun this weekend after all.

Bronwyn turned her cheek back into her pillow. It was funny how, despite the best efforts of Miss Felicity Parker Prescott, 'High Society' events had always produced the same desire in Bronwyn: the desire to run the other way as fast as she could! *Must be the McCarthy in me.*

She closed her eyes.

Bronwyn Prescott-McCarthy had been raised in a Brattle Street mansion filled with the antique trappings of wealth and faded Prescott glory, but had never had much of a stomach for the natural snobbery that surrounded the Prescott social circle. She'd always laughed, discreetly of course, at the large numbers of her mother's friends and their snooty offspring, who delighted in stringing together long, preposterous old family names in an effort to show the rest of the world how important they were. Names like Jennifer Regina Walton-Cavendish, her first roommate freshman year at Radcliffe. They hadn't gotten along well. Or the boy who had taken her to her first cotillion, Brandon Myles Goodrich-Rutherford. Brom and good old "Brad" had *definitely* not gotten along. Perhaps that's why Bronwyn had always shied away from using all of the affected-sounding names with which the Prescott heritage had sprinkled her baptismal papers.

Only once had she used the entire string, and that was in the third grade, when a particularly spoiled little WASP princess, whose outrageously expensive and excessive birthday party she was attending, announced to the dozen other eight-year-old heiresses sporting *real* pearls and *real* diamonds, that she was so happy to have such good friends from all the *best* families. And then added, with a little-girl simper that would some day grow into an upper class woman's sneer, "I mean, *most* of you come from the best families. Some girls only come from *half* of the best."

Bronwyn knew who she was talking about, even without the room full of giggles and pitying looks.

She got up slowly from the dining room table set with Wedgewood china and Tiffany silver, and carefully folded her napkin. She walked with perfect posture to the head of the table and looked at the little blond girl occupying the hostess seat, whose cheeks were turning a bright crimson.

"I'm going to leave now, Amanda," Bronwyn had said. "My mother told me to always thank the hostess. So, I would like to extend my thanks for a lovely and *gracious* time, from Miss Bronwyn Amelia Parker Prescott … McCarthy."

That night, she told her mother that she'd changed her mind about the use of hyphenated names. For once, Felicity Parker Prescott didn't argue.

June 1966   Somewhere north of Firebase Bravo

"Sergeant!" the colonel snapped out. "Report!"

Sergeant Michael Prescott McCarthy, Mick to his friends, shook his head, but his feet carried him into the center of the village.

The colonel smiled at him. "Your squad is waiting for you, Sergeant."

"What do you want me to do, sir?" Mick heard his voice answer.

The colonel gave the same answer he always did.

"You know what to do, Sergeant."

Mick shook his head as his men crowded around him.

"Come on, Sarge, they're coming at us."

Mick bit back a scream because he knew what *they* were, those black, misshapen lumps crawling out of the smoldering huts.

"C'mon, Sarge," pleaded Private Begley, just as he had that first night in the jungle two years ago.

"Give the order, Sarge. They're coming for us."

"Give the order, man," Henderson yelled. "Waste 'em, Sarge!"

Mick stood rooted to the spot, M-16 clutched in shaking hands, moving his head back and forth, whispering again and again, "No, no!"

The smoldering, blackened lumps that had once been the people of the village crawled forward.

His men shouted, "Give the order, Sarge. We have to open up—waste the V.C. bastards before it's too late."

"Report, sergeant! Report!" The colonel shouted. "This village has got to be cleared."

The shadows were moving in. Closing in again.

"Report! Report!" the colonel shouted.

He shone a flashlight in Mick's eyes, dim at first, then brighter and brighter, and hot, very hot. This was no flashlight.

Napalm!

Orange. Orange and red and hot… "No!"

Mick sat bolt upright and threw up his left hand to block it.

The sun rose over the dunes on Cape Cod Bay and struck him full in the face.

Where was he? Last night… the club… the chase. The black Bonneville. The gunshots and… Bridget.

Where was she?

He half ran, half crawled to the top of the dune. The early dawn sea breeze of salt, sea grass and incoming tide hit him full in the face. He shaded his sleep-filled eyes against the rising sun and… there, at the water's edge. She sat huddled in his denim jacket, knees drawn up to her chin, staring out at the water.

Mick walked down the seaward side of the dune and dropped down beside her. Was she okay? Was the drug still floating around in her brain?

She looked up at him and smiled. It was okay. She was back.

"Hey, babe."

"Hey, luv."

"You okay?"

"I think so."

"Do you… do you remember last night?"

"You mean my dance to the moon? I remember."

There was silence except for the sound of the incoming waves then Bridget slowly smiled and said, "Did you like it?"

Her smile ripped away the last spiderwebs of his nightmare, and he grinned. "You bet your ass, even though for a minute I thought I was gonna have to fight half the horny guys on Cape Cod!"

"Oh, darlin'," she sighed, and put her head down on his bare, cold shoulder. "What the bleedin' hell would I do without ya?"

"I don't know, and I don't ever want you to try to find out."

Mick pulled her down next to him as the rising sun warmed them and the incoming tide washed against their feet.

Chapter 12

Falmouth, Massachusetts | Cape Cod | Father's Folk and Jazz Club

July 29, 1968 | 9:14 a.m.

"Mickey," Bridget said in a soft but tense voice, "I don't want to go back in there."

She stood next to the bike in the deserted parking lot at Father's club, like a pale green-eyed waif shivering in some cold Dickensian alleyway.

Mick knew it wasn't the cold that made her shiver—it was late July, and the summer sun had already burned away the early morning fog. No, it was something else. Something he didn't often see in those sea-green eyes. Fear.

And it took a lot to scare Bridget Connolly.

He took her small, cold hand in his. The events of last night had subjected Bridget to something she didn't experience very often, and hated worse than death. Loss of control.

Even though there was no way she could have resisted the drug, she felt embarrassed. Used. Violated. Less of the person that she'd been twenty-four hours ago. The thought of not being able to control your own actions, to do things you'd never do, or maybe you would if the dark demons of your subconscious were let loose, was terrifying.

He knew. He'd been there. That night in the village, in the jungle in 'Nam.

He'd lost control. Dark demons had been unleashed. All thanks to Sloan, the rogue CIA agent and his mind-wrenching drug. Even after two years, the nightmares were still with him. He couldn't let that happen to Bridget.

"C'mon, Bridge," he said, putting his arm around her and leading her up the steps to the club. "We're gonna ask our music-loving friend inside a few *questions*. And he better have some damn good answers."

THE BARTENDER WAS LOADING longneck bottles of Miller High Life beer into a stainless steel cooler under the bar.

"Hi," Mick said, leaning his elbows on the bar, "Where's Manny this morning?"

"What do I look like, the friggin' Yellow Pages?" the bartender snarled, hunched over the cooler.

Mick let the back of his hand sweep across two half-empty bottles of Schlitz. They tipped over, spilling flat, cold beer down the bartender's neck.

"God damn!" he yelled, straightening up and cracking his head on the edge of the bar.

"Sorry," Mick smiled. "I'm always really clumsy before I've had my morning coffee. Who knows what else might happen while I'm in this state?"

"What the hell do you want him for?" the bartender asked, rubbing his head and dabbing at his shirt with a handful of wet napkins.

"Well," Mick continued, "I left my guitar with him last night, when we had to leave in kind of a hurry." Mick's eyes locked on the bartender's. "I thought he might have some information about a few of the nice new *friends* we made here last night."

MANNY SILVA had a headache, and it wasn't even 10:00 a.m. yet.

The two reasons, Mick and Bridget, were standing in front of his cheap old steel desk in the club's back room. The room did double duty as office and storeroom for the more expensive, halfway decent booze that he didn't want his spaced-out performers and second-shift waitresses stealing.

He looked up at the pair in front of him and tried to keep his expression neutral.

They'd come in escorted by his shit-for-brains, lunch-shift bartender, who was gonna find himself an unemployed bartender before the night shift.

Mick, the kid with the don't-mess-with-me eyes, pulled one of the metal and vinyl folding chairs out, and with a deceptively gentle expression, motioned to his girlfriend to sit.

She sat down and smiled at Manny. He responded with an equally insincere smile.

What the hell game were these two playing? He was afraid he knew.

Mick stood behind his girlfriend's chair and put both hands on her shoulders. He smiled at Manny again.

Manuel Silva held up the big aluminum coffeepot near the edge of his desk. "You kids want coffee?"

"Thank you, no," the pretty green-eyed girl smiled, "I prefer tea meself."

"Yeah," her boyfriend smiled, not quite as nicely, "me too."

Sure you do, Manny thought.

He knew what had happened last night, and he knew that by now this pair of 'folk singers' was starting to figure it out, too.

Damn! Why the hell had he let those bastards talk him into... yeah, he knew why. And even worse, he knew who. And he wished he didn't. But Manny Silva, son of a Portuguese fisherman and a mother who had to clean bathrooms up at the Chatham Bars Inn, knew all about sucking it up and doing whatever had to be done. Whatever.

"So, what brings you two back? Oh, I know."

He got up from behind the desk, walked to the corner of the room, and pulled out a black padded canvas guitar case with a shoulder strap.

"You forgot this when you split last night."

"Yeah," Mick answered. "We were kind of in a hurry."

Manny Silva carefully leaned the guitar case against the desk and sat back down.

"So, you want to come back tonight? You guys are pretty good."

And it was almost true. Except he had a strong hunch they weren't any frigging folk singers.

He looked around at the booze-crowded back room. He had parlayed a small outdoor food stand in P-Town, serving *Linguica*, the spicy Portuguese sausage, and onions, into a restaurant. And then he'd bought a rundown clam shack on Route 28 in Falmouth, and ridden the folk music craze into a successful nightclub.

Every night, hundreds of college kids lined up with mommy and daddy's money in hand, to drink pitchers of watery beer and see the folk acts that he got for almost nothing. In another year or two, he'd be out from under *them*. Then he'd be free and clear. So, if he had to look the other way now and then, well...

"So, what d'ya say? Last night was audition night. Tonight it's fifty bucks and free beer. What d'ya think?"

"I think," Mick said, as he walked around the desk and sat down on the edge, still looking at Manny with his cold half-smile, "that I'd like some answers first."

"Like what?"

"Oh, maybe like, who do you suppose those guys in the black suits with pointy-toed loafers were?"

Manny tried to look puzzled, but the sweat started in his armpits.

"Shit, kid, if I paid attention to everyone who comes in here, I'd never get a single act on stage."

"Don't know 'em, huh?"

"Sorry."

Mick kept smiling and picked up a letter-opener off the desk. It was shaped like a miniature sword. He tried the point against his thumb.

"Sharp."

"I guess," Manny said warily.

"Never saw 'em before, huh?"

Manny shrugged.

"Want to see a trick? I learned it from a Viet Cong guerrilla, almost the hard way."

Manny pushed his chair away from the desk. He eased the left top drawer open and slid his hand in until it touched the butt of the .32 caliber Browning automatic, and—

"Shit!" The drawer slammed on his hand, and in the same instant, the needle-sharp point of the letter opener pressed against his throat.

"Anh chět," Mick grinned.

"Damn you!" Manny yelled.

"You know," Mick continued, "that's exactly what I said to the V.C. guerrilla when he did that to me. Anh chět."

"What the hell does that mean, you son of a bitch?"

"It means," Mick said, increasing the pressure on the letter opener at his throat, "you're dead."

"I'M SO SORRY, Mr. Silva," Bridget said as she finished wrapping a bar towel packed with ice around his rapidly swelling left hand. "He just gets a bit rambunctious when he's after something he feels needs knowing."

"Bastard," Manny mumbled under his breath.

"I'm sorry," Mick said smiling even wider. "This is my bad ear, so I'm afraid I missed the answer to the question I asked you. Would you mind repeating it?"

"Mick," Bridget said with mock severity. "Will you let the poor man collect his thoughts?"

"Collect away," Mick grinned.

"Look," Manny said. "I don't know the names of those guys." He sighed. "All I know is that I got a phone call right after you two played."

"From whom?" Mick said

"A guy. A guy in Providence, Rhode Island. A guy who owns a lot of property on the Cape."

"Including this club?"

"Yeah, part of it."

"What did he say?"

"He said to keep you kids around here until the two guys in black suits got here. You know, like have you guys play another set. Some free beers. Stuff like that."

"Stuff like slipping something into those free beers?" The grin was gone.

"No!" Manny shook his head. "I never did that. That was—"

"That was our new friend and fan, Marcy." Mick said. "The one with the long brown hair that falls over the table when she leans forward. Very pretty. Sort of like a light brown curtain. We could hardly even see the glasses when she filled them."

Manny's mouth closed into a hard, tight line.

"I want her full name and address," Mick said, picking up the letter opener again.

"I don't know her last name," Manny muttered.

Mick stood up.

"Bridge, why don't you go back out to the bar and see if the bartender can find you a cup of tea."

Manny stood up.

Bridget looked up at Mick and her expression turned worried.

"Mick. Mickey darlin', please, it's okay. We should just go. You don't need to do this on account of what happened to me."

She got up and put a hand on his shoulder.

Mick took her hand off his shoulder, but he never took his eyes off Manny.

"Yes," he said in a flat, cold voice. "I do."

THE SUN WAS almost fully overhead when Mick pointed his right forefinger toward the faded green signboard up ahead, warning the Chevy station wagon behind him that he was about to make a right turn.

He leaned the bike right and slowed as they entered a sandy, narrow blacktop lane, flanked by stunted sea-pines. He slowed and stopped in front of a gray-shingled, rambling Victorian farmhouse, surrounded by a sagging porch. He killed the motor and Bridget slid off the back.

He looked at the house and decided that it might have once been painted green. Now it was sea-gray.

"Who the hell would live in a house smack dab in the middle of Cape Cod?" he said, shaking his head. "Christ, this is about as far as you can get from any beach on the whole damn Cape!"

"People who can't afford to live anywhere else, I guess."

As it turned out, Manny didn't know Marcy's last name, just that she hung out with a lot of rich kids from Newport. But after Mick offered to show him another 'trick' that he'd learned from the V.C.,

Manny suddenly remembered that he did know one of the kids at the table, the heavyset girl with the red hair. As a matter of fact, she worked for him off and on, filling in when a waitress or one of the kitchen staff called in sick. He had her full name and address.

And this was it. Mick took off his jacket. It was hot here in the interior of the Cape, and getting hotter.

This was Dennis. Not Dennisport, where cool breezes blew in off Nantucket Sound, just Dennis, ten miles from the Sound to the south and from Cape Cod Bay to the north.

There were no sea breezes here, just the sound of crickets, the smell of scraggly pines, and sand.

Mick and Bridget climbed two gray, warped wooden steps and knocked on the faded screen door. Bare feet shuffled on the wood floor inside.

A figure appeared behind the screen, barely visible against the house's dark interior.

"Oh, like, wow! It's you!"

Chapter 13

Providence | Rhode Island

July 29, 1968 | 11:52 a.m.

"Siddown, kid," the heavyset man behind the big walnut desk said.

Cody Ewing looked around him.

Everything that had happened since that fast-talkin' Yankee lawyer had showed up in front of the cell yesterday afternoon and bailed him out was sort of a blur.

Hell, he thought for the hundredth time. *I'd have to be some dumb friggin' bastard to stay sittin' in that cell when there's some slick old boy with bail money in hand.*

So he'd gone with him.

Him and that lawyer had got into some big old limousine with dark windows and ridden up to a city that he thought must be Providence, 'cause that was the only city that was close to Newport.

He thought that maybe he'd get a chance to see it, but the limo had gotten off Route 195, turned down half a dozen side streets, and into a small underground parking garage.

The lawyer, still wearing a smile as bland as his gray pinstripe suit, had taken Cody into a small elevator and up to a big penthouse apartment.

The blinds had been drawn, and when Cody went to the bathroom to take a whiz and pulled the blinds up, the window underneath had black coverings on the outside.

The lawyer told him to make himself comfortable, that he was the guest of a really important man who he'd meet the next morning. And until then?

"Well," the lawyer said, "I think you'll be happiest staying right here. Nice and quiet."

He left a fella named Bobby to keep Cody company.

Bobby didn't say much and never smiled at all, so pretty soon, Cody gave up trying to talk to him.

Around the time his growling stomach told him it must be suppertime, a man with slicked-back hair and a white waiter's jacket brought him a great big old T-bone steak and a bottle of Jack Daniel's.

He finished the steak and the bottle, and that was all she wrote, until the lawyer woke him up this morning and brought him here to this man.

Wherever 'here' was. And whoever this was.

Then, 'whoever this was' spoke.

"So, kid, did you like the place? Chow okay? Booze?"

"Yes, sir," Cody answered. "Hell, I'd have to be pretty damn hard to please not to like T-bone steaks and J.D." Cody grinned. "But I gotta admit, I'm more used to drinkin' Rebel Yell."

"What the hell is that?"

"Just some old down-home Kentucky sour mash bourbon that's about all we can afford."

The heavyset man snapped his fingers. "Bobby, go pick up a couple bottles."

"Sure thing, Mr. C." The unsmiling man who shared the apartment with Cody last night left the room.

Mr. C. looked back at Cody.

Who the hell was he? What was this all about? Mr. C. sure didn't look like anyone from Harlan County. For one thing, his suit was too expensive. For another, he was too fat. Most everyone from down home was lean and rangy and rubbed raw from the elements and hard, dirty, unforgiving work.

No, they didn't look like this guy at all. Except around the eyes.

Yeah, he'd seen eyes like that before. On those old granite-faced moonshiners, way back up in the hills. They always kept one hard eye on the copper coil that dripped 'white lightning' corn mash, and the other on anyone stupid enough to cross their path without their say-so.

Yeah, that was where he'd seen eyes like these.

"Siddown." Mr. C. pointed to the lone chair in front of his desk.

It was not an invitation.

"So," he began with a smile that wasn't really a smile, "two nights ago, you met a hot-to-trot little blond chick. A rich broad, named Blair Prentiss Vanderwall."

Chapter 14

Dennis, Massachusetts | Cape Cod
July 29, 1968 | 12:12 p.m.

"Do your friends want anything to drink, Janet?" The tired-looking woman in the pink waitress uniform with the name *Sally* on her Clam Shack Bar and Grill name-tag stopped in the middle of the hot, dark living room and looked at her daughter.

"No, mom, we're fine."

Sally, the Clam Shack waitress, shrugged.

"Suit yourself. I'll be lugging drinks soon enough anyway." She paused with her hand on the screen door. "Don't forget to do the dishes."

"Sure, ma."

Another shrug, and the screen door slammed behind her.

Janet frowned and then brightened as she looked back at Mick and Bridget.

"Like, wow, you guys were really far out last night. And you know, you've got that thing going together, you know, like that chemistry thing. I mean, like, you give off these really good vibes, cause everyone can see that you really dig each other. It, like, comes through in your music. It makes me feel good. You know, like all warm and mellow."

She paused and looked down at the worn, sandy floorboards.

"Sometimes, I wish I had someone I could sing with like that. Or just maybe someone who…"

Mick shifted uncomfortably on the faded flower print couch.

Janet looked back up and asked, "So, why did you come here?"

"We're looking for someone," Bridget said.

"Who?"

"Two girls," Mick answered.

"I've been told they're very pretty," Bridget added.

"Yeah," Mick said. "Cody Ewing, who could wind up hanging out in the Newport lock-up on a permanent basis, said they were with Blair Vanderwall when he met her at Father's. It seems that Miss Vanderwall could have been a model. Drop-dead gorgeous, beautiful, and—"

"And," Janet said in the sad and bitter voice of the picked-on-once-too-often, "one of the cruelest little bitches that ever drew breath."

Bridget got up and sat down on the edge of the small, worn hassock, next to the dumpy, red-haired girl in the faded 'Flower Power' T-shirt.

"Was she mean?" Bridget whispered. "Did she say things that she knew would hurt you? In places that she knew would hurt most?"

"How did you know?"

"Because I go to a school that's chock full of Blair Vanderwalls, darlin'," Bridget said.

She put an arm around Janet.

"Once," Janet began in a barely audible voice, "we were having this party at Jackie Trainor's parents' house up in Chatham. Oh, it's so beautiful up there," she sighed. Then her eyes hardened again. "Anyway, in case you haven't noticed, I got kinda this weight problem."

Bridget squeezed her shoulder.

"So I bought this new kind of dress that's sort of loose and all. It's called a muumuu. Hawaiian, I think. It was all red, flowers and birds and everything. And I thought I looked really nice."

A tiny drop of water oozed from one of her eyes and trickled down her chubby cheek.

"Everyone was dancing to the records and having fun and everything. And then this song came on."

She stopped and looked past Mick and Bridget. She shook her head, in the manner of people who seem to know that they were born to be hurt, but don't know why.

"And Blair, beautiful, 'drop-dead-gorgeous,' popular, golden-girl Blair Prentiss Vanderwall said in front of the whole party, 'Why, Janet, this must be your new theme song. "Red Rubber Ball."'"

The tears made their way down Janet's face and collected at the corner of her mouth. She turned to Bridget and said in a bewildered voice, "Why did she have to do that? She had everything. Why did she have to make me feel bad?"

Bridget shook her head and said bitterly, "There's some people who, no matter how much they have, can't live in this world without crushing small things underfoot."

"And if it's any consolation," Mick added grimly, "Miss Vanderwall isn't gonna be crushing anything underfoot anymore."

"Mickey, don't," Bridget said.

"It seems that someone else, maybe even someone in your group, wasn't a fan of Miss Vanderwall's brand of humor," Mick said looking pointedly at Janet.

"You don't think I… I mean, that I would have… I mean, even when she was mean and made fun of me, all I ever wanted was for her to like me."

She turned toward Bridget.

"Don't you understand? I would have given my life gladly to be her for just one day." The tears squeezed out from behind her eyelids again. "I still would."

Bridget reached into the pocket of her jeans and brought out a crumpled pink tissue. Janet blew her nose then wiped her eyes on her T-shirt.

"Janet," Bridget said, "we need your help. Cody's been charged with the killin' of Blair. We need to find the people who were with her that night when she left the club."

"That's easy," Janet said. "I left the club early two nights ago, but I can tell you who was with Blair. She never went anywhere without the co-presidents of her own personal fan club. If you're looking for suspects in our group, start with the two 'runners-up' to Blair for queen of the bitches. Valerie Cortland and Jackie Trainer."

"Was there anyone else, Janet?" Bridget asked.

"Yeah," Mick said. "Preferably someone a little more open and a little less sleazy than the bunch you were with last night."

Janet frowned for a moment then smiled. "As a matter of fact, yeah. You ought ta go see Suzy Cantrell. She's a real talker. She's okay, I guess, just blabbers to everyone about anything almost non-stop. She used to spend a lot of time there and was at the club that night."

"What do you mean 'used to'"?

"Her boyfriend Chet always brought her there and they sat with a bunch of really snooty, obnoxious prep school and Ivy League types. But I don't think she'll be hanging out there any more."

"Why?"

"She and Chet had a big fight that night and he dumped her. She started crying and yelling so two of the guys at the table took her outside to calm down. A few minutes later, Blair and that cowboy left the club together."

"And the two guys that went outside with Suzy?"

"Only one of them came back in."

For a moment the only sound in the hot dim room was the buzzing of a bluebottle fly beating its wings against the screen.

Then Mick said, "Who were they, Janet? Do you have names?"

"No—sorry." She said a little too quickly.

Bridget leaned forward. "Janet, this is really important."

"I told you." She mumbled looking at the floor, "I—I don't know 'em."

Mick clenched his fists and then forced himself to relax. "Okay, then how about this Suzy Cantrell. Do you know where she lives?"

"No-o-o..." Suddenly she brightened. "But I do know where she works. At a funky new club down on the waterfront in Newport. The White Rabbit."

"That's almost back where we're staying, Mickey."

"What about Valerie and Jackie?"

"Valerie lives in Newport but I'm not sure where Jackie is living for the summer. You could try her parents' place in Chatham."

"Do you have that address?" Mick asked

The expression on Janet's face darkened.

"Yeah," she said bitterly. "How could I ever forget it?"

Bridget turned her head slightly, motioning Mick to go outside.

"Ah, I think I'll fire up the bike and..."

Bridget's eyebrow lowered a fraction in agreement.

"And, ah, give me a minute or two to adjust the carbs, and then we'll be good to go."

"Sure luv," Bridget smiled.

Mick pushed open the old screen door and let it slap shut behind him.

Bridget turned back to Janet.

"Let's give him a few minutes to play with his machine. Sit with me, please."

Bridget touched her hand and Janet shuddered uncertainly.

"Janet. Can you help us? Me?"

She sensed that something smoldered just beneath the surface of this wary, wounded girl. "Is there anything else you can tell me about

Blair? Especially how she was with the boys she loved and—"

Janet drew a great ragged breath. "She never loved a boy!" she burst out.

Bridget pulled back. "Really? But I'd heard—"

"No," Janet said, "not really. Not love the way that… the way that you and Mick… No. Blair Prentiss Vanderwall was incapable of love. But… but," she bent her head and beat her pudgy fists on the old chipped coffee table, "she had the power to make others love her. Oh yes, she could sure as hell do that."

She leaned forward and let the tears flow. Bridget put both arms around her. "Shush darlin', it's all right. I understand. Love's sorta like a lobster pot, isn't it? Easy to get into, but kinda tough to get out of."

Janet smiled through the tears and then wiped her eyes on the sleeve of her T-shirt. "Thanks, Bridget."

"Now, tell me how Blair treated the boys she went with. Did she make one of them desperate and mad enough to murder her?"

Janet laughed bitterly. "You could say that. She played with them, like a cat with a mouse. First the teasing, the torment, and then when the fun of torture turned to boredom, the humiliation and destruction."

"When, where?" Bridget asked.

Janet sighed. "The last time was that night in the club. The last night any of us saw her alive."

"Who was the victim that night?"

Janet looked into Bridget's eyes as if searching. Then her eyes dropped and she looked at her chewed-down fingernails.

"I can't tell you his name. But in typical Blair fashion, she did her best to make him feel bad. She sashayed by his table and blew him a kiss as she left arm-in-arm with your friend the banjo player."

Chapter 15

Chatham, Massachusetts | Cape Cod

July 29, 1968 | 2:11 p.m.

"Sorry, Mrs. Trainor," Sam Jordan said. "But that little foreign job you bought your daughter is gonna need a whole new clutch assembly."

"And how much is that going to be?"

"Well," Sam said, scratching the back of his balding, sunburned head. "Probably around three to four hundred dollars."

"Well," Mrs. Sarah Bennett Trainor said in her 'I-am-not-pleased' voice, "I would hope that with all the business my husband gives you with that silly Jaguar machine of his, you could put one tiny little sports car in proper working order for less than that."

Sam Jordan, owner of Mid-Cape Sports Cars, decided not to launch into his standard speech about having to 'baby' British sports cars and said instead, "Well, that white MGB you bought Jackie is a beautiful little machine. Just like her owner, if you don't mind my saying so."

Mrs. Sarah Bennett Trainor's expression told him that she did mind.

"Please take it away, and bring it back when it's all fixed."

"Ah, sure, Mrs. Trainor. And what do you want me to do about the stripped clutch?"

"Whatever is necessary, Mr. Jordan. Good day."

Sam knew when he'd been dismissed. "Frigging rich people from New York," he muttered under his breath as he marched down the long, crushed seashell driveway. Everyone south of Rhode Island was a snotty New Yorker, as far as Sam Jordan was concerned. But what really pissed Sam off was that he had to take it, play the humble tradesman to the

Trainors' money and power, when what he really wanted to do was to tell that arrogant bitch Mrs. Trainor that she could take her daughter and the little white MGB and shove them up…

Sam jumped back as a big metallic blue motorcycle roared up the driveway.

"Goddamnit. Watch where the hell you're going, you goddamn hippies!"

The guy on the motorcycle pulled up sharp, ten feet past Sam.

"Hey, man, sorry," he called over his shoulder. "I thought you were one of them."

Sam looked to where the guy with the insolent grin was pointing, and his face became as red as the coats on the jockey statuettes that flanked the long driveway.

Sam Jordan shook his head and continued on down the driveway.

"DO YOU REALLY THINK Mrs. Trainor will tell us anything?" Bridget asked, gracefully sliding off the BSA's rear seat and smoothing her skirt.

"Well, I don't know where else to find Jackie and Valerie's whereabouts. According to Janet, Mama Trainor is another 'Cliffie' Alumnus. So all you've gotta do is give out with a little snobby high class chit-chat while I—"

"May I help you?" a frosty-cold voice behind Mick and Bridget asked.

Mick climbed off the motorcycle. "Mrs. Trainor?" he asked.

"And who are you?"

Mick drew a deep breath. This was going to call for strategy. Time to trot out the big guns.

"Good afternoon, Mrs. Trainor," Mick enunciated, calling on almost sixteen years of Harvard and Andover private school education. "My name is Michael Parker Prescott," he said, with the almost natural snobbery of the best of the Boston Brahmins. "And this," he said, taking hold of Bridget's hand and lifting it as if to escort her to the dance floor, "is Miss Brenda Wexford."

Bridget's eyebrows shot up.

"Brenda met your charming daughter at the Harvard/Yale game last fall, and Jackie said that if we were ever down in Chatham, we just had to stop by."

"Well, of course," Sarah Trainor nodded as a lifetime of carefully controlled breeding and good manners took over.

"YOUR HOME is absolutely divine, Mrs. Trainor," the newly christened 'Brenda Wexford' commented in a low, throaty, and decidedly English upper class accent.

Oh, Bridge, Mick thought, *you should be on the stage.*

Bridget sipped her iced tea and made inane upper class chitchat with Mrs. Sarah Trainor.

"Ah, excuse me Mrs. Trainor," Mick asked, "but might there be a washroom that one could use?"

"Of course," she replied with an airy wave of her hand. "Straight through the living room, down the hallway and the third door on the left."

Mick got up and nonchalantly strolled through the elegantly decorated living room of the gigantic 'summer house.'

"So, you go to Radcliffe, Brenda?" He heard Mrs. Trainor ask sweetly.

"Oh, yes," Bridget/Brenda answered with an insipid smile. "It's lovely, and I do enjoy it so."

Mick laughed soundlessly behind Sarah Trainor's back and blew Bridget a big, phony kiss. She was gonna kill him when they got out of here.

Better make good use of the time and find what they'd come for. He slowly backed up to the mantelpiece and worked his way along. Lots of expensive, useless knickknacks, tarnished silver trophies, tennis—mixed doubles—1955; Newport Mid-Class Regatta, July 4, 1957.

Newport. Hmmmm…

"And then, of course, there's the wonderful lecture series on Renaissance and Baroque art."

Atta-girl, Bridge. Keep the old Ivy League trout occupied.

He blew Bridget another kiss. Yep, she was definitely gonna kill him.

Get going, Mick, he told himself.

He moved to the end of the mantelpiece. There they were. High school—strike that—*prep* school graduation pictures of Jackie (Jacqueline) Trainor.

Nice lookin' chick. Familiar?

He shook his head. Not what we're here for. He moved on from the end of the mantelpiece, to the floor-to-ceiling bookcase.

Mick ran his hand over the rich cherry wood. It smelled of beeswax, polish, and decades of wealth and salt air. Mick moved down the bookcase. He knew what he was looking for.

Every parent kept photos of their kids in the living room, and sometimes, when a kid had a really special group of friends—

Bingo! A graduation photo of Jackie Trainor next to two other beautiful, privileged and pampered heiresses to all the best that life had to offer. Valerie Cortland, and, of course a girl who could only be Blair Prentiss Vanderwall. Mick picked up the photo and studied it for a moment. Blair Vanderwall had a beautiful face, no question about that. Flawless, creamy complexion with the bare minimum of makeup. Sparkling white teeth set off by provocative hot pink lipstick and the entire dazzling package crowned by what he was sure was completely natural honey-blond hair.

But it was the eyes. He couldn't not look at them. They were *electric* blue.

Those eyes must have had the power to turn every man, woman and child who fell under their spell into her willing slave. Yeah, and she knew it too. There was something else in those electric blue eyes.

Cruelty.

The expressions of the two girls on either side of her showed that they acknowledged her power. Interesting. A group photo in the Trainor home of three best friends at graduation. All very normal.

Except that the person in the middle, dominating the photo, was not Jackie Trainor, but Blair Vanderwall.

He forced himself to study the expression on Jackie Trainor's face. Was that admiration and worship behind her eyes, pale and washed out by the radiance of Blair's? Or was it something else? Like envy.

Chapter 16

Newport | Rhode Island | Nickerson Way
July 29, 1968 | 7:16 p.m.

"God damn you, McCarthy," Bridget yelled. "I'm gonna bloody kill you!"

"I know," he whispered, kissing her on the tip of the nose.

Her anger ran out of her like air from a punctured balloon.

She shook her head and sighed. "Brenda Wexford? Where in the name of all the saints did you ever dig that one up from?"

"From you! Didn't you tell me about visiting your old man when he was being held by the 'specials' in Wexford prison? And the Brenda part, well, I just threw that in for free."

"Lord give me strength." Bridget shook her head.

"But, my divine Miss 'Society' Brenda Wexford…" Bridget made a face and he kissed her on the nose again. "Your forty minutes of inane conversation were worth it. Look!"

Mick produced a color photo from the top pocket of his denim jacket.

"So, that's them?"

"Yep."

"You stole it!"

"Yep again."

"Well, all right, Mr. Smart Tough-guy Detective, then just give a listen to what I found out about them three friends from Mrs. Trainor, and especially the earful she gave me about our Miss Blair Prentiss Vanderwall!"

"Okay, let's hear it." Mick stripped off his denim jacket, rolled it into a ball, and tossed it into the tiny closet of their tiny bedroom. "What dirt did you dig up while I was checking out their living room?"

"Stealin' their family photos," Bridget sniffed.

"Gathering evidence," Mick said piously. "Now what did Mama Trainor have to say about the late and strangely unlamented Blair Vanderwall."

"Well," Bridget began. "Mrs. Trainor told me as how her older daughter Jackie seemed to worship the ground Blair walked on. Did everything Blair told her to do. Even things that weren't very nice."

"Like what?" Mick asked, pulling off his T-shirt. He held it up to his nose and frowned. He held the worn, olive drab piece of cloth in front of Bridget's nose. "Do you think this smells too bad?"

"Yes!" Bridget snapped, pushing his hand away. "Change it, fer pity's sake. I swear, McCarthy, fer a lad raised in prep schools, you've got the hygiene of a barnyard animal."

"Ha," Mick responded. "You've obviously never smelled a boy's prep school on Saturday night."

"No," she made a face, "and I hope I never do! Now, will you bloody pay attention!"

"All right, so Jackie Trainor was Blair's little puppet. Which, by the way, sounds like the perfect recipe for some serious resentment."

Bridget sat back down on the edge of the narrow bed and paused for effect.

"Well, first of all Mrs. Trainor let it out that she never had been able to 'warm up' to Blair. Even though Blair was very polite and came from the best of families, she always felt there was something cold and calculating about her. As though she knew everyone's secret weakness and how to use it to manipulate them—especially Jackie—to get what she wanted. And then it was like Mrs. Trainor realized she was saying more that she'd intended and tried to gloss it over by talking about how she'd been schoolmates with Blair's mother, so she was sure that deep down Blair was really all right."

Bridget stuck her nose in the air and did a perfect impression of Mrs. Trainor's affected finishing school accent. "After all, Miss Wexford, she does come from one of the best families in the Northeast."

Mick clapped his hands and Bridget giggled.

"Bravo *Miss Wexford*, splendid performance. Now if you could please get back to the juicy tidbits about the 'not very nice things.' You've got me panting with anticipation."

Bridget raised one eyebrow. "Really? You pant mighty easy, McCarthy."

"Must be your proximity, sweet thing." Mick sat down on the bed and began walking his fingers up her leg.

"Do you want to hear the story or not?"

"Can we make it a bedtime story?"

Bridget took his wandering hand off her leg and smiled. "Maybe later—if you're a very good boy and pay attention to all the lovely clues I'm about to lay out…"

Mick sighed.

"Well," she continued, "whenever Blair wanted to break up with a boy, it seems she wanted him to suffer. So she'd tell Jackie to go flirtin' with the boy and get him to kissin' her and makin' out, and then, just when he was nicely on the boil, Little Miss Blair would walk in on the two of them, give the poor lad a brutal dressing down, and then tell him she never wanted to see him again."

"Mrs. Trainor told you *that?*"

"Well, no. She kind of clammed up when she realized that she'd probably said too much about the daughter of one of her 'dear friends.'

I got this part from Janet. When you went out to start the bike, she told me that she thought it might be someone Blair had hurt real bad, someone who could have been mad and jealous enough to kill her."

"Did she have any idea who?"

"I got the feeling she had someone in mind but was afraid to say."

"Afraid to say or just didn't want us asking any more personal questions that might have hit too close to home."

"Mickey, you don't really think Blair's devoted little acolyte could have done away with the object of her affection."

"Let me ask you a question," Mick countered. "When does love turn to hate? And how long does a 'sock puppet' stay docile and dependant, before she decides to cut not only the strings that bind her, but the cruel puppeteer herself?"

"I'm sorry but I just can't believe that poor little Janet had it in her to murder Blair. Now on the other hand, her mate Marcy—well that's a different story isn't it then? She was only too willing to play her part in getting rid of us."

"Did Janet say anything else about Blair's staged break-ups?"

"Yes. Blair would laugh at the boy and tell him that he was pathetic and a loser and that she'd never loved him anyway."

"A first class bitch," Mick shook his head, still staring at the electric blue eyes.

"And that's not the worst of it," Bridget said, leaning forward. "She always pulled this little trick in a very public place, so that her victim would feel utterly humiliated. Places like a party, a dance, or in a club!"

Mick raised his eyebrows.

"A club like—"

"Father's! And not less than the night before she was murdered!"

Bridget laughed and clapped her hands. She jumped up from the bed and pirouetted on the left toe of her tiny black boot. She dropped into an elaborate curtsy in front of Mick, and said, "So there, Mr. Detective McCarthy, I practically solved yer case for you."

"Not so fast, Agatha Christie." Mick paced back and forth. "We've got no proof. We don't even know the jilted mystery boy's name."

Bridget sat back down on the bed.

"No," she said slowly. "Janet insisted she didn't know. But if he was at the club that night, one of the Valerie-Jackie crowd's bound to know. We've just got to keep after those kids. Now just listen up to what I put together," she said leaning forward. "You know you're not the only one who can find things out from photographs."

"Come on," Mick smiled. "Give."

"Well, while we were talkin', I happened to notice this nice photo on the coffee table of two girls who looked enough alike to be—"

"Sisters." Mick finished.

"Yes!" Bridget cried, jumping up from the bed. "And of course you know what that younger sister's name is."

Mick nodded his head. "Marcy. The girl with the long brown hair at the club in Falmouth."

Bridget's normally warm, sea-green eyes turned into hard, sharp emerald chips of ice as she said grimly, "She and I have got a score to settle."

"Leave that kind of crap to me," Mick said, setting her back down on the bed.

"Michael McCarthy, I am the daughter of an IRA Major, and we settle our own grievances, in our own way."

Mick looked at the woman he loved and thought, *Christ, I wouldn't want to be Marcy Trainor.*

"Okay, but first, we've got to find the Trainor sisters. So, I'm afraid it's back to Falmouth, and Father's."

"Maybe not, McCarthy," Bridget smiled.

"What? Your crystal ball's working overtime tonight?"

"No, but I can be just as good as you when it comes to ferreting out clues."

"I'm all ears."

"Well, it just so happens that when I was chitchattin' with Mrs. Trainor, she let slip as how she'd be a whole lot happier if Jackie wasn't spending the summer so far from her mama's place in Chatham."

"Where is she?" Mick asked.

"Right here in Newport!" Bridget answered triumphantly.

"Nice work, Nancy Drew," Mick smiled. "However, there's a lot of people in Newport for the festival, and it's not like we have an—"

"Address?" Bridget gave Mick a Cheshire cat grin as she held up a pale yellow envelope with pink and blue flowers on it.

"Is that what I think it is?"

"Well, if you're thinkin' that it just might be a letter from one of the Trainor sisters to their mama, and that it just might have a return address in Newport on it, well, then, you just might be right."

"And how did you happen to come by this fortunate piece of correspondence, my dear, amazing Miss Connolly?"

"Why, I just took a lesson from my own true love." She smiled and threw her arms around Mick's neck. "I stole it!"

Chapter 17

East Providence, Rhode Island
July 29, 1968   8:02 p.m.

Cody waited outside Mr. C.'s office. He hadn't enjoyed their first meeting earlier that morning, and he was pretty damn sure he was going to enjoy this one even less. He had a jittery feeling in the pit of his stomach, and sitting around the apartment with the blacked-out windows all day hadn't done much to improve his state of mind.

He got up from the single wooden chair in the bare hallway and paced. He never could stand to be cooped up, even as a kid. He remembered how this girl from Covington he'd gone out with a few times had told him once that he had claustrophobia. And he supposed it must be true. After all, she'd gone to the community college for close to two years, so she must've known what she was talking about.

He paced faster. Damn! What was this all about, anyway? Why had that Mr. C. asked him about Blair Vanderwall? They didn't think *he* killed her, did they? His heart beat faster. He wiped sweat from his palms on the legs of his jeans.

He looked at the bare gray cinder-block walls. Not even a window. The narrow hallway was close and small and mean. It made him feel like one of those cats that the two piggy-eyed, narrow-foreheaded Garnett twins had used to catch back in Gravel Switch, Kentucky. They sat there behind the feed and grain store all day long, knowing that the town's stray cats would come sniffin' around after the rats that the grain attracted. Them Garnett boys would grin and slobber after they caught half a dozen cats and locked 'em in that big wooden feedbox without any light or air. And they'd giggle and poke one another as the poor ol' cats yelled and screeched inside. And then they'd taken it down to the creek, and…

He'd fought them once.

He was just ten. And even though Pa didn't like cats around the house, Cody had picked up a little gray and white cat out back of the feed and grain store, and made it a little bed on some old sacks, and brought it milk in a cracked teacup he found in the barn. He even made it a collar, using some red ribbon from his Ma's sewing basket. And he wrote the kitten's name on a piece of cardboard from a crackerjack box. He named the kitten Toby. He didn't know why, he just kinda liked the name.

And the scrawny little kid that he was had loved the scrawny little cat. They seemed right for each other. That is, until the Garnett twins had found Toby.

He'd come straight from school to the back of the feed store, just in time to see the Garnett boys moving off with their box of mewling, howling things.

He'd known right away.

"Where's Toby?" he asked in a voice too high and thin to carry much menace.

Vance Garnett answered him back in a voice that carried plenty. "Who the fuck wants to know, you little piss-ant?"

"You got 'im in that box," Cody said, curling his small hands into fists. "You let 'im out, or I'll…"

"You'll what, you little piece of pig shit?" Willard Garnett laughed.

"I'll smash your stupid face in. You… you goat fuckin', inbred son of a bitch!"

Cody had heard his daddy call a guy that just before he'd gotten stomped outside of the Lucky Spot Bar and Grill up in Parkersville.

It hadn't been a good idea for his daddy, and it hadn't been a good idea for Cody either. They both got the tar wailed out of them.

As a matter of fact, the only thing that kept Cody from getting his brains beat out by those sadistic mothers was his cousin Smitty showin' up.

Smitty had kicked Vance in the balls and broken a two-by-four over Willard's head.

Damn, Cody thought. *I do love that ol' boy.*

And he wished like hell that cousin Smitty was here right now.

The door opened and Cody jumped. A squat, nasty looking little guy motioned for Cody to come in. He wiped his hands on his jeans again and walked into the room.

"C'mon in, kid, siddown," the harsh nasal voice rumbled. "Christ, you look as nervous as a friggin' virgin on prom night."

Cody didn't know if he looked nervous or not, but decided that if he wasn't, he probably should be. So he shut up and sat down. It had been a very strange and spooky day.

"So, Codeine."

"It's Cody, sir."

"Yeah, whatever."

Mr. C. made a small gesture with his diamond-ringed pinkie, and two of the guys in the shiny dark suits with pointy-toed loafers appeared on either side of Cody's chair.

"So, how would ya like to make some big bucks, kid?"

"I'd like it better than a poke in the eye with a sharp stick." Cody shrugged.

"The kid's a comedian," the fat man said to the two suits. "Okay, Mr. Comic, want to see something that will really crack you up?"

Mr. C. paused and reached into the top drawer of the desk. "This will put a big friggin' grin on your face."

He pulled out an envelope and pushed it across the desk. Cody picked it up slowly and looked inside. It was filled with hundred dollar bills.

"What's this for?" Cody asked.

"For keeping your goddamn mouth shut!" the fat man snarled.

"I don't get it," Cody said.

"Then listen up, cracker. On Monday morning, you're gonna show up in the Newport County courthouse, with our own Mr. Parmenter here." He smiled up at the distinguished looking, silver-haired man standing behind Cody's chair.

"The judge is gonna ask you how you plead to the charge of murdering this Blair Vanderwall chick. And you know how you're gonna plead, kid?" The close-set eyes narrowed as they bore into Cody.

Cody shook his head.

"You're gonna plead 'nolo contendere.'"

"What the hell is that?"

"It means you ain't saying yes, and you ain't saying no. You know why?"

"No, sir."

"Cause you was so messed up with booze and dope that you don't know nothin.' And anyway, kid, that's about right, ain't it?"

Cody mumbled, "I don't remember much, but I know I never could've killed that girl."

"Who the fuck said you did? Listen, you do like you're told, our friend, lawyer Parmenter there, will plead you down to six months in the county lockup, and when you get out, there'll be another envelope waiting for you with another ten grand in it. That's a total of twenty grand for laying around some county joke jail and watching TV all day. Think about it, kid."

"I don't know, Mr. . . ."

"Mr. C., kid."

"Well, Mr. C., it's just that I don't much like bein' cooped up."

Mr. C. looked at Cody and compressed his lips for a moment. Then he smiled and snapped his fingers.

"Bobby, bring our young friend here a drink. What was that booze I told you to get when he was in here this morning?"

"Re-Rebel—Screamer?" Bobby answered.

"Did you get it?" Mr. C.'s voice was softer, more menacing.

"Ah, no, Mr. C. I tried, but, uhm, they were all out of it."

"How could they be all out of it, if you didn't even know what the fuck it was called?"

Bobby took a step backwards.

"I… I dunno, Mr. C."

"Hey, kid," the fat man looked back at Cody. "You said you don't like being cooped up, huh?"

Cody nodded slowly.

Mr. C. looked from Cody back up to Bobby and then returned his gaze to Cody.

"You wanna know something that's a whole lot worse than bein' cooped up?"

Cody didn't want to know, but Mr. C. continued. "Whadda you think it is, Bobby?"

Sweat ran down Bobby's forehead, but he didn't raise his hand to wipe it. "I don't know, Mr. C.," he whispered hoarsely.

The man known only as Mr. C. smiled and raised his right hand from underneath the desk. It held a .380 automatic with a two and a half inch silencer screwed into the barrel.

He locked eyes with Cody as he pulled the trigger, blowing a fist-sized hole in Bobby's chest.

"Being dead," he whispered.

Chapter 18

Newport, Rhode Island | Christie's Wharf
July 29, 1968 | 9:07 p.m.

Janet wondered if she had made another mistake, in a long line of stupid mistakes that seemed to be the story of her life. She'd gotten tired of driving her beat-up old VW around the waterfront bar area, looking for that elusive, probably nonexistent, parking place.

So she'd said, "The hell with it," and parked in the deserted boatyard lot halfway between the restaurant on Christie's Wharf and the welcoming lights of the bar where she was supposed to meet Marcy and Paul and the rest of the group.

Even though it was the end of July, Janet shivered as a fog-cool wind blew in off the harbor. The dank salt wind carried the smell of low tide, old used-up fishing boats and rock-strung seaweed.

Black-green seaweed. Just like the seaweed that had been covering up the beautiful, bone-white body of—Oh, God! The memory was sharp and jagged like broken glass in her stomach.

How could she have let… or gone along with…?

God, she thought, now shivering for real. *I know she was a horrible bitch to me most of the time. But every once in a while, she would almost act like she liked me.*

Oh, how Janet had lived for those brief, sweet moments when Blair's cruel-cat persona would drop away, and she'd smile and put a beautiful perfumed arm around her chunky shoulders and laugh, "Oh Janet, my little pudge-bunny. I do love you so. You just crack me up."

Then she'd kiss Janet on the cheek and giggle, "Incense and peppermints."

And Janet's heart would almost break with love as she whispered back, "Incense and peppermints, Blair."

Janet stopped and leaned her forehead against the fog-slimy bricks of the alley wall that separated the boatyard parking lot from the street.

"Oh, Blair," she murmured, the name catching in her throat, "I'm so sorry. I should have warned you. I could see it coming. I thought you knew. You always seemed to know everything and how to handle everyone. I should have said something. Oh, please believe me Blair. I never wanted… I, I just loved you."

Almost blinded by hot, bitter tears, she stumbled down the alley toward the street. She moaned softly, "Blair, I'm sorry, so sorry. I just loved you. I'll always love you."

She looked up at the dim, crescent moon that poked in and out from behind wisps of fog.

"Can you hear me, Blair? Oh, Blair," she moaned to the dank, sea-bottom wind that followed her down the alleyway. "I wish I could be with you!"

The half-prayer, half-curse froze on her lips as a hollow sounding voice answered out of the fog.

"I think that can be arranged."

110 Chestnut St. | 9:33 p.m.

"There it is, Mickey, number 110," Bridget said, leaning close to Mick's ear and pointing to a three-story, faded red clapboard building.

Mick slowed the bike and coasted to a stop in front of a psychedelically painted storefront window, covered with images of peace symbols and hash pipes. A red and gold hand-painted sign over the door read The Trucking Turtle Head Shop.

Mick looked up at the image of the winking cartoon turtle holding a joint and laughed. "Well, I guess this is the perfect location for that bunch of burnout hippies we met at Father's last night."

"I'm not so sure about the burnout part," Bridget murmured as she walked past him to a recessed door on the far side of the building. "Here it is." She pointed at the faded blue card decorated with flowers. "Apartment 3-B." She held up the 'borrowed' envelope and matched the return address.

"Temporary home of Miss Marcy Trainor and friends," Bridget said in a cold, soft voice.

Mick stood quietly beside her for a minute then put his arm around her rigid shoulders.

"Okay, babe, let's go have a nice little chat with Miss Trainor and 'friends.' Who knows, maybe we can pour her a drink."

"SHE'S NOT HERE."

People were dancing in the room behind the half-open door. The smell of pot and sandalwood incense wafted out past the stocky kid in a dirty Arizona State sweatshirt who was blocking the door to Apartment 3-B.

Mick stiffened but Bridget squeezed his hand and shook her head in a gesture of warning.

Mick let his breath out slowly. "That's cool," he shrugged. "Mind if we come in? Actually, we were looking for Marcy's friend too, you know, tall, long blond hair."

"You mean PJ?"

"Yeah," Mick smiled. "That's right, PJ."

"Hey, Paul!" the stocky kid called back, "you got some friends here."

The only response was a blast from the stereo as Country Joe and the Fish asked the musical question, 'what are we fighting for?'

Mick paused halfway through the door and thought bitterly back to his never-to-be-forgotten nightmare in the jungles of Vietnam. "Yeah, what the hell were we fighting for? For the colonel and 'Black Ops', and…"

Bridget's arm slipped around his waist and she pulled his head down close to her lips. "Don't, Mickey. Leave it there, darlin'. Cody Ewing needs you to be here, to help clear him. And I need you, too. And Mickey?"

"What, babe?"

"I'll always be here for you. Always."

"C'mon. Let's find our 'pal' PJ."

THE SHADOW STOOD over the lump of flesh that had been a sad, red-haired girl. The dark fluid that leaked out from a dozen knife punctures looked like puddles of black tar in the fog-shrouded alley gloom.

She had only screamed once, and barely fought back, almost as if she welcomed death. The alley shadow was only too happy to supply it.

The shadow shook a long, silver stiletto which it held in its left hand, and drops of black blood splattered the damp alley walls.

The shadow bent down to the corpse and almost tenderly ran the bloody blade through the frizzy red hair. When the blade was clean, the shadow pressed a large silver button on the stiletto's ivory handle, and the five-and-a-half-inch blade retracted with a soft *snick*.

The shadow paused for one more moment over the body, whispering to the dead girl.

"Give my love to Blair when you see her."

Clouds covered the moon again, and when they passed, the figure had faded back into the fog.

MICK AND BRIDGET made their way through the tightly packed living room of apartment 3-B on Chestnut Street.

"Have you seen PJ?" Mick yelled at a girl in a long black velvet dress and a 1920s beaded hat and scarf.

"In the kitchen, man." She pointed to the rear of the apartment without missing a beat as she danced.

Mick turned around to take Bridget's hand. She was trying to disentangle herself from a kid in a URI T-shirt. Mick moved closer.

The kid said, "C'mon. Just one dance. Like, you really turn me on." The guy clamped one sweaty hand on her butt and pulled her close with the other.

"Oh, I'd love to, darlin', just let me ask my old man here. You know, he used to ride with the Hell's Angels, and gets so terrible jealous. Why, do you know what he did to the last guy that asked me to dance?"

URI T-shirt shook his head slowly and started backing away, but Bridget leaned forward and whispered in his ear. The guy mumbled something back and disappeared into the crowd.

Mick hooked his thumbs into his brown, hand-tooled leather belt as Bridget looped her arm through his.

"What the hell did you say to him?" Mick asked.

"Why, nothing much, darlin'," Bridget answered breezily.

"Then why did he turn that pasty green color and make tracks for the door?"

"Well, I just told him what my Hell's Angels boyfriend had done to the last guy who'd asked me to dance."

"And?" Mick raised an eyebrow.

"And," Bridget's eyes twinkled, "I told him that my nasty old boyfriend had cut the guy's you-know-whats off and made them into earrings for me. And then," she giggled, "I asked him if he'd like to see them!"

"SO, PJ, REMEMBER ME?"

PJ did remember that voice, and barely had time to mutter "shit" under his breath before an arm clamped down, just a little too hard, on his shoulders.

PJ turned around slowly, telling himself to keep cool, and looked into a pair of gray-blue eyes just a few inches lower than his own.

The face that looked back at him was, at first, an ordinary face. Curly brown hair spilled over the forehead. Eyebrows looked like they'd been bleached by tropical sun more than once. And the nose looked as if it had been broken, also more than once. A mouth framed by weather-beaten, chapped lips smiled without warmth or humor. The thin, blue-white line of a scar ran from just under the left cheekbone down to the corner of the mouth. He had a feeling that it wasn't a scar left over from some childhood playground accident.

But it was the strange, shifting gray-blue eyes that got to him most of all. It seemed like they could be nice, friendly eyes. Could be, but weren't. They were cold as a pair of granite tombstone chips.

The cold-eyed guy grabbed his arm and squeezed. PJ winced and looked at the petite pixie standing next to him. Her eyes were almond shaped, a deep emerald green with tiny flecks of gold, almost like a cat's eyes.

The green eyes were neither warm nor cold; they just watched him.

"Like I was saying, PJ, you must remember us. At the club last night? Why, hell, didn't you buy us a round?"

Sweat trickled down PJ's back.

"As a matter of fact, that cute girl you were with, the one with real long brown hair, even poured it for us. Didn't she, Bridge?"

"That she did."

Despite the screaming of Vanilla Fudge from the stereo in the living room to set them free, the three people in the crowded kitchen seemed to be encased in their own cocoon of silence.

Finally PJ cleared his throat. "Hey, man, ah, Mick, right? And Bridget?" His eyes darted around the room before they settled back on the pair in front of him. "Listen, man, like, I don't know what kind of weird shit was going down last night. Hell, I didn't buy that pitcher, that came from the dude who owned the club, uhm…"

"Manny," Mick said. "Manny Silva."

"Yup, that's right. So you know what a sleaze ball he is. Hell, I don't know why he put something in your drinks. And I wasn't even—"

"How'd you know there was something in our drinks?" Mick asked quietly.

"Well, you said, ah, didn't you just tell me that someone had…?"

"Nope."

"But it wasn't him that put that *thing* in our beer, was it?" Bridget said in a soft voice laced with steel. "It was your girlfriend, Marcy Trainor. Sister to Jackie Trainor, best friend of Blair Vanderwall!"

"You know, we had a nice little *chat* with Manny this morning," Mick said, "and he got me to thinking about some nasty little tricks that I learned from the VC back in 'Nam. Would you like to see some?"

PJ shook his head.

"Funny," Mick smiled a cold smile, "that's just the way Manny felt at the end, too."

He steered PJ to the back door and out onto the rickety porch.

"Your turn," Mick said. "Tell us about the Trainor sisters. Jackie, and your girlfriend Marcy, and especially Blair. I want the names of every guy who was madly in love with, and got his heart stomped on by, little Miss Blair Vanderwall." Mick looked PJ hard in the eyes.

PJ slouched against the broken railing. Finally he said in a low monotone, "Then I guess you better start with me."

Chatham, Massachusetts | Cape Cod | Hardings Beach
July 4, 1968 11:53 p.m.

"PJ, stop it!" Blair Vanderwall giggled, pushing his hands away. "You're getting sand all down my bellbottoms. Do you want me walking around with sand on my butt for the rest of the night?"

"Mmm-m, ah, Blair. You're so frigging beautiful. C'm'ere, babe!"

"No, PJ. We've got to get back to the party. I mean, after all, what is your girlfriend Marcy gonna say? Or is it Jackie? I can never remember which. Or…" Blair touched her left index finger just below the cheekbone of her perfect, soft cheek, and whispered, with her perfect innocent-erotic giggle, "is it both?"

"Oh, Blair!" PJ moaned, shifting over on to his knees. "Please, I'm begging you. I don't give a crap about Jackie or Marcy, or anyone. It's you. It's always been you!"

"Aw, PJ, that's sweet," Blair said as she tucked her peasant blouse into her denim bellbottoms and re-tied the maroon macramé sash around her hips. "And you've always been my big old puppy dog friend."

PJ looked up at Blair as if he'd just been punched in the stomach.

"Is that all I am? Just a 'big old puppy dog friend?'"

Blair took both his hands and looked deeply into his eyes, and PJ felt the ache in his chest start to fade.

She does care! he thought as she leaned forward and kissed him on the lips, his heart ready to burst with hope.

She held his hands for a moment longer and then burst into a tinkling little laugh as she kissed him on the nose and said, "Woof, woof, puppy!"

Her laughter mingled with the hiss of the incoming waves as she ran off down the beach.

Chapter 19

Newport | Rhode Island | 110 Chestnut Street
July 29, 1968 | 10:08 p.m.

"So, PJ, I didn't know you were sick."

PJ whirled around, half expecting to find that Mick and Bridget had returned, having realized that there was a part of his story that PJ had left out.

But it wasn't them.

Two expressionless men in dark suits ascended the last two wooden stairs and stepped onto the small porch.

PJ took a step back, until the base of his spine bumped against the rickety, warped railing.

A third person, the one who'd spoken, walked up the last two steps and past the two men in dark suits.

"Hey, man," PJ said, as recognition was accompanied by a sinking feeling. "I… I'm real sorry about everything. I mean it, man."

"Well, maybe that's the reason you've gotten sick."

PJ shook his head.

"I don't know what you're talking about, man. I'm not sick."

The man's voice drifted out from the darkness that seemed to cling to him. It had a cruel, mocking undertone.

"Yes, PJ, you are. It seems you've developed a bad case of 'motor mouth.'"

PJ's hands shook, and his heart was beating like some small, trapped animal.

"Hey, listen, man. I didn't tell them anything! No shit, really!"

None of the three figures facing PJ made any sound or movement.

Finally, the man in the shadows said in a cold, amused tone, "No shit, PJ? Really? Well, you know what I think? I think that you're *full* of shit!"

The man stepped quickly from the shadows and jabbed him with a short, savage punch just below his rib cage, knocking the breath out of him and doubling him over against the railing.

"Jesus... I..." PJ gasped.

He grabbed PJ by his dirty, long blond hair and twisted his head until he was looking up at him.

He bent down slowly and murmured in PJ's ear, "We've been following that motorcycle-riding cretin and his slut girlfriend for the past two hours—with only a brief stop for an occasional diversion." The face relaxed into a strange, almost ecstatic smile that was even more chilling. A wisp of fog passed over the moon for a moment and when the dim light returned the smile was gone and pitiless eyes glittered crueler than before.

"We were standing on the porch below the whole time, you worthless piece of garbage. We heard the whole thing. Including your sad little story about how Blair broke your asshole hippie heart. Christ," the speaker said with disgust, "just the thought of her kissing you makes me want to puke!"

He twisted PJ's hair harder. PJ moaned and tried to stand, but the speaker pushed him back against the railing. "As a matter of fact, you weren't even good enough to be her puppy dog!"

PJ's breathing became more labored. They'd heard everything!

"And since you saw fit to blab about your pathetic love life to those two snoops, I'm sure that if they came back for more information, you wouldn't hesitate to tell them about your little trip to your van to bring more of your stash back into the club that night."

"I—I, no man, I didn't. I mean I'd never tell them…"

The voice got harsher. "I don't give a crap if you want to play the 'nickel bag' dealer to the rest of your brain-numbed crowd, but you should have stuck to dealing over-priced grass."

The voice hissed from the shadows. "Too bad you had to stare when you saw me walk to my car after Blair left with that cowboy."

PJ tried to swallow.

"No, man. You got it wrong. I never saw… I mean I was just walking into the club and I never even saw you go after Blair."

"Then how do you know I went after her?" His voice softened. "Why would I do that? That would be very wrong of me, wouldn't it, PJ? Very, very wrong."

His face was turned away, staring into the darkness, but PJ could almost sense a smile on that handsome but terrifying face.

"Why, that would almost make me seem like a 'boyfriend.' Or a jealous lover. But that couldn't have been me, PJ, now could it?"

PJ croaked, "No."

"From what I heard you telling that pair, it seems you were the one who wanted to be her 'boyfriend.'" The voice rose again as an iron-gripped hand shot out and grasped PJ's throat. "Her lover!"

PJ couldn't breath. He tried to struggle but was frozen into immobility when the face with the insane eyes leaned close to his and hissed, "She broke your poor little heart, didn't she, PJ? Oh yes, she's very, very skilled at that."

He snorted contemptuously and stepped back into the shadows.

"But you know what?" he said, almost pleasantly. "I believe that I can help you out. You see, I know just the cure for a broken heart."

PJ painfully pushed himself upright and took two desperate steps toward the back door to the kitchen.

The two men in dark suits grabbed him by either arm and slammed him back into the railing.

"The cure is really quite simple," the voice in the shadows continued. "We just make sure that the rest of your body matches your broken heart."

He made a small gesture with his right hand, and the men on either side of PJ pushed. PJ went backwards over the railing and fell with hardly a sound.

Half a second later came the *thunk* of the body hitting the asphalt parking lot, three flights below.

The two men in the dark suits melted back into the shadows with him, and all three disappeared down the back stairs.

Chapter 20

Newport, Rhode Island   Bellevue Avenue
July 29, 1968   10:27 p.m.

Mick's bike coasted to a stop in front of the four-story rambling beach 'cottage' at the end of Newport's "Millionaires Row," known to the rest of the *'have-not'* world as Bellevue Avenue.

He pushed his wind-tangled hair out of his eyes and stared up at the imposing house. Bridget shifted her weight on the rear seat.

For a moment, they were silent, the only sounds on Bellevue Avenue the far-off bark of a cranky watchdog and the low rumble of 650 cubic centimeters of British pistons and valves moving at a slow 800 rpm idle.

"Ready to meet the next Queen Bee in the Newport hive?"

"Just so long as she doesn't sting us both in the butt," Bridget mumbled into his back as he put the BSA into first gear and rolled up the long driveway.

"Oh, Christ, McCarthy," Bridget whispered as Mick climbed up onto the front porch and rang the doorbell. "I look a bleedin' fright."

She shifted her ever-present compact mirror around, trying to get a glimpse of the back of her head. She tugged her small brush through her thick black hair for a few seconds, then smoothed her wrinkled denim skirt down over her black tights.

As Mick rang the bell again, the door swung open. A distinguished but annoyed looking fifty-something, squash-and-tennis-fit, jet-set type man, said coldly, "Yes, may I help you?"

"Must be the butler's night off," Mick cracked to Bridget out of the side of his mouth. The pale, cold blue eyes looked at Mick and Bridget as though they were specimens of a new, unpleasant kind of bug laid out under a microscope.

"If you're selling something or collecting for the newspaper," he sniffed, "kindly come back tomorrow when Arthur has returned, and he'll take care of it."

Mick turned back to Bridget and winked with a grin, "I told you it was the butler's night off."

He said it just loud enough to make sure he was heard by the uptight dude in the tennis sweater, who was holding the door half closed.

"Good night!" came the clipped and definitely not-amused reply. The big white door slammed shut. Almost. It was hindered by the thick pointed toe of Mick's cowboy boot, which inserted itself into the last two inches of space between the door and the jamb.

"Yeah, hi." Mick smiled through the two inches of open space like a traveling salesman. "We're friends of your daughter, Valerie, and her friends, the Trainor sisters. And another good friend of theirs, PJ, asked us to stop by and return something to them."

"They aren't here. And if they were, I certainly wouldn't let you see them," he said from between gritted teeth. "Now kindly remove your goddamn boot from my goddamn door!"

"Just a few more questions if you don't mind. Mr. Cortland, is it?" Mick smiled as if nothing was happening.

The man tried to push the door closed again, and when it became obvious that Mick wasn't about to move, he jabbed his finger down on a button mounted on the inside of the doorjamb. There was a crackle, and a static-garbled voice spoke over the tinny speaker. "Yeah, Mr. Cortland?"

"Daniel? Come up to the house." He paused for half a second and looked at Mick with malicious satisfaction, adding, "Bring Blitz and Krieg."

Mick hadn't done well in German his junior year at Andover. As a matter of fact, his professor, Herr Gunter Wolff Kriebst, had told him at the end of the semester, "Your 'F', Herr McCarthy, is one of the most satisfying I have ever given."

Despite the mutual dislike between Mick and that unrepentant exile of the Third Reich, he had, almost in spite of himself, picked up a pretty fair German vocabulary. So, when he heard this unpleasant looking man in front of him tell someone to bring up two 'somethings' that were named 'lightning' and 'war,' he knew that they were definitely not going to be invited in for tea.

Less than ten seconds later, his pessimistic view was confirmed in spades, when a grizzled, tall, thin man with greasy gray-black hair stumbled up the driveway, pulled by two snorting, growling Doberman Pinschers.

Mick pushed Bridget toward the alcove where the porch angled toward the front door.

"Don't move!" he hissed back to her without taking his eyes off the two slobbering dogs and their nastily grinning handler.

"You just give the word, Mr. Cortland," the skinny man rasped with a sadistic grin.

Mick looked at the man and the dogs and then at his bike and the saddlebags. Especially at the left saddlebag. That's where Big Mike's snub-nosed .38 Police Special had rested ever since he and Bridge left Cambridge, which now seemed like a thousand years ago.

Could he make it to the bike and root through mounds of clothes, tools and empty potato chip bags before those two dogs ripped his throat out?

As Bridget would say, "Not bloody likely."

And what about Bridge?

What would happen to her after Mick became "Puppy Chow" for the two Kraut canines?

Uh uh. He needed a better plan. Only problem was, there wasn't one. And they were all out of time, 'cause out of the corner of his eye, Mick saw Mr. 'Tennis Anyone?' give a slow nod of his head, and 'Bad Dog Danny' bent to unsnap the chains of the choke collars.

"Bridge!" Mick said sharply without turning his head. "When I say 'run,' you run for the gate. Don't stop and don't look back. No matter what!"

"Mickey, I..."

"Just do it!" he yelled, and tensed himself for the first ripping bite.

The dog chains rattled and spring-loaded leads *snapped* ready to release.

"Gilbert? What's going on out here? Please, dear, either conclude your business or invite your friends in. Remember, we have guests."

A bland-faced, middle-aged woman, with expensively coiffed auburn hair and a thick strand of choker pearls, pulled the heavy door halfway open.

"Please go back inside, Bunny," the man said with a strained attempt at a smile. "I'm handling this."

"Well, if you say so, Gil."

Mick tensed again.

A familiar voice called from behind the woman and man. "Gil, Bunny? Whatever is going on? Are you having a party on the front porch? And if so, may Bronwyn and I come, too?"

The big front door was suddenly pulled all the way open, and Mick stared at the cool, elegant figure looking back at him from the cavernous, oak-paneled front hallway.

"Mom!"

"WOULD YOU LIKE a soft drink, dear?" Felicity Parker Prescott asked Bridget when they'd all seated themselves in the Cortlands' grand, chastely white living room.

"No, thank you, Mrs. Prescott," Bridget said, carefully enunciating each word. She sat perched on the hard edge of a brocaded wingback chair.

Mick's mother smiled indulgently at Bridget and turned to her long-ago college roommate. "Bunny, this is Michael's little friend from school, Bethany."

"It's Bridget," she corrected.

"I'm sorry, dear. What was that?" Felicity Parker Prescott smiled blandly.

"It's Bridget, mom!" Mick said loudly, half rising out of his chair. He added with a snarl, "Bridget!"

"My goodness, Michael. You needn't bite my head off," his mother answered, never losing her patrician poise. "He has a temper like his father," she said to Bunny.

"Yeah. But my bite is all verbal, unlike your friend's little pets, 'Flopsy and Mopsy' out there, which were getting ready to chow down on me and Bridge."

Everyone ignored Mick's statement, as if the recent unpleasantness had never happened.

"I'm sorry, dear," Felicity said to Bridget. "Now I remember. It's Bridget. Weren't you at one of our house parties at Brattle Street?"

Mick ground his teeth, and Bridget looked at the floor. He knew just as well as Mrs. Felicity Parker Prescott (McCarthy) that Bridget had been at the party. As a waitress for the catering service.

Mick was about to explode when Bridget sat up very straight and said, in a perfectly modulated upper class English voice, "Yes, Mrs.

Prescott, that is quite true. You see, the terms of my scholarship to Radcliffe, your alma mater I believe, require a specific number of hours spent in menial labor. I presume that it is so that in case I should fail to marry well," she looked at Felicity, "or marry money," and she looked at Bunny Cortland, "then I will have a useful trade to fall back on."

Bridget sat very still and folded her hands carefully in her lap. She remained expressionless as the three upper class faces turned bright crimson.

Applause from a shadowed corner of the cavernous living room broke the silence.

Mick smiled, having almost forgotten that his sister, Bronwyn, had been sitting silently in the corner ever since they'd been reluctantly ushered in.

Bronwyn, apparently relieved at having been snapped out of her bored-out-of-her-mind stupor by Bridget's comeback, stood up still clapping, and said, "Right on, Bridget!"

"Damn straight! Right on, sister!" a voice called from the top of the stairs. "That's telling the old fossils!"

A blond, long-necked, younger version of the bland-faced Bunny Cortland glided gracefully down the long staircase.

"And would you be Valerie Cortland?" Mick asked.

"Right on, brother!" the tall girl in embroidered hip-huggers answered from the doorway.

Mick scanned the faces in the room.

Bunny Cortland looked bemused and confused at the same time.

Her husband, the nasty dog-man, looked mad.

His sister Bronwyn looked like she'd been rescued from drowning in a sea of terminal boredom.

His mother's face was a china mask of perfect, inscrutable correctness, and he had never really been able to see behind it.

And Bridget? Well, Bridget wasn't someone who schemed or hid behind anything or anyone. She didn't settle things with her fists the way Mick did, but she never ran from a fight either. She'd draw strength into her tiny frame from God knows where, and stand up to trouble like a frigging rock!

And Mick didn't think that he'd ever been luckier than that wintry night in Harvard Square, Cambridge, when he'd met the feisty little green-eyed pixie from County Cork.

"NICE CAR," Mick said with a low whistle as he looked at Valerie Cortland's shiny red two-seater TR-3 convertible.

"Thanks, man," Valerie Cortland smiled back. "I guess rich daddies are good for something, right, Bronwyn?"

"I wouldn't know," Bronwyn answered with a shrug. "Our father was a cop."

Valerie raised her eyebrows.

"Okay," Mick said, "so you think you know where the Trainor sisters are hanging out tonight?"

"I *know* that I know where Jackie and Marcy are hanging out tonight, 'cause I'm supposed to meet them there in one hour. They're at that new folk club down by the harbor."

Mick rose up on his left foot and kicked the BSA's starter to life as Bridget slid on behind him.

"C'mon, Bronwyn," Valerie said as she lifted her long legs into the TR-3's low bucket seat, "you can ride with me."

The little red sports car spun around in the gravel of the driveway and sped through the gate, followed closely by the metallic blue motorcycle.

The two chained guard dogs watched the small procession and whined.

Two more eyes watched the twin taillights and single motorcycle taillight disappear up Bellevue Avenue.

But there was no whine.

These eyes knew they would get what they wanted. And soon.

Chapter 21

Newport, Rhode Island | Bowen's Wharf | White Rabbit Café
July 29, 1968 | 11:28 p.m.

"This way," Valerie Cortland said, pushing her way through the crowd that shuffled inside the Thames Street bar and music club.

The crowd didn't so much part for Valerie as allow her to slither through. Bronwyn went through the same cosmic personality hole, dragged by the self-assured force of Valerie's charisma.

"Funny," Mick said to Bridget , "Bronwyn lets these smug little rich girls lead her around by the nose. And then you look at our Mom, 'Miss Felicity.' She's always in control, never lets anyone push her around. Ha, go figure. Where the hell do you suppose all that disappeared to?"

"Can't imagine, luv." Bridget said, winking. "But I've a feeling you know who inherited that better-not-push-me-around' gene."

"Hi, guys," Valerie Cortland called through the haze of tobacco and pot smoke to the two girls at the table against the wall. "This is Bronwyn. Her mom is a friend of my mom's."

Jackie Trainor barely looked up.

"And this is her brother Mick, and Bridget."

Marcy Trainor looked like her heart had stopped beating.

"Well, aren't we lucky, running into you this way," Mick said, pulling up a chair next to Marcy. Marcy kept her eyes locked on the band.

"I'd really like to talk to you about a few things," he said.

"I'm sorry," she tried to smile. "I was kind of zoned out listening to the band."

"Yeah? Well, I guess I can dig that. Me and Bridge sure as hell know what it's like to be zoned out, don't we, babe?"

"Oh, yes," Bridget answered. "We certainly do."

Dead silence covered them amid the noise and music. It stretched on and on until Mick slapped a ten dollar bill down on the table, turned to Marcy's older sister and said, "Jackie, would you be a real doll and get us all a beer?"

She frowned, looked like she was going to say 'no way,' then smiled. Obviously she wasn't used to being spoken to like this. After a moment of looking into Mick's eyes, she got up and headed for the bar.

Valerie Cortland leaned forward in her chair and put her elbows on the table. She intertwined her long thin fingers under her aquiline jaw and said, "Oh-o-o, this is getting interesting."

"Bronwyn?" Mick said, never unlocking his eyes from Marcy's.

"Mick?"

"Don't you need to visit the ladies' room?"

"Ah-h-h, sure."

Bronwyn's chair scraped back from the table.

"And Valerie?" Mick continued in the same expressionless voice. "I'd consider it a very great personal favor if you'd show my sister the way to the ladies' room."

"You're kidding!" Valerie laughed.

The laughter died on her lips as she saw the expression on Mick's face.

"She might get lost, and I wouldn't want that. Get the picture, Valerie?"

She shrugged.

"As a matter of fact," Mick continued, pulling another crumpled $10 out of his pocket and laying it beside the other one, "why don't you guys go keep Valerie company at the bar and have a couple of beers on me."

Valerie gave Mick an am-I-missing-out-on-something look, but

Bronwyn took her arm and pulled Valerie in the direction of the bar.

Mick waited until Valerie and Bronwyn lost themselves in the crowded room. Then he turned back to a withdrawn, pale-faced Marcy and said, "Now tell me about you and PJ and Blair."

Chatham, Massachusetts | Cape Cod | Hardings Beach
July 5, 1968 | 12:28 a.m.

Two of the guys at the July 4th TKE / Tri-Delt roaming summer beach party had brought their guitars and were mellowing out on a set of Dylan, Donovan and Peter Paul and Mary songs as the hour got later and the couples started looking for a little 'mood music.'

Until Blair Vanderwall suddenly emerged from the darkness behind the sand dunes and said, "Hey, this party is really starting to suck. C'mon, guys, enough with all this downer crap. Hey, Chip!" Blair's gaze fastened on Jackie's on-and-off, old standby, always-there-and-taken-for-granted boyfriend. "C'mon, dance with me. Tommy, Eddie," Blair called to the two guitar players, "step it up. Do 'Midnight Hour.'"

The two guitar players grinned at one another, shrugged, and launched into the Motown beat of the Wilson Pickett song.

Blair jumped into the center of the campfire circle, pulled Jackie's boyfriend to his feet, and swayed seductively to the throbbing soul beat. Her Hot Pink lips pouted.

Marcy looked at her sister. Her mouth was trying to smile, but it didn't look like a smile of amusement. More like helpless frustration, as if to say, *What can you do? It's Blair.*

Marcy might almost have agreed with her if, at that same moment, she hadn't seen the love of her life, Paul, aka PJ, stumble over the crest of the dunes, a hopeless, frustrated fire in his wild eyes. With stinging eyes and an aching heart, she watched the boy she loved stare in anguish at Blair, shimmying seductively in the driftwood firelight.

PJ, in a daze, his mouth hanging open, came closer and gazed at Blair.

Marcy could hardly see through the tears that welled in her eyes. But one thing came into crystal-clear focus.

The smear of Hot Pink lipstick on PJ's gaping mouth.

"Oops, looks like you lose again, little sis," Jackie laughed.

PJ's face flushed with lust as he watched Blair's perfect white body writhe in the firelight.

"Tsk, tsk," Jackie mocked, "that's one more score for Blair and once again, zip for Marcy!"

Jackie walked toward the firelight and joined Blair.

Chapter 22

East Providence, Rhode Island

July 30, 1968   12:03 a.m.

"Siddown, kid, you're making me nervous."

Cody Ewing stopped right in the middle of his hundredth journey between the couch and the apartment's blacked out picture window. He hadn't realized he'd been pacing for the better part of the past hour!

He was going plumb, frigging, bat-shit stir-crazy. He'd never been able to take being cooped up.

Even as a kid, the teacher in the old rundown, warped-board, single-room school he'd attended with his brothers, sisters and assorted cousins had regularly whacked him up on the side of the head 'cause he couldn't sit still.

And he'd been caged up in this gold-plated chicken coop for over twelve hours now.

But worse than even that was the memory he couldn't get out of his head, no matter how much Jack Daniel's he tried to wash it away with. His hands shook again. He reached for the bottle and took a long shuddering pull. All he could see was that guy Bobby, with his guts blown all over the mobster's office, and everyone just standing around like it was something that happened every day. Cody stopped pacing. Damn! It probably was.

That fat I-talian hood—"Mr. C." they called him—had told Cody to take some time to think over his offer.

And he had. Over and over and over. In the apartment with the steak and the Jack Daniel's and the blacked out windows.

At first he couldn't even look at the steaks and just concentrated on the J.D. But after a while the Tennessee sippin' whiskey had dulled the bloody image of Bobby's staring corpse around the edges and well, now the steaks were gone, along with half of the Jack Daniel's and he was going damn stir-crazy from clostra-whatever-it-was.

If he could just kick down that imitation oak door and run like hell. And he would, except for a very bored, very mean looking, acne-scarred, greasy-haired, stockily built guy in a silvery sharkskin suit sitting two feet to the left of the apartment's only exit.

Even so, Cody was almost ready to try it. He played it out in his mind. Three running steps, one, two, three. Knock the little dago off the chair with a kick in the head. Then one good kick to the door, down the stairs and…

The unopened bottle of Jack Daniel's exploded on top of the bar.

Cody jumped.

"Don't even think about it, kid," Cody's watchdog said with a quiet sneer.

The semi-sweet hickory odor of Jack Daniel's mingled with the acrid sulfur smell of gunpowder and cordite drifting up from the silenced muzzle of the 9 mm Ruger automatic, which his smirking jailer now pointed at Cody's stomach.

He grinned mirthlessly at Cody with his snake's-head sneer and said, "The next one goes right through your friggin' gut, pal. So just sit the fuck down and keep thinkin' over what Mr. C. said."

Chapter 23

Newport, Rhode Island | The White Rabbit Café, rear entrance

July 30, 1968 | 12:05 a.m.

Suzy Cantrell hated her job, which was almost funny, she thought, considering how hard she had worked to get it, and how excited she'd been when she finally had.

She had sent perky but professional-sounding letters to the Newport Chamber of Commerce, detailing her experience, which included three summers working as a waitress and hostess at the Steak Palace in Bowling Green, Ohio. She had outlined her summer goals in the most businesslike manner she'd learned in Mr. Pender's Business and Commerce 201 class.

She'd explained that she was planning to go into Food Service Management Administration and was anxious to gain as much practical experience as possible.

But what she had really wanted was some fun and excitement on the free-flowing, far-out East Coast. And to get as far as possible from the dull, deadly-boring, up-tight, no-fun, stifling environment of the Steak Palace and Bowling Green, Ohio.

Oh, she liked Bowling Green State University okay, especially her sisters at Alpha Chi Omega, but this was the last summer between her junior and senior year and, well, all she wanted was a little fun! If that wasn't too much to ask, for goodness sake!

And maybe, just maybe, a little summer romance thrown in.

Well, that was how she'd felt when she'd shown up to start her job as a cocktail waitress (read 'barmaid', she thought bitterly) at The White Rabbit Café in June.

At first, it had been exciting. There'd been music and high energy and lots of cute boys!

But now, a month and a half and one failed romance later, well, The Steak Palace back in Bowling Green was starting to look better and better.

The 'high energy' job (and the high energy romance) had drained her, and she was heartily sick of people yelling in her ear to bring them another pitcher and of getting her butt pinched by every table of drunken fraternity boys that she walked by.

That's why she really looked forward to these cigarette breaks out behind the club.

She smiled and shook her head when she remembered how she'd been the only one in her sorority who didn't smoke, and now here she was, up to almost two packs a day.

It was all that jerk Chet's fault. Boy, had he ever taken her for a ride, in every sense!

"Chet the Vet", as she and her sorority sister and fellow waitress Marty, had nicknamed him for his shiny red Corvette.

And it had been so great! For a while.

He took her to great parties, out on his daddy's sailboat, and he was so, so good-looking and rich and cool and all the things that the sweaty-handed boys that she'd gone out with in Bowling Green were not. And they looked great together. Everyone said they made the perfect couple. And everything between them had been perfect too. That is until that night on the beach. A little pot, some music, and a lot of beer, and good old Chet the Vet got what he wanted (and yeah, she wanted it too).

After that? The bastard dumped her.

Well, she thought, *as Grandma told me when I was sixteen, who's gonna buy the cow when he gets the milk for free?*

She shook her head and said to herself, "Well moo moo, Suzy Q, better get your little cow butt back to work before Mr. Baxter has a cow himself!"

She flicked her cigarette butt into the dark water underneath the pier which the café rested on, and turned toward the back door of the club.

And froze.

Three men moved through the back door.

They weren't employees, she could tell, they were dressed too nicely.

Before she could think better of it, she blurted out, "Hey, you guys aren't supposed to be using that door. It's like, for employees only, you know?" The first two of the trio turned around and looked at her. They were dark, swarthy and mean looking.

She took a step back.

Then the third man turned around.

He smiled slowly and said, "Hello, Suzy."

"Oh, like, ah, hi. I didn't know it was you. What are you doing back here?"

He smiled back at her. "We just wanted to surprise a friend inside."

He motioned to the other two men. "Go on, I'll be with you in a minute."

The back door closed.

"So how have you been, Suzy?" he asked, walking toward her.

She shrugged.

"I was really sorry to hear about you and Chet."

"Yeah, well, his loss," Suzy said, tossing her long blond hair back.

Suddenly, she stopped.

"Wait a minute. What do you mean, 'sorry to hear?' You were there.

You were sitting at the same table when Chet dumped me Tuesday night. You even came along when Barry took me outside because he thought I was gonna throw a fit, or throw the drinks at that creep, Chet."

She looked at him with the beginning of suspicion. "That's right, you came outside but you never came back in. You got in your car. Barry even said 'where the hell is he going?' That was right after Blair left with… How could you not remember that night? You especially! Oh my God!" She shook her head in confusion.

"You're right," he said softly, putting his arm around her. "I'll never forget anything about that night."

He sighed sadly. "And apparently, you haven't either, Suzy."

The arm around her shoulder grew tighter.

"You know I do agree with you about Chet. He always was a fool. Did you know that we were at school together for a semester? That was when I was twelve. I had to leave school… unexpectedly. So we never got to know one another that well. But the several times that I saw Chet at the club, he did mention to me that he thought that you had a really 'dynamite' personality." He chuckled.

"He said that you were an exceptionally extroverted conversationalist. Loved to talk. Yes, he said that you would talk to just about anyone, about anything and… everything. Is that right, Suzy?" The arm continued to tighten around her shoulders.

"Yes. Unfortunately there were some very inconvenient and nosey people at the club that night who saw me leave. Like you and Barry—and PJ. You, Suzy, definitely fall into the 'nosey' category. Barry, fortunately for him, has left for his uncle's ranch in Colorado for the rest of the summer, and PJ, I'm sad to say, has succumbed to a terminal case of 'broken heart.'" He chuckled. "But you're still here, aren't you, Suzy? Still here with your 'Chatty Cathy' mouth."

The face was smiling but the pressure increased on her shoulders

"Ow. Knock it off. You're hurting me!"

"Yes, Suzy. I'm afraid so."

"Listen, listen," she stammered, "I've got to go. Please…"

"I know you do, Suzy," he said softly.

He leaned forward and kissed her on the cheek.

There was a sharp intake of breath. A snapping sound, as with the breaking of branch.

A splash.

And then, silence.

HE STARED DOWN at the blood dark water below the pier. The body of the blond waitress from Bowling Green, Ohio floated, rocking gently on the incoming tide. Her blond hair spread out from her like a fan, like the delicate sea anemone he'd seen while scuba diving in Aruba many years ago with his family… his loving family.

He snapped his fingers at the man who slouched against the black car waiting in the parking lot next to the pier. The man in a dark suit raised his head and looked back.

"Bring her," he called. "Suzy will need to join the others for one last party. *Her* party."

He smiled and chuckled, "and you know how she hates to be kept waiting."

Newport Police Department | 12:08 AM

Assistant Desk Sergeant Jonathan Fahey had just gotten up from the well-worn leather chair behind the booking desk in the NPD and was on his way to the coffee machine when the telephone perched on the corner of the desk rang. He paused, the cold dregs of his coffee cup swaying in his hand, and briefly considered continuing on to the coffee pot and basket of stale crullers and letting whoever was on the other end of the line go bleep themselves. Then he noticed Larry Daniels, one of the summer cop kids they hired every year to help out with traffic and beach patrols, watching him from across the room. *Damn, the little college prick would probably rat him out if he didn't answer it.* So he turned back to the desk and grabbed for the phone, knocking his coffee mug against the open drawer and spilling the contents onto his leg. "Aw shit!" he muttered snatching up the phone.

"Newport PD, whadd'a want?! He snarled into the receiver.

A tired woman's voice on the other end said, "Ah, I'm calling from Dennis. Ya know, on the Cape?"

Dennis, Fahey thought, not even one of the wealthy taxpayers of Newport. No need even to pretend to be polite.

"Yeah I know it, lady, so what's yer problem?"

"Well, my daughter—ah, her name is Janet. She told me she was going to a bar or a club up there last night and—"

"And what lady?"

"Well, it may not be anything. I mean she's not a little kid or anything and it's not like I ever tell her she can't go where she wants and do what she—"

"Get to the point lady."

The tired voice on the other end said tonelessly. "She never came home last night."

Chapter 24

The White Rabbit Café | 12:13 a.m.

"You know, Marcy, we can sit here all night, if that's what it's gonna take," Mick said, almost pleasantly.

Marcy continued shredding napkin after napkin and staring down at the scarred tabletop. After another full minute of silence, she raised her head slightly and blew a long strand of silky brown hair away from her left eye.

"Why don't you two just stop being so uncool and split? I don't want to talk about her any more."

"Uh-uh," Mick said, shaking his head. "Not until we get some answers."

"Ask my sister. She was Blair's big buddy."

"That's why I'd rather ask you. Because you weren't."

"You got that right."

"Marcy," Bridget said in a tight voice, "we both know what you did. And I think you know what it did to us, to me especially."

Marcy looked up and shook her head. "I didn't want to put that… that stuff in your drinks. Well, I mean it wasn't my idea. I swear to God. You've gotta believe me."

"But you know whose idea it was. Don't you?" Mick said. "Your sister."

"And you never even gave us a word of warning," Bridget added, her voice shaking.

Marcy shook her head, the long brown hair swaying back and forth.

"No."

Mick reached out and took Marcy's chin between his thumb and forefinger, raising her face up till it was level with his own. "Then you owe us one, don't you? A big one."

She nodded and answered quietly, "Yes."

She looked around the noisy, crowded barroom. He looked, too. Jackie, Bronwyn and Valerie were still at the bar. Marcy's jaw stiffened as if she'd finally made up her mind.

"Okay," she nodded again. "I'm gonna tell you something about that bitch Blair that very few people know. Most of it I've overheard from bits and pieces of gossip between Jackie and Valerie. The rest I've sort of pieced together myself."

She stared across the table with bitter eyes.

"It wasn't just my boyfriend PJ that Blair took and used, and ruined for anyone else to love."

Marcy stared fiercely at Mick and Bridget, rasping out from between gritted teeth, "Believe me when I say that she had a power. A kind of evil, sexual power that she used to get everything and anyone she wanted. Anyone!"

Mick and Bridget leaned closer.

"Some things about Blair I know from experience." She looked up at Bridget and added, "Bitter experience. Other things were teenage gossip and rumors. But knowing Blair, and the effect she had on everyone, well, here's what I know, and you can make up your own mind."

The sounds of the club seemed to drop away as Marcy continued. "It was almost ten years ago, I was just a kid hanging around my older sister and Blair, whenever they weren't yelling at me to get lost. I really didn't know what was going on. Blair had just turned twelve. She was starting to understand the kind of power she had, and was looking for new places to try it out. That summer, a young art student came to

Newport. He'd been hired by Johnathan Vanderwall to paint several paintings of the child he doted on."

"Blair." Mick said flatly.

Marcy nodded then murmured almost to herself, "Yes, he always favored Blair over her brother Jack, but then so did everyone."

"But why an art student? Surely he could have afforded a master artist."

Marcy nodded again. "He could and did. He hired a professor of fine arts from the academy in New York, but Blair, typically, made a fuss and said she didn't like him. He was too old and ugly and made her feel 'icky' when she was around him. The professor didn't want to lose out on the entire commission, so he sent for his prized pupil, a handsome young man named Emil."

"And I'll bet Blair liked him just fine." Mick smiled wryly.

"That would be an understatement."

Marcy continued. "By the time Emil had finished the first painting, the one that hangs in the Vanderwall library, he had become Blair's tennis partner. After the second portrait of Blair on the family yacht, he'd become her sailing partner as well. But by the time he finished the third painting, the one that was supposed to be secret, he and Blair were intimate—"

"Whoa, back up a second." Mick leaned forward. "You said she was only twelve."

Marcy nodded. "She was."

Bridget broke in. "Oh my God. Marcy, you don't mean that at twelve she could…?"

"Oh yes, she could and did. She was Blair. But that's not even the wildest and grungiest part of the story. It seems that painting—"

"How did you hear all of this?" Mick interrupted.

Marcy smiled. "I became very good at eavesdropping when Jackie and Valerie got together. And Valerie swore that she'd heard it from Blair herself. The third painting was, as they say in polite circles, an 'art study.' In other words, the human form. The unclothed human form."

"Commissioned by her own father," Bridget said, shaking her head.

Mick whistled. "Man, sounds like Blair could have given lessons to Lolita."

Marcy stared at the tabletop and muttered to herself again, "They're a very strange bunch up at the Vanderwall house. Very strange."

"I'd like to talk to this art student," Mick said.

"Good luck with that," Marcy said.

"What do you mean?"

"He never showed up in New York for the fall term."

"Jesus H. Christ!" Mick whistled.

"But, but," Bridget stammered, still shaking her head in disbelief, "how could she, I mean, even with everything I've heard, I never…"

For once, Bridget Connolly ran out of words.

Mick had one or two, but he decided he really didn't want to say them. Instead, he stared hard at Marcy and tried to see what was going on behind her long brown hair and guarded expression. Was this the real Marcy telling the truth, or was this something that you came up with after taking one too many freshman psych courses?

Marcy's gaze traveled back and forth between them. She looked down at the table and let her long hair hide her face again.

Mick turned Marcy's story over in his mind. Could anyone, especially an "innocent" twelve-year-old girl, be that kinky and twisted? And what did that say about her family? And especially her…?

A waitress walked by in black bellbottoms and a T-Shirt sporting a cartoon white rabbit toking off a hookah. Mick reached out and snagged her wrist. "Hey, do you know if Suzy Cantrell is working tonight?" The waitress paused and said with an impatient smile, "Do you guys want any drinks?"

Mick shook his head. "No thanks, for now just information. Is Suzy here?"

"She's on break," she called back before losing herself in the crowd. "Probably out back having a ciggy."

The waitress flipped her hand toward the back door.

Marcy's voice dragged Mick's attention back to the table.

"Do you want to know what I think?" she said, still not looking up. "I think that last Tuesday night, all of the bad karma that Blair had been throwing out collected in the club up in Falmouth. That's why, when she met Cody, and she put the moves on him, her—oh my God!"

Marcy sat bolt upright and clapped her hands over her mouth. What little color she had drained out of her face as she stared across the room to the back door.

"I've got to go," she gasped.

"What? Why?" Mick reached for her arm.

"It's—him! If he sees me talking to you—"

Marcy knocked her chair over as she got up and bolted from the table.

"Marcy!" Bridget called and started after her.

Mick looked behind him. A man stood near the back entrance, his face obscured in the shadows. But after seeing the effect he had on Marcy, Mick knew he needed to find out who 'him' was.

As Mick walked toward him, the man in the shadows slipped out the back door. Mick pushed through the sweating, gyrating bodies on the tiny dance floor, and pulled the heavy wood and steel door open. A figure stood by the trash barrels and five-gallon soft drink containers.

"Ah, you must be the famous Mick McCarthy we've been hearing so much about." The voice seemed old and young all at once.

The darkness and fog hid his face until a breeze blew the clouds away from the moon. A pair of lifeless, china-doll blue eyes glinted at Mick.

They shifted slightly to over Mick's shoulder and something crashed into the back of Mick's skull. The image turned inside out, like a black and white negative. And then all the lights went out.

VOICES CAME TO HIM from a long way off. Where was he? He tried to get up, but a foot stomped down on his shoulders and pushed him back onto the rough surface.

He forced one eye open and raised his head half an inch. He saw cracked and pitted planks of wood. The foot pushed down harder on his back. Then it came to him.

V.C.! He was in a V.C. interrogation center.

He scrambled for the Fairbairn combat knife strapped to his right calf. It was gone. They'd taken his weapons. They were going to interrogate him. Hard interrogation. And then, of course, they were going to kill him. Hopefully, quickly.

"Okay, so we got 'im. Now, what the hell do you want we should do with him?"

Wait, this was English, sort of, not V.C. Mick's head was spinning.

"Something special, I think," answered a voice that definitely was not V.C.

No, it was the same kind of voice that Mick had heard at Harvard and Andover. Well-spoken, well-educated, privileged.

The voice continued. "He's caused a lot of trouble over the past two days, and caused me a lot of painful memories. Very painful. Memories of things that I want to put away. Things that should be put away… forever."

MARCY TRAINOR PUSHED a sweaty lock of long brown hair from her right eye. She had to get the hell out of the club!

PJ should have been there by now. He said he'd meet her at the Rabbit at midnight, 12:30 at the latest. It was now 12:45. He might not always have been faithful, but he'd never stood her up before. Something was wrong. Something had happened. Something was going down at the club tonight, something bad. Very bad.

She'd seen *him*.

She shivered. She needed to split but she wasn't going out onto Thames Street alone. Not with *him* around.

And she had a very horrible feeling that PJ wouldn't be coming.

She scanned the room until she saw her sister at the bar.

"Jackie!" Marcy yelled over the band's high-decibel version of the Stones' "Satisfaction." She rushed over and put her hand on the pale violet, hand-embroidered silk blouse covering her sister's shoulder.

Jackie jerked the shoulder down and out of Marcy's grasp.

"Watch it! You're gonna make me spill my drink"

"I need your car. Where is it?"

"Where's yours?" Jackie answered irritably.

"At PJ's"

"And where is 'lover boy' tonight?" Jackie sneered.

Marcy looked at the floor for a moment, then looked up at her sister with a smoldering hatred. "I'll tell you one place he isn't. He isn't getting the moves put on him by your bitch friend, Blair. I mean, 'late' friend."

Jackie's face turned chalky white. She reached out and slapped her sister across the face.

Marcy put her fingertips to her face. It hurt, but it wasn't unexpected. This wasn't the first time that Jackie had hit her. When they were kids, she'd tried to tell her mother, but her mother hadn't wanted to hear it because Jackie, pretty and popular, had been her favorite. So she had just said, "Oh, Marcy, don't squabble and don't tell tales. Just try to work it out, dear."

Marcy never had.

And Jackie's friendship with the domineering Blair had only made things worse. Marcy had learned to lie low when Blair was around.

Her cheek stung, more from anger than pain. She leaned into her sister's face and hissed, "Give me your goddam car keys. You owe me!"

Jackie backed away from the bar. "I owe you nothing."

"Oh, yes you do." Marcy stepped in front of her. "Because—"

"Because you, Jackie," a sharp Irish brogue broke in, "were the brains and yer sister Marcy the poor stupid little pawn. You two set us up to be drugged and shot! And I want to know what you're hiding about Blair Vanderwall. Who told you to put that drug in our beer?"

"I'm not telling you anything," Jackie snapped. "You can't prove anything."

"*He's* here," Marcy whined. "I saw him. That means he's looking for me. For *us*. We've got to get out of here."

"Shut up, Marcy."

"No, I won't! You got me into this and you've gotta help me now. He came here to find us and…"

"Will you shut your goddamned mouth, you idiot!"

Marcy lowered her voice. "Do you think you're safe? After what happened to Blair? You know how crazy he is. He won't stop now."

Now it was Jackie's turn to look shaken.

"My car is parked in the town lot, where's Valerie's?" she said.

"Right outside the door," Bridget lied.

"All right," Jackie said, moving toward the front door, "let's go."

Marcy followed. Bridget laid a hand on her arm. "Stay close to me, luv. There's something I think you need to know about your sister."

As Bridget spoke, her mouth smiled companionably at Marcy but her eyes were sharp and brittle as two little chips of emerald green glass. It was time to take care of this little 'problem' in her own way.

Chapter 25

Bowen's Wharf | The back of The White Rabbit Café | 12:51 a.m.

Mick struggled to get up from the dark well of unconsciousness that someone had thrown him down, but each time he got near the surface, something smacked into his ribs and sent him spiraling back down to the bottom again.

At the top of that well he knew was the shadowy face he'd gotten just a glimpse of and desperately needed to see again. There was a connection there that floated just out of his grasp. He needed to come to, get up, see that face again…

A dull ache throbbed in his side. Something heavy on his back pushed down on him. He struggled to his knees. The thing on his back slid off then smashed up into his stomach, knocked the breath out of him and sent him sprawling into the damp muck of the Vietnam jungle.

He squeezed his eyes shut and shook the water from his face as he forced himself to open them. Wiping his eyes with the back of his left hand, he stared into the mud a few inches below his face. Except it wasn't mud. It was cracked asphalt. And it didn't smell of heat and the jungle. It smelled of fish and tar… and the sea.

He rubbed his stomach where the pointed heavy object had crashed into it, and that same object hit him again, this time in the side, and rolled him over on to his back.

He looked up and saw the object a few inches from his face. Oh, yeah, the pier off the rear entrance of The White Rabbit Café. He was on his back, and the pointed object was a polished black Italian loafer. Right now it was drawing back to kick his teeth in. A cultured, well-modulated voice caused the owner of the black loafer to pause the kick in mid-air then slowly draw back the foot.

"I'm going to ask you one last time," the voice drifted down to him, "and I strongly suggest you answer while you still have enough teeth left to frame an articulate response."

Mick struggled to raise his head as the voice from the shadows with the unmistakable prep school intonation said softly, but with an edge to the words, "What did Marcy Trainor tell you?"

"Nothing," Mick rasped, trying to draw air into his aching lungs.

The shadow voice sighed. "Still trying to play the macho man, huh?"

"Go to hell!" Mick snarled, regretting the words almost in the same instant he uttered them.

"You first," the voice whispered back.

There was another sigh, and the voice said, in an almost disinterested tone, "Gentlemen, he's all yours. Enjoy yourselves."

Footsteps faded away toward the parking lot flanking the pier, and a high nasal voice above and behind him said, "Yeah, I'm gonna enjoy this."

Mick steeled himself for what was coming next and called out in his confused, pain-fogged mind to the one solid figure who'd been there at his side every time he'd been on the losing end of a bar fight in Saigon or a firefight in the Mekong Delta. The guy who'd been his rock in the horrors of the jungle battlefields. Smitty.

The image of the coalminer's son from Kentucky, his corporal, best friend, and the guy who'd saved his ass more than once, floated in his fading consciousness. God help him, he needed Smitty now.

He fell back down the well of nightmare, but this time he had someone with him. Someone he'd die for—and almost had.

A SHORT BURST of 7.62 mm AK-47 slugs tore through the tender green bamboo shoots, and the 244th re-con patrol's noncoms threw themselves flat into the mud of the Mekong Delta infiltration trail.

A steel jacketed slug hissed as it cut through the rotted edge of green canvas on the corporal's flak jacket. The bullet burned and buried its way into the muscle under the corporal's armpit and knocked the breath out of him, pushing his face into the mud of the trail.

"C'mon, man… Get the hell up!" the baby-faced sergeant pleaded with his corporal.

The corporal tried to raise his face out of the mud but fell back.

"I'm all messed up, man. Just go," he gasped.

"I'm not fuckin' leaving here without you, dude," the sergeant said from between gritted teeth.

He caught hold of his friend's flak jacket, and dragged him, inch by inch, into the tall grass off the edge of the trail.

Another burst of AK slugs ripped up the soft dirt of the muddy Vietnam jungle. One of them smacked into the corporal's leg, just above the calf muscle, and another creased the 19-year-old sergeant underneath his third rib.

The two young noncoms lay there on the jungle trail, panting with the same rhythm that pumped their blood into muddy, red rivulets, which would nourish the uncaring greenery while their bodies decomposed into jungle mulch.

But not now. Not just yet.

Bowen's Wharf parking lot 12:52 a.m.

Jackie Trainor sprinted across the parking lot leaving Bridget and Marcy.

"Where are you going?" Marcy asked Bridget as she slowed and stopped, looking uncertainly around the parking lot.

"To the car," Bridget snapped, continuing across the broken, bleached shells imbedded in the worn asphalt.

"But it's right here," Marcy whispered, pointing to the bright red TR-3 parked under the flickering street light.

She was right. There it was.

Marcy looked at her. "Valerie didn't give you her keys, did she?"

Bridget shook her head.

"Why did you bring me out here?" Marcy asked.

Bridget shook her head again, trying to clear it. Trying to clear it of images from nearly a decade ago, on a cold, drizzle-filled night on the southwest coast of Ireland. Of another time when the thought of revenge and all of its consequences sat like a cold, bitter pill at the pit of her stomach.

St. Thomas School | County Cork, Ireland
March 21, 1959

"Bridget Ann Connolly!"

With a guilty start, Bridget snapped her gaze back from the gray-misted window to the formidable figure of Sister Margaret.

"I'm s—sorry, sister," she mumbled.

"I said," Sister Margaret repeated with barely controlled impatience, "translate the third paragraph of Caesar's Commentaries from the Latin into English."

Bridget looked down helplessly at the text in front of her. The words swam on the page like tiny mocking fish. All she could think about was the crumpled figure lying at the end of the High Street turn, and—

Smack!

"I said translate, Miss Connolly. Not woolgather. Now!"

An angry red welt rose on the back of her left hand. Sister Margaret loomed over her, ruler poised for a second strike, and the image of the bleeding figure on High Street faded into a cold, sharp negative of black and white.

"Yes, Sister Margaret," the small, thin thirteen-year-old girl answered back. She sat ramrod straight in the hard, wooden chair, and looked up at her red-faced, scowling Latin teacher.

Then the girl lowered her eyes to the pages of her Latin textbook, and in a steady, perfectly enunciated voice that was cold as the County Cork rain sullenly falling outside the classroom window, began to translate.

"BRIDGET?"

A palm brushed across the back of Bridget's left hand, just where that humiliating welt had fallen a decade ago. She spun around, raised her right hand into a fist and looked into Marcy's stunned, frightened eyes.

"Bridget, what did I do?" Marcy asked, taking half a step backward.

Bridget looked at her cocked fist and then back at the frightened girl with the long brown hair

What was she doing? Why had she lured Marcy out here? Snippets of images crashed through her brain like lightning flashes. The cold wind blowing through the cracks in the wall of her curtained-off corner of her brother's bedroom. The threadbare skirt of her school uniform on the third turn-down when the other girls had a new one each year with polished shoes to match. The snickers and pitying looks from Kathleen Walton and Denise Kiernan when she had to tell them that she couldn't go to the picture show again this Saturday because her father was in jail again and there wasn't even a spare shilling in the Connolly household.

All of these things flashed across her memory in an instant and she wanted to hurt as she had been hurt and strike as she'd been struck and take out a lifetime of frustration and endurance on the privileged rich girl cowering in front of her.

Then she looked at her own angry image through Marcy's frightened eyes and whispered to herself, "Oh, my God, what am I doing?"

Bowen's Wharf | The back of the 'White Rabbit Café | 12:54 a.m.

Mick was jolted to a painful consciousness. He curled into a ball but a second kick knocked the breath from his lungs. The third kick, however, broke through the numbing pain and tripped the little switch in the back of his brain that cut loose the "red McCarthy rage" that was legendary in Southie, and Mick vowed, as he struggled to his knees, that there wouldn't be a fourth.

There wasn't.

But not because of Mick, or the "red McCarthy rage."

Because as the foot drew back for another kick, and Mick pushed himself shakily to his knees, a voice said, "Hey, Cuz, how's it hanging, man?"

The meaty *thwack* of a baseball bat smacking into the head of the taller of the two hoods toppled him face-first into a brackish puddle with a satisfying thud.

The second of the pair slid his hand inside his black suit coat and pulled out a steel-blue Smith and Wesson automatic. Before he could raise the gun and fire, the bat shattered the wrist bones of the hand holding the gun.

As the gunman grabbed his wrist, a wiry, well-muscled body stepped into the weak light of the restaurant's back door, and with a small, sharp gesture, pushed the end of the bat into the gunman's stomach. He staggered to the edge of the restaurant pier, gasping for breath. The compact figure in the faded black leather jacket turned toward Mick and grinned. Then he winked and, almost casually, swung the bat around again. It caught the thug on the side of his head, and he dropped over the side of the wharf like a sack of empty beer bottles in Southie on Saturday night.

"Oops," said the wiry, stringier version of Mick as he held out a hand.

Mick woozily grabbed the strong, scabby-knuckled hand that reached down to him. The world started spinning again, and just before it spun Mick back into his half-conscious jungle-nightmare universe, he could have sworn that he saw the cynical, smiling face of his cousin, Daniel Patrick McCarthy.

Bowen's Wharf Parking Lot | 12:55 a.m.

The flickering beams of the municipal parking lot lights reflected off the cherry-red hood of Valerie's TR-3 and onto the pale faces of the two girls who leaned against the polished fender.

"What did you want to tell me about my sister?" Marcy asked, looking at Bridget out of the corner of her eye. Bridget shook her head. No, she wasn't going to make this weak, frightened rich girl pay for a lifetime of standing at the end of the line. It wasn't right. Even if Marcy had played a part in drugging her and propelling her into a night of terror and humiliation, it still wasn't right to take it all out on Marcy.

"Bridget..?" The helpless, whining tone in Marcy's voice set Bridget's teeth on edge. "I need to know. What were you going to tell me?"

Bridget shook her head. No, she had to let it go.

"Please, you've got to tell me."

What she had meant to tell Marcy, the pampered little rich girl, back when her rage was fresh and clear, was something calculated to cut and tear. She was going to tell Marcy that—

"What?" Marcy said, grabbing Bridget's left hand again, just where, all those years ago, that red welt had been raised. Bridget spun around, all of her good resolve burned away in a hot blast of remembered rage. The face of Sister Margaret scowled down at her and she spat out, "I was gonna tell you that yer sister and her bitch friend Blair played ya fer the fool that you were!"

Marcy's eyes told her that the knife had struck home. Good! Bridget gave it a final twist. "Mick and I saw yer precious PJ tonight. He told us that he loved Blair. And he always had, all the time he was with you!"

Bridget looked at the rich little pseudo-hippie girl and thought, *yes, it hurts doesn't it! Serves ya right. That's fer livin' in luxury and comfort while I was shiverin' in the rain, waitin' outside of the Four Foxes Pub to pay back that fat bastard who—*

Small trickles of tears leaked from Marcy's eyes and collected around the yellow and amber beaded necklace that circled her pale throat.

Bridget watched her for a moment then silently began to cry.

THE SHADOW FIGURE paused halfway across the municipal parking lot, edging out of the overhead lights and watching silently as the scene between the petite black-haired girl and the willowy girl with long brown hair played itself out.

The words drifted across the parking lot. Now angry. Now hurt. And then the tears. The shadow figure drew in the emotion and the pain. It was nourishing. Satisfying.

The girl with the short black hair put her hands on her hips and rounded on the slender girl with the waist-long hair. She screamed out her pain and pent-up rage before dissolving into quiet sobs.

Yes, this was sweet.

Hate. Pain. Rage.

They all had to be let out.

When the rage and jealousy became intolerable, when you needed to do something, anything, to make it stop.

The overhead light reflected dimly in the eyes of the shadow figure, which had already started to glaze over, remembering.

Remembering when, finally, all of the artificial taboos had fallen away, and the pain and the poison had been let out to flow free.

And oh, how they had flowed on that night.

Like warm, red blood.

He motioned to a long, black Bonneville parked in the shadows at the dark end of the lot, shadows that he had now embraced like a lover. Shadows that had once held fear, humiliation and loneliness, but now shadows that he had made his own.

The black car moved slowly toward the two girls still locked in their embrace. He smiled. Soon his own dark shadows would stain those two pretty faces with the only kind of tears that mattered—pain and terror.

Chapter 26

Bowen's Wharf | The back of the 'White Rabbit Café' | 12:57 a.m.

Someone grabbed Mick with both hands. He struggled up out of woozy semi-consciousness and instinctively lashed out. He pushed at the hands and tried to roll over into a defensive posture. The hands fell away and a voice chuckled. "Hey, man, take a chill."

Man take a chill?

The little worm of consciousness and remembering slithered across the front of Mick's cerebellum and whispered, *I was just about to get my teeth kicked in.*

Mick's eyes opened again, and he looked up into the grinning, sarcastic face of his cousin from South Boston.

"Jesus, Mick," Danny laughed, reaching down to help him up, "those two punks looked like they were starting to kick your ass. What's the matter, kid, you losin' your touch?"

With Danny's help, Mick rose to his feet unsteadily.

"Yeah," he smiled, "must be, so thanks for the assist, Grandpa."

They went into the club. Mick looked around for Bridget. He walked unsteadily back to the table they'd been sitting at.

"I've got to find Bridge. Make sure she's okay."

"Relax man, hang easy," Danny said. "I saw her leave with some skinny chick with long brown hair."

Marcy. Bridge had seen the thugs and the strange young man at the back of the club and had made tracks with Marcy. Probably back to Sparrow's. Smart girl. Mick breathed easier, then turned back to his cousin.

"What the hell are you doing here, anyway?" He asked, gratefully swallowing the beer that Danny had shoved into his hand.

"Well," Danny said, draining his bottle of Carling Black Label and motioning the bartender for another, "a little birdy from Southie, by way of Harvard Square—or, make that a big tough junkyard birdy—told me as how his favorite little 'peeper' was down in Rhode Island on a case. And as how he hadn't heard from this bad little bird in four days."

Mick winced.

"So, I decided I just might want to fire up the D Street pony," Danny said, referring to his beloved '65 Mustang, "and slide on down to the land of the rich and famous to see what was up with my big shot detective cousin."

"Well, Danny-boy," Mick said, raising his glass, "I'm damn friggin' glad you did."

"That's nice to hear, Cuz, but when you hear what else old cousin Danny has got for you, you're gonna be even gladder."

Mick raised his eyebrows and took another pull of his beer.

"You see, yer old man, my lovin' Uncle Mike, told me to be careful about poking my nose into places where it could get flattened."

Mick smiled, "That's Pop."

"Well anyway, he said that just in case I decided to take a ride down here—just on my own hook you understand—I should tell you that he got a couple of snitches that owed him, to cough up a name or two. One is a fat guinea who's got his fingers in every dirty pie from Fall River to Rhode Island. A Mr. C. And the other was that kid from down south that you're trying to help. The one who got himself snatched, probably by the Italian, yer Pop says."

"Cody."

"Yeah, that's it. Well I got some good news for ya, Mickey boy. While you were sleeping on the job facedown on the pier out back, yer lovin' cousin had a little 'chat' with that one greaseball that I didn't heave off the pier." Danny finished his beer and belched. "Friggin' tough guys." He shook his head in mock sadness and turned back towards Mick. "Do you know that I only had to break two of his fingers before he started singing like the choir at Sunday Mass?"

"And?" Mick looked up over the rim of his glass.

"And he told me that he works for the guy yer Pop was telling me about. Mr. C. The one who runs all the rackets in Rhode Island. Some guinea name like Costello or Cabrillo or…"

"Cataldo?"

"Yeah. You know him?"

"Naw. Back about five years ago, Pop helped the Feds break a stolen car ring in southeastern New England. Cataldo and his crew were heisting them for some rich dude who pulled the strings out of New York. Pop said Cataldo was a bad-ass and a stone-cold killer."

"Yeah? Well 'bad-ass' or not, he must be losin' it cause his 'muscle' gave it all up to me by the time I got to his third finger."

Mick shook his head. He was about to give Danny some grief about going overboard with his interrogation techniques. Then he remembered his 'chat' with Manny Silva and shut his mouth.

"Learn anything useful?"

"Oh, not much." Danny stretched and examined the broken thumbnail on his left hand. "Just an address."

"Yeah? Where?"

"East Providence. Where we can find Cody Ewing."

Chapter 27

East Providence | Rhode Island
July 30, 1968 | 2:47 a.m.

Paulie Oliverio was having a nice dream. A very nice dream. It had to do with the platinum blond waitress who worked down at the High-C Club on Binney Street, doing talented things to him with her luscious, red lips.

"Oh-h-h, Paulie," she cooed, "I never been with a guy as good as you. You're fantastic, baby."

"You better believe it!" Paulie grinned in his dream.

She pulled him closer and moaned as she ran her fingers through his long, greasy hair. Her fingers wound themselves tighter. Too tight. It was starting to hurt.

"Hey, you dumb bitch, loosen up with the fingers," he snarled. Instead, she grabbed a full handful, pulled his head all the way back, and shoved something hard and cold under his chin. Then she whispered in a flat, nasal South Boston accent, "Wake up, Sleeping Beauty, nap time is over."

"What the fuck?" he sputtered. His eyes flew open and looked up at the upside-down image of a tough Irish face grinning down at him.

One scar-knuckled hand was clamped tightly in his hair, pulling his head back, while the other pushed the sharp, cold muzzle of a snub-nosed .38 revolver under his chin.

The smile was still there, but the eyes got harder as the words drifted down to him. "Okay, greaseball, we want to see Cody Ewing. Now!"

Newport Harbor | 22-B Nickerson Way
July 30, 1968 | 3:36 a.m.

"Is this it, Mick?" Danny grunted.

Mick nodded. After dragging drunk, half-conscious Cody Ewing up two flights of narrow stairs, it was easier to nod than speak. Cody could crash on their floor tonight. They could come up with a plan tomorrow. He smiled. *Oh man, Bridge is gonna love this!*

"Okay then, pal," Danny muttered as he maneuvered Cody's other limp shoulder toward the chipped door of Mick and Bridget's room. "In you go!"

The last syllable was punctuated by a muted crash as Danny's size eleven work-boots kicked open the door.

"For Christ's sake, Danny!" Mick hissed. "Why don't you put a couple of those brain cells you keep in those goddamn big feet back up in your head? Do you want to wake her up?"

Mick scanned the small room. No Bridget. Maybe she was with Sparrow, doing some more of that Tarot stuff.

"Wake who up, Cuz?" Danny asked with a total lack of interest as he squeezed Cody through the narrow doorway and let him fall heavily on to the tiny room's single bed.

"I guess he means me, bright eyes," answered a sleepy, half amused voice from the hallway behind them.

"Oh, hi, Sparrow." Mick smiled weakly.

"Hi yourself, Mick," she said with a lopsided grin. "And your rather large, red-haired friend with the talented, if somewhat loud feet, is…?"

"Ah, yeah. Sparrow, my cousin Danny. Danny, meet Sparrow."

Danny hitched up his belt and ran a hand through his wiry, red hair.

"Sparrow, huh? Great name for a great looking chick. Now, answer old cousin Danny one question, little bird. Does a cute little canary like you fly alone, or do you sometimes like the company of big old red-haired buzzards?"

Danny grinned at Sparrow and winked at Mick.

Mick shook his head. "Jesus, Danny, I'm getting out my hip boots, it's getting deep in here."

Sparrow laughed. "Well, hey, 'Cousin Danny,' why don't you come on down to my room, and maybe you could make sure this little birdy doesn't have to spend the rest of the night flying solo."

She stopped halfway out of the doorway and winked back at him. She pulled a small plastic bag out of her red velour nightgown and dangled it in front of Danny. "Who knows?" she said in a throaty voice. "After a few tokes of this stuff, we may not have to fly on one wing, either."

Danny's grin widened as he stepped through the narrow doorway, put an arm around Sparrow, and said, "Sparrow Baby, like that good Irish kid, Jimmy Morrison's song says, come on baby, light my fire!"

"You got it, handsome," Sparrow chuckled and wrapped her arms around Danny's waist.

As the pair moved down the hallway, Mick called, "Have you and Bridge been doing more crystal ball gazing tonight?"

"Uh-uh," she answered. "And tell your friend he can crash on the couch downstairs if Bridget comes back. If she doesn't, he can crash in your room."

Bridget? Not here?

He was out of the bedroom door and down the hallway just as the door to Sparrow's bedroom was closing. Mick pushed the door open, catching Danny in the back. "Hey Mick, what the—?"

"Shut up, Danny."

Mick took hold of Sparrow's shoulders. His eyes bored into hers.

"Do you mean you haven't seen Bridget tonight?" A hard little knot of dread was forming in his stomach.

She shook her head. "Nope. The last time I saw her was when you guys left here earlier."

"God damn! Where the hell is she?"

"Don't sweat it, Mick," Sparrow said. "Maybe she's visiting a friend, or caught last call down at the wharf."

Mick looked at his watch. It was almost 4:00 a.m. "She doesn't have any friends here and last call was over two hours ago."

He ran down the hallway, took the stairs two at a time, and rushed out into the darkness.

Mick's foot was poised over the BSA's recoil starter. He wiped the sweat from his eyes after his headlong rush down the two flights of stairs and out onto Chestnut Street. He fumbled with the padlock, cursing his shaking fingers, until at last, it dropped free, and he pushed the bike off the curb, straddling the seat as the front tire hit the cobbled paving stones. Pushing open the gas tank's petcock, he flipped the round pedal of the recoil starter until it fit between the heel and sole of his boot. He raised himself up onto the bike to push down with his right leg.

A big black car screeched to a stop half a block in front of him. That car again! The same black shape, silhouetted against the moon, reflected in the silver surf of an outgoing tidal stream.

Except that then there had been a man on the hood, taking aim with a sniper's rifle.

Mick's foot came down hard on the starter, but before the bike's engine could catch, the Bonneville gave a sudden lurch forward then ground to a stop. The right rear door flew open, and something rolled out onto the pavement.

Mick dropped the bike and ran. The 4:00 a.m. wind blew thick black clouds over the moon, and the street was plunged into shadows and darkness. Mick ran to where the Bonneville had been and looked up just in time to see the tail lights disappear around the corner.

The street was empty.

Shit! He must've been seeing things. He turned around and drew a deep breath to sprint back to the bike.

Then he heard a small noise, a catch in someone's throat.

There, under the elm tree that lifted the crumbling red bricks up off the uneven old sidewalk, a small figure crouched, huddled against the rough bark.

"Bridge!" Mick rushed over and lifted her to her feet. He pulled her thin, shaking body toward him. She twisted away and spun out of his grasp.

"Don't! Don't look at me!" she hissed, turning her head away.

"What's wrong, baby?"

"Just go away, go inside for a moment and let me be."

"No," Mick said. "I can't do that."

He stepped up to the curb next to her and put his arms around her. She stiffened.

"I can't do that," he whispered. "Any more than you could go away and leave me alone if something bad happened."

His voice shook as he asked the next question. "Did something bad happen?"

"Just go, Mickey, please."

"Bridget, I swear, nothing could ever happen that would make me stop loving you."

He pulled her tightly against his chest and felt her resistance loosen as her shoulders shook. He lifted up her face to kiss her. She stiffened again and jerked her head away.

"No!" she cried. "I told you, don't look at me!"

But Mick didn't let her go. He pulled her back and kissed her wet cheek. She struggled weakly in his grip and sobbed.

"It's all right, baby, it's all right," Mick soothed as he kissed her cheek, then her jaw line, and bent lower to kiss her smooth, ivory white neck.

She screamed. Mick pulled back. On the beautiful white neck of the girl he loved, the neck that he had covered with thousands of kisses, was a deep, blood-red oozing wound from just beneath her jaw all the way down to her collar bone.

A COLD, GRAY LIGHT crept across the warped window pane of the back bedroom, but Mick was no closer to sleep than he'd been two hours ago, when he first wrapped his arms around Bridget and told her that it would be all right.

But it wasn't. And probably wouldn't be for a long, long time. Right now, his only concern was to heal his poor wounded lady, hurt deep down where her soul met her bright, proud spirit. Mick was very much afraid that that's where the deepest scar would be.

She refused to let him take her to the hospital, turning on him with tears running down her face. "No! No one touches this—no one!"

But in the end, he did. *You don't go through seven major actions and thirteen months in the bush without learning some basic first aid*, he thought as he dabbed antiseptic cream from Sparrow's medicine cabinet. She sat at rigid, straight-backed attention with gritted teeth as he wound a long strip of gauze around her neck. He cursed his thick blunt fingers as they brushed against the long red line leaking through the first layer of the gauze. "Sorry, babe," he whispered. But she never flinched.

"Cover it. Just cover it up!"

When the last trace of the wound disappeared under the final layer of gauze, she lay down on the bed and turned her face to the wall. Her shoulders shook with unshed tears.

Mick lay down beside her. She stiffened in his arms and whispered, "Don't look at me. Don't."

But Mick didn't let go of her. "It's okay, baby, it'll be okay. I love you, and that'll never stop. No matter what."

She turned to him and the tears began to flow as pieces of her spirit fractured and washed away.

It wasn't the pain that caused her iron will to crack. Not even the terrible red wound, which looked as if it would always scar her beautiful white neck, could crush her spirit like that. No, it was being thrust helplessly into someone else's power, for the second time in as many days, that made her break.

All he knew was that she'd been taken, and he was pretty sure he knew by whom. But he'd find out all that soon enough, when she was ready. But first, he had to do everything he could to help her get through this.

They'd made a small start. She wasn't vain, but she knew she was damn good to look at! When she'd screamed and tried to keep him from seeing that red, raw wound, he knew she wasn't thinking about her image in a mirror, but about her image in Mick's eyes.

When her sobs finally settled into soft hiccups, he kissed her on each wet eyelid and lastly, on her throat, next to the gauze that covered her wound.

She tensed for a moment then relaxed as he whispered, "You're beautiful, always. And I love you, always."

She gave a small shudder, then pressed her cheek tighter against his chest and drifted off to sleep.

Mick lay that way, with his back against the hard wooden headboard, Bridget's head on his chest, but sleep wouldn't come.

He meant what he'd said. She was beautiful, and he'd always love her, but they'd taken something away from her, and from him. And he was going to pay them back.

With interest.

Chapter 28

Newport | Rhode Island | Crest View cemetery
July 30, 1968 | 4:22 p.m.

It was almost the first of August, and it should have been cut-offs and T-shirt weather, but instead, the thermometer would be lucky to nudge the high 60s today. A cold damp fog blew across the cracked asphalt track that led to the cemetery overlooking Newport harbor.

Mick turned the bike left and headed around the outside of the ornate wrought-iron fence. A gust of wind off the ocean blew a breath of forlorn fog into his face. "Perfect friggin' day for a funeral," he muttered.

Mick half turned and looked at Bridget. She pressed her cheek tighter into the back of his jacket.

He stared into the wind-wet fog and let the moisture coat his face and mingle freely with his sadness.

Bridget hadn't said much of anything since she'd spilled all of her fear and despair into his T-shirt in the tiny hours of the morning. It seemed like this last random kick of fate had finally succeeded in breaking a small chink in the self-confident armor that the diminutive Celtic Princess-warrior from County Cork had forged to protect herself.

They'd gone downstairs to Sparrow's bright, canary yellow kitchen, with its brightly painted murals of birds floating above psychedelic clouds, all designed to loosen the mind and let the spirit soar. But it did nothing for theirs. They drank their tea in silence, while Mick held Bridget's hand. Or tried to. She let it rest coldly in his for a few moments before she slowly pulled it back across the table.

Should he have held onto it? Carried her back upstairs and made love to her? He didn't know. He just didn't know what he should do, or feel.

He had been staring helplessly at the tabletop when he heard Bridget's sharp intake of breath. Then the morning newspaper was pushed across the table, and Bridget had said a single terse word. "Look!" Her finger stabbed a notice on the obituary page.

Mick read. "Services will be held today at St. Ann's Episcopal Church for Miss Blair Prentiss Vanderwall, followed by interment at Crestview Cemetery."

He looked up. Bridget, white-faced and shaking, said in a rasping voice, "When that black Mariah hell-car pulled down this street last night, just before he—" She squeezed her eyes shut and looked back into her nightmare memory. "Marcy whispered to me, 'The funeral tomorrow. Go there. You'll see.'"

BRIDGET'S HANDS gripped the tabletop.

"I could never get a good look at his face, it was always hidden in the shadows, in the corner of the back seat. But Marcy recognized him. She wanted us to go to the cemetery because she knew this 'Shadow Man' was gonna be there. I asked Marcy "who?" but he pulled her head away by the hair. I got a glimpse of his face then, but it's all a blur in my mind. All except the eyes." Bridget paused and stared through Mick. "Those eyes. They were like nothing you can imagine. A flat bottomless blue. Like looking into a deep cold lake, with nothing underneath but miles and miles of madness."

She began to shake. "Then he hit Marcy, hard, and the other one grabbed me."

She paused, took a shuddering breath, her eyes staring off over Mick's shoulder, and said in a wooden monotone, "As the car turned down Chestnut Street, the one in the front seat, the fat one, said, 'I'm gonna give you a message to take to your boyfriend. And I'm gonna stamp it in a way that you and him will never forget, not as long as you live.'"

Mick sat frozen, helpless, watching her relive the horror.

"Then the fat man said, 'Go ahead, kid. Do it. I know how much you want to.' And he laughed." Bridget looked from her distant vision back into Mick's eyes. "He looked at the one in the shadows. A cigarette lighter lit, and I could almost see his face and the terrible mad eyes. Then it was gone again. Only the glowing red tip of a cigarette remained." Her voice dropped to a whisper. "The fat man in the front seat said, 'You and your boyfriend get your noses out of where they don't belong and leave Newport tonight!' And then the pock-marked greasy one sittin' beside me grabbed hold of my arms and pulled them behind me and held me."

Bridget's eyes searched his and she choked, "He held me so tight I almost couldn't breathe. And the other, the 'Shadow Man,' he drew and drew on that cigarette until it seemed like the whole back seat glowed hell-red. Then the Shadow Man whispered 'I'm going to leave something on your pretty white face. A warning and a judgment on you and every other beautiful girl who uses her body and her face to…'"

She looked up at him. "Mickey, he's insane. He pushed the tip of his cigarette toward my face. He meant to scar me, right here." She pointed to her right cheek. "But at the last minute, I saw my Da after they'd let him out of Wexford Prison. They'd beat him something awful. I was only twelve, and I cried so as we carried him back home, but he said to me, 'Look at me, daughter, and remember this. You are a Connolly and the daughter of an IRA Major, and you never give up ta the bastards without a fight.' And so, at the very last moment, just as I could feel the heat of that burning tip on my cheek, I twisted and the cigarette burned down my neck. But not my face!"

She looked up and whispered one more time, "Not my face. It's still—is it still all right?"

"God, yes, Bridge." Mick took her hand in his and kissed it. "It'll be all right."

Now all they could do was to take this last clue that Marcy had given to Bridget in that final, terrible moment, and run with it.

So half past four on a fog-damp Newport afternoon found them looking through the iron bars of a hillside cemetery as a polished mahogany coffin with gold handles began its final descent.

Mick killed the motor, pulled up the kickstand, and turned to help Bridget off the bike, but she was already off and starting for the open gate.

She paused, and Mick's heart broke one more time as she pulled up the collar of her black turtleneck sweater. Sadly he wondered when, if ever, he would see that beautiful, white neck, without the black turtleneck.

Bridget was already through the gate by the time Mick pulled the big bike up onto the kickstand. The wind off the cold, white-capped waves in the distance blew through the pale green stems of the wild beach plums that grew against the iron fence. But inside the gate, everything unruly and untidy had been banished. There were no wild beach plums or tough sea grass, or anything untamed. It was as though those who were now putting away that strange, wild, selfish and self-indulgent spirit that had been Blair Prentiss Vanderwall had needed to confine whatever essence had been hers to some place tidy and controlled. Somewhere where she couldn't get out and make their ordered lives unpredictable again.

Unpredictable, like the things that were happening to him and Bridge, spinning their lives out of control, making them doubt. Making them fear.

Bridget stood at the edge of the crowd that was slowly dispersing from the graveside. She stared at a group of men about fifteen feet from the hole that the bored-looking groundskeepers were filling in.

She looked from one to the other, marking them. The fingers of her right hand went to her throat, and he knew who they were.

Mick walked toward the gravesite. He stopped as a trio dressed in black passed in front of him. Blair Vanderwall's family, Mick guessed. The mother, a thin, elegant woman with short blond hair and finishing school bearing. Her face, obscured by the black lace veil that hung from her pillbox hat, was still attractive.

The two males were dressed alike, in somber Brooks Brothers suits and white, button-down oxford shirts. The older was tall and fit, with haunted, sleep-deprived eyes, and baggy eyelids. The younger, shorter and baby-faced, had the bearing of one destined to sit at the head of boardroom tables and wield power.

A nagging feeling of déjà vu came over Mick. That face. He'd seen it before—in a dream. A very bad dream. It hovered just outside of his consciousness.

As the three walked toward the gate, a fat man in a shiny suit, purple shirt and bright flowered tie, detached himself from the group by the grave. He hurried over and laid a hand on the older man's arm.

"Not now!" Mr. Vanderwall snapped and pushed the hand away.

As they approached their black limo, the younger man looked back at Mick for a moment then climbed into the car. The limo driver shut the heavy back door and drove away.

"What the hell are you looking at, bitch?" A low-pitched, nasal whine blew across the salt-damp graveyard.

Mick turned. Bridget stood on the seaward side of the grave, behind the pile of freshly turned earth. She stared across the hole at a sneering, acne-scarred face that called out again, "I'm talkin' to you, bitch."

Mick came up behind her and put his arm around her shoulders. She didn't move toward him, or even acknowledge his presence. She just stared, her fingers clenching and unclenching.

"Was he the one? Did he do that to you?"

Mick dug the toe of his right cowboy boot into the soft ground. He opened and closed his right hand, the hand that was going to rip that mother's heart out and stuff it down his—

Bridget's head slowly swiveled right to left.

No? Mick's body froze. If not him, then who?

A hand fell on his shoulder and pulled him around. A fat but powerful looking 'hard case,' the same who had approached Mr. Vanderwall, said, "McCarthy, right?"

Mick pushed Bridget behind him and answered, "Who wants to know, Porky?"

"Funny kid," the fat man said without smiling. He raised his hand and pointed at Bridget's neck. "Do you think that's funny? Cause if you do, then you're gonna bust a gut at the next one. It's gonna go right across that pretty white face."

Mick reached out and grabbed a handful of the purple silk shirt and bright flower print tie, but a fist came out of nowhere and smashed into his stomach, doubling him over.

Bridget dropped to her knees in the soft dirt beside him and hissed, "Leave him alone, you bastards."

Three other black-suited thugs stood behind their leader, while the one who'd sucker-punched Mick grabbed him by his jacket collar and pulled his head back. The fat hood straightened his tie and bent down until his face was level with Mick and Bridget's.

"What happened to your lady last night was just a warning, pal," he whispered. "You don't want there to be a next time."

He stood up, brushed off the knife-sharp creases on the knees of his expensive Italian suit, and said, "So listen up kid, 'cause I'm only gonna ask this once. Where the hell is Cody Ewing?"

Mick mustered his best 'screw-you' grin. "Sure, I'll tell you Porky—when fat pigs like you sprout wings and fly."

The skinny, acne-scarred punk holding Mick's collar snarled, "shut up, asshole!" and drew back his fist. But the fat man in the purple shirt shook his head and smiled at Mick instead.

"I like your girlfriend's choice of wardrobe. The turtleneck looks good on her. It would be a real shame if we ever had to *chat* again. Then the neck of that sweater might have to be stretched up to cover her face."

Mick lunged for him but didn't get far. One of the men grabbed him from behind, pinned his arms and pushed a knee into the small of his back. The fat man gripped the collar of Mick's T-shirt.

"This is the last time I'm gonna say this. You tell me where you stashed that banjo playin' cracker, then you take your broad, while she still got a face left, and climb on your little motorbike, and get the fuck outta my state."

He grinned. "I know all about you, tough guy. Friends of mine up in Boston told me about you and yer old man. He used to be a tough guy, too. Maybe he still is. And maybe that's the only reason that I'm talking to you now and not shoveling dirt onto you and your bitch's face in that grave over there."

Mick was breathing hard.

"It's almost five o'clock," the fat man said, looking at his gold Rolex watch. "In one hour, Paulie and Sammy, here, are gonna pull up in front of that hippie broad's place, and you're gonna bring out that skinny, bourbon-drinking son of a bitch, or tell us where he is, or," he reached down and lifted Bridget's white jaw between his right thumb and forefinger, "I'm gonna let the boys do things to this cute little face that will—"

Mick bit down on the wrist of the arm pressed against his throat. There was a scream, the arm whipped back. Mick lunged, grabbing for the fat boss, but the sound of the hammer being drawn back on the pistol at Bridget's head stopped him cold.

"Yeah, that's right, tough guy, you better think twice. You got one hour."

THE ROAR OF 650 cc of British pistons drowned out Mick's muttered curses as he wound the BSA down the windswept sand and asphalt track toward Newport harbor. Bridget's fingernails dug into the back of his denim jacket.

He shifted into neutral with his left foot and coasted up to a four-way stop sign at the corner of Nickerson Way and the east end of Main Street.

He seethed every time he thought about how that fat, greasy thug had looked down at him crouching in the dirt of Blair Vanderwall's freshly filled grave. His fingers ached to wrap themselves around that fat neck and squeeze out some long overdue payback.

But first he had to warn Cody, Sparrow and Danny to get the hell out before the goon squad showed up.

He pulled up in front of number 22-B Nickerson Way. Bridget hadn't said a word since they'd left the cemetery. Truth be told, Mick didn't feel much like talking either, but he also knew that action was gonna be the best medicine—for both of them.

He drew in a breath of the dank sea air. "Okay, Bridge, here's the plan. We're gonna be waiting for those bastards when they come here, but we're gonna change the rules of the game. First, we're gonna make sure Cody and Danny and Sparrow get out of here. And then," Mick put his arms around Bridget's shoulders and whispered into her sweet, soft hair, "I'm gonna kill the bastard that hurt you."

MICK AND BRIDGET rushed through Sparrow's front door, expecting to find her and Cody and Danny smoking a joint, listening to music, chilling.

They stopped dead in their tracks.

"Oh, no," Bridget said. "The bloody bastards!"

"I should have known," Mick said. "Only an idiot would take the word of a pig like Cataldo."

They stepped into Sparrow's main-floor studio. With her fingertip Bridget traced the slashes in one of the hippie woman-child's bright seascapes, littering the floor and hanging askew on the walls. Mick reached out and pushed away the shattered remains of Sparrow's pottery wheel. The remnants of her latest psychedelic coffee mug fell off the worktable with a plop.

"Obviously his goons were on their way here to snatch Cody while we were having our friendly little chat with the boss. But he was wrong. There was nobody here when they arrived."

"How can you tell?"

"They did this," he swept his arm over the destruction around them, "to scare us, break our spirits. Make us think the game was over and we'd lost. Well we haven't!" Mick slammed his hand on the table. A few shards of broken pottery fell off and joined the others on the floor.

"You know," Bridget said, "I've been thinking ever since Cataldo said he'd be coming here in an hour. How did he know where we were staying? Who would have told him? The only answer I can come up with doesn't make any sense."

Mick frowned. "One of two people in Newport who know. Sparrow, or—"

"Her brother, Sergeant O'Donnell."

"Christ," Mick said through clenched teeth. "I hope you're wrong."

"And who tipped Cody off to get out of here?"

"Nobody. I'm betting he headed for the only safe haven he knew on the whole east coast."

"The Newport Folk Festival," Bridget said.

"Right. His band's performing tonight. Those guys are friends and relatives. He's counting on those 'down home' boys to protect one of their own with their lives. I know, I had a corporal like that. Cody likely offered Sparrow the protection of his Kentucky clan, and old cousin Danny would follow Sparrow and her stash of Acapulco Gold anywhere."

"So when we find Cody's band, we find them all."

Bridget slowly nodded her head and the old fire started to come back into her eyes. "We've got to find them and keep Cataldo and his filthy bunch from getting their hands on them."

Her eyes widened, she covered her mouth with her hand. "Mickey, I've been so... so... rattled by what happened to me that I never even thought about... Sweet saints, what if they still have Marcy?"

"I thought you hated Marcy and were gonna call for an IRA 'action' on her."

"Michael McCarthy!" Bridget snapped with an echo of her old fire.

"Don't you go jokin' about things like that!" She looked at him with a ghost of her County Cork pixie smile, and shook her head. "No, boy-o, I've sent the word out to all the loyal sons of Erin that the 'action' against Miss Marcy Trainor has been suspended."

"Very commendable, Miss Connolly. And may I ask why?"

"Because," she answered, her face serious again, "while I was with her last night, in the parking lot and in that car, I came to realize that even though she was a little rich girl, brought up with all the trappings and privilege of the bloody gentry at home, she'd been the odd one out in her family and social circle. The runt of the litter, so to speak. She was abused, knocked about. Not in the way you think of it, or in the way I knew it as a girl back in County Cork, but abused all the same." She gave a snort of disgust. "Especially by her nasty excuse fer a sister and her bitch friend, Blair."

Bridget got that hard look that Mick knew all too well. "The two of them took a positive delight in tormentin' the poor girl."

"So," Mick said, "Marcy finally had enough of being made the kick ball for those two, and decided to eliminate one of her tormentors."

Bridget shook her head once more.

"No. Marcy didn't kill Blair."

She looked around her at the ruins of Sparrow's studio.

"She was too scared to tell me, but she knows who did, and the ones who took us know, too. The one who sat in the shadows of the car last night, the one who—" Her voice choked. She shuddered. "You have no idea what he's capable of," she whispered. "Oh dear God, if he's got her now, the things he could be doing to her!"

Bridget stared past him at a horror only she could see. "What he's capable of doing would make death welcome."

She balled her hands into fists and pulled away from Mick. "How are we going to find her? She could be anywhere. She could be…"

"All we can do is get down to the festival and look out for Cody. Cataldo's smart enough to figure out that's where he'll be, and he's bound to show up looking for him. With Cody and his band's help, we take out Cataldo and his hoods, and they tell us where Marcy is."

"Let's go then. God help us, I hope we're not too late, for Marcy's sake."

They left Sparrow's house and ran to Mick's bike. He swung his leg over the teardrop gas tank and Bridget climbed on behind.

They made a right turn onto Chestnut, a left onto Thames and headed east toward the Newport Folk & Blues Festival.

Chapter 29

East Providence | Rhode Island | Binney Street
July 30, 1968 | 6:37 p.m.

Smack!

The sound of flesh striking flesh filled all corners of the small room.

"What did you tell them, Marcy?" the polite, almost pleasant voice asked the girl with the waist-long hair, bound to the wooden chair at the center of the dank, stone-walled room.

Marcy was not a brave girl. Most of her well-to-do life had been spent letting others—the hired help of the wealthy and privileged—solve her problems for her.

But she had been hit before. Many times. And almost always by her older sister, Jackie. Her pretty, popular older sister.

And despite all the wealth and privilege that being a daughter of Sarah and Walter Trainor brought with it, there had never been any redress for that particular problem. No servant interfered. No trusted old family retainer said, "stop." No parent gathered her in her arms and kissed away her tears. Not a disinterested and only occasionally there father, and most certainly not her own dear mother.

"Oh, Marcy, don't squabble, and don't tell tales. Just try to work it out."

And so she had. She avoided it whenever she could. She ran whenever it got too close. And when she couldn't avoid it, when there was nowhere to run, then she just took it.

Like now.

Smack!

This one struck her right cheek and threw her head back against the chair. She let her head roll back with the blow. She was used to rolling with the punches.

The third grade. Mrs. Nelson's art class. "Marcy, this drawing is totally unacceptable. Why, you haven't even colored inside the lines like all of the other girls."

Smack, went the words into the small, mousey brown-haired girl's eight-year-old ego.

Miss Alicia Seymour's Dance Academy for Young Ladies, June of 1960.

One by one, each of the girls in their taffeta dresses and patent leather shoes were chosen by awkward, sweaty-palmed boys for the sixth grade's final session of dancing school. All except for the shy, skinny, brown-haired girl sitting alone in the corner.

Miss Alicia even approached the awkward boys standing along the opposite wall, poking one another, and said something to the best looking of the pack, a boy with bright blue eyes and curly dark hair. His name was Mark Richardson, and Marcy had had a quiet crush on him since the first grade.

"Mark," Marcy could just make out Miss Alicia's words from her corner, and her heart jumped.

"I think it would be very nice," Miss Alicia continued, "if you asked Miss Marcy Trainor to dance."

"Uh-uh," Mark shook his head.

"And why not?" Miss Alicia asked.

"Because," answered the boy that little Marcy loved with all her twelve-year-old heart, "she's a dope and she wears braces."

Marcy had clapped a white-gloved hand over her mouth and run crying from the dancing hall.

Smack! Marcy's head hit the back of the chair again.

Blood trickled down the left side of her chin and spotted her long-sleeved paisley dress.

She looked up at her tormentor. Sweat beaded on the old acne scars of his cheeks and forehead. He frowned, unsnapped his tab collar and loosened his dark, narrow tie. "Hey, Mr. C.," he called over his shoulder. "This is either one tough or real friggin' stupid bitch."

"Keep your mouth shut and your mind on your job," the fat man behind the bare wooden table growled.

"Yeah, sure," the young man called Sammy grunted. He hit her across the mouth again.

Smack!

"Marcy!" the voice from the shadows called, this time almost plaintively. "What did you tell them? Mick and Bridget?" The voice rose again. "Tell me! How much do they know?"

Smack!

"What did you say?"

Silence.

Smack!

"Tell me!"

Smack!

The voice of the one who stayed hidden in the shadows added almost softly, "Please."

Marcy smiled and slowly shook her head from side to side as she tasted the coppery blood that leaked from numerous small cuts inside her cheek. Because now she knew, fully, finally, and with absolute certainty, exactly to whom the voice belonged.

Chapter 30

Newport Harbor | Rhode Island
July 30, 1968 | 7:36 p.m.

The sun dipped toward the horizon and turned the water lapping the pier upon which the Newport Yacht Club restaurant rested a shimmering blood red. It sent chills up and down the spine of Bronwyn Prescott-McCarthy.

She stared out at the crimson water, turning darker red with each passing moment. She shivered despite the summer-like temperature within the lounge adjacent to the club's main dining room.

There was something about that water, or maybe just this place, Newport, and her mother's creepy, plastic friends, that freaked her out.

"Bronwyn, did you hear me? I asked you where you went with Michael and Bridget. I don't know why in heaven's name he has to drag that little Irish waitress along with him everywhere he goes!"

Bronwyn was in no mood for her mother's probing and condescending put-downs. Not after last night at the White Rabbit.

"Do you always have to put down anyone who doesn't live on Brattle Street or Beacon Hill? Mick loves Bridget and she loves him." She looked at the blood red water. "And they could both be in real danger."

Felicity Parker Prescott grabbed her daughter's arm, for once losing her cool patrician poise. "What do you mean 'in real danger'?"

"I… I don't know."

"Bronwyn Prescott, tell me this instant! Do you understand me?"

Bronwyn pulled her arm away and snapped. "Stop it! Stop bossing everyone around like they were your servants!"

Her mother's face turned white, her lower jaw quivered.

"Mom, I'm sorry, but I don't know the details. I just know that they're after Blair Vanderwall's killer, and the closer they get, the more shit keeps happening to them."

"Bronwyn!" Her mother said. "Your language. I—I don't know what's come over you."

Bronwyn shook her head. She spoke softly, more to herself than her mother. "I don't know either, Mom."

But I've got a horrible feeling that things are going to get a whole lot worse before they get better.

Fifteen minutes later, Bronwyn was still staring at the almost black water when a cool, slender hand brushed across her shoulder. She jumped. It was her mother, and she had apparently decided to do what she usually did whenever there was anything remotely resembling an unpleasant scene. She blotted it out of her mind and returned to the banal and safe.

"Bronwyn?" Felicity Parker Prescott murmured. "You mustn't mope, dear. It makes you unattractive. You look like you've just lost your invitation to the Junior Miss Debutante Ball."

Bronwyn turned away from the hypnotic pull of the ocher red sea and said, "I really don't think that would spook me all that much, Mother."

As a matter of fact, I think I'd prefer a long swim off the end of this pier to an invitation like that.

She tried to push the feelings of foreboding out of her mind as she remembered why debutante balls had never really mattered very much to her. As the ominous sun set, she made a decision to stop playing 'the good little girl' to her mother and do something wild and or irresponsible that *she* wanted to do. And she was going to do it tonight! She was going to the festival and let whatever happens happen. But for now? Play the dutiful daughter. So she smiled the smile of the doomed and the damned and the too-comfortable-to-do-anything-about-it, and said, "Oh, look, Mother, Mr. and Mrs. Cortland are waving to us. Our table must be ready."

But as she followed in the self-satisfied, self-centered wakes of the Cortlands and the last of the true Prescott ladies, she allowed herself a small smile and sent out a secret thought to the old bear sitting in his smoke-filled cave of an office in Cambridge.

Dad, I hope you're thinking of your 'little girl', 'cause I've got a feeling that before this night is over I'm gonna need every bit of McCarthy I've got in me!

WHEN THE BORING dinner finally ended Bronwyn stood up, kissed her mother on the cheek and said, "Okay, Mom. See you later." She walked toward the door.

As expected, Miss Felicity said in the voice that had been coached almost from the cradle to command servants and lesser beings, "Bronwyn, dear. I really think you should stay with me tonight."

Bronwyn stopped and turned. "Sorry, Mom, no can do."

Her mother turned up the saccharine meter in her voice, but underneath was pure poison.

"Bronwyn, I'm not about to let you go off all by yourself to—"

Bronwyn struck. "Oh, don't worry Mom, I won't be alone." She smiled and gave it to her mother between the eyes. "I'm going to the Festival with," she looked at Gilbert and Bunny Cortland, "Valerie."

Miss Felicity took Brom's verbal sucker punch right in the gut and sat back down. "Oh."

Gil and Bunny looked at each other then at Felicity. Then they looked back at Bronwyn, then at Felicity again and then back at each other. In unison, they said, "Oh."

Bronwyn mentally carved an unaccustomed notch into the 'win' column of the epic and unending verbal battle with her mother for the domination of her soul, and gave a cutesy little wave with her fingertips.

"Bye. Thanks for a great dinner, and—don't wait up."

Cambridge | Massachusetts | Harvard Square
July 30, 1968 | 7:41 p.m.

"McCarthy?"

The 56-year-old former Boston police department sergeant and detective grade cop held the old black rotary dial telephone to his ear. Someone murmured on the other end of the line.

The ex-cop heard muffled words then a raspy, nasal voice—southeast New England: New Bedford, Fall River, or East Providence, yeah, that was it, East Providence—came on the line and said, "Mike McCarthy?"

'Big Mike' McCarthy let the seconds tick away on the old Seth Thomas wall clock, one of the few quality items in his Harvard Square office. Finally, he answered in a voice mangled by whiskey and Lucky Strike cigarettes.

"Yeah, and how the hell are you, Cataldo, you slimy piece of crap?"

There was a pause and then a heavy breath on the other end of the line. "Still the tough guy, McCarthy?"

"Tough enough to cut your balls off and stuff them down your throat if you're calling about what I think you're calling about."

The voice on the other end of the line paused again then went on. "Listen, I'm doin' you a big favor. Givin' you a heads-up. Get your fuckin' kid out of Newport. Tell him and his broad to get their long noses outta my asshole and get the fuck back up to Boston. Or the next time, they—especially her—won't get off so easy."

Michael Francis McCarthy sat bolt upright in the hard old wooden chair next to the battered rolltop desk that took up most of the space in the one-room office. He snarled into the receiver, "Cataldo, If you've done anything to Mick or his girlfriend, I'll rip your—"

"Not much yet, McCarthy. Not like what's gonna happen if you don't tell him to play it smart."

Mike heard a wheezing intake of breath and the voice continued, "This is a friendly, professional warning. For old times' sake. There won't be another." The line went dead.

Chapter 31

Newport | Rhode Island | Newport Folk and Blues Festival
July 30, 1968 | 8:24 p.m.

Mick pulled up about five hundred yards from the festival entrance and cut the engine.

"Wha'dya think, babe?"

Bridget shook her head. "I think if we're right and Cataldo's waiting for us, he'll be watching the entrance. So we leave the bike here and sneak in behind the stage."

Mick nodded. "Good plan."

Bridget nodded and started to climb off the bike. Mick reached back and put his hand on her arm.

"All except the part about leaving the bike."

"Oh?"

"We may need to get out a whole lot faster than we came in, and the BSA has never let us down."

He stamped down on the starter and the big machine roared to life.

The festival grounds sat in a natural amphitheatre. On one hillside, Mick spotted a crumbling stone wall. A narrow path snaked up to it, overgrown with sea grass and littered with bricks and stones. At the top end of the path, where it bent close to the breach in the wall, a section of hillside on the seaward side of the trail had broken away and fallen into the surf at the bottom of the cliff. There was a gap of maybe twenty feet between the path and the wall beyond. There was no fence around that side of the field. Only a suicidal idiot or a mountain goat would want to climb it and try to jump that gap. That is, unless they had a machine that had already made an impossible jump less than forty-eight hours before.

"Ready Bridge?"

"Absolutely not!"

He turned back and grinned at her.

She nodded once and wrapped her arms around his waist.

"Lead on McDuff, and damned be him who first cries, 'hold enough'!"

"Huh?"

"Paraphrase of an Englishman I do like. Shakespeare. Let's do it!"

Mick popped the clutch and leaned the bike around toward the back of the festival grounds.

"HOLY SHIT!"

A back-to-nature couple who had pitched their small tent out at the far end of the festival field where they could listen to the music, smoke a little weed and enjoy one another's company without the up-tight, middle class encumbrance of clothing, were rudely jolted back to reality when a large hunk of blue metal screamed almost over their heads and landed in a skidding cloud of dust not ten feet away.

The big motorcycle spun around 180 degrees and the driver called back over his shoulder as he headed for the area in back of the stage, "Sorry for the interruption."

The couple looked at each other and when they looked back again, the guy, his motorcycle and the girl on the back, had disappeared in the dust and the darkness.

Festival Grounds | 8:46 p.m.

Mick and Bridget paused at the bottom of the stairs leading up to the back of the stage.

"Stop, Mickey," Bridget said, clasping his arm.

"What is it?"

"I thought I saw a black suit in the crowd, just over there. Now it's gone. They're already here."

Mick chewed the inside of his lip. "Okay, let's make this quick. We'll find out what time Cody's band goes on and then hide out in one of those parties behind the stage where we can keep an eye out to see if we're being tailed."

He took her hand and winked at her. "Come on, Miss Watson. The game's afoot."

They bounded up the stairs.

THE SINGER/POET on stage inclined his head slightly toward the crowd; the volume of cheers rose higher and higher. He smiled at his roaring sea of fans and nodded to his hybrid electric/acoustic band. The third headlining group at the 1968 Newport Folk and Blues Festival launched into the title song of their newly released *Elektra* album.

Standing off to one side of the fifteen-foot high backdrop of psychedelically painted canvas, the group's newly appointed A&R man looked around at everything and nothing.

It was his first big assignment, to monitor the newly signed folk/rock group on their first big tour. His boss, Phil Moscone, had said, "Be cool. Act cool. Let it all seem effortless. But don't ever, *ever* let it get out of your control."

"Take it to frigging heart, man," he muttered under his breath. He raised his shoulders under his camelhair sports jacket and lowered them again to ease the tension. "His" group's hit song built to the slide guitar and tambourine crescendo and the festival audience was on their feet, screaming.

Yeah, he was gonna knock this thing off just fine, go back to L.A. and tell old Phil that he'd shepherded their new soon-to-be-number-one group through a successful tour and—

"Excuse me."

Christ! What now? He looked at the grey-eyed guy and the very attractive green-eyed girl in the short denim skirt, black tights and black turtleneck.

"What?" the A&R man asked, looking at the green-eyed girl.

"Sorry to interrupt," the grey-eyed guy, who really didn't seem very sorry, said, "but you know what time The Rounders go on?"

"Who?" he snapped

"The Rounders."

Mr. L.A. thought for a moment then snorted. "Oh, those hillbillies from Kentucky."

"I guess you could call them that," the quiet voice responded.

"Well," the future record 'Desk Jockey' answered, watching the band on stage, "probably later tonight. When all the good acts are through, they let the 'hicks and hacks' on stage to wail away for the burnouts and the 'half-in-the-bag' crowd. If you want my advice," he turned toward the pair, "you'll—"

Standing where the guy and girl had been a second ago was a man with a pockmarked face, in a black suit and shirt. His snake-black eyes stared back without expression. In a high, nasal monotone, he said "My boss, Mr. C., wants to know whatcha told them two you was just talking to."

"What two?" His mouth was suddenly dry.

A fist slammed into his stomach.

"I'm not gonna ask you again, pal," the black suit snarled.

All of the neophyte A&R man's dreams of glory whooshed out with his breath, and he gasped, doubled over, "They were looking for… a band… called The Rounders."

"BRONWYN PRESCOTT!" a voice called through the crowd.

Bronwyn Prescott-McCarthy turned. "Laney Hewitt. I was hoping I'd run into you."

"I had no idea you were a festival type. Last time I saw you was in Grendel's Den in Harvard Square, just before school got out."

"Oh, Mom decided we needed a 'girls' weekend' away, so she dragged me down here to stay with a bunch of her old fogey friends up on Bellevue Avenue."

"Oh, barf," Bronwyn's Radcliffe friend said, making a face. "What a bummer!"

"Tell me about it," Bronwyn sighed. "You have no idea what I had to go through to ditch Mom and make it down here."

"Well, I'm glad you did," Laney said, grabbing on to Bronwyn's arm and pulling her back to the row of wooden seats that she and her friends had staked out as their own little bit of Cambridge at the '68 Folk Festival.

"Hey, Buzzen," Laney called to her boyfriend, known in other upper-class circles as Warren Busby III. "Look who's here."

"Hey, Brom," 'Buzzen', a.k.a. Warren, answered in a voice made way too mellow by way too many tokes on way too many joints. "What's up?"

"Not a whole lot, Buzzen," she giggled then whispered to Laney,

"I mean, 'Warren,'" and Laney giggled back and passed her Buzzen-Warren's soggy joint as Brom finished with, "I just came to hang out with you guys for a while and feel some peace, love and really good vibes."

Festival grounds | 8:57 p.m.

"Walkin' down Beale Street, turnin' up Main / Lookin' for that little gal who sells cocaine. Cocaine—all ramblin' round my brain.

The girl with long, braided auburn hair pushed a wayward strand back up under her beaded headband and looked adoringly up at her boyfriend as he finished the last notes of the hard-blues song with an accompanying harmonica solo. He strummed out the final chords to another one of the small crowd's generational anthems, and favored the impromptu hootenanny with a cool, indulgent smile.

"Oh, Mitch, like, wow, man," the singer's girlfriend exclaimed. "That was, like, so far out!"

"It's just another damned cover. Everybody does that," whispered a voice on the other side of the trash and charcoal briquette campfire behind the festival stage.

"Shush, Mickey!" Bridget hissed from beside him. "We're just blendin' in, remember?"

"Blend away, babe," Mick yawned, stretching his arms up over his head.

Christ, he was tired. It seemed like all they'd been doing for the past four days had been chasing, being chased, running, hiding, fighting, getting beat up and generally knocked around. And he was getting damned tired of it. So damned tired.

He hadn't slept at all last night and that was something else he was going to pay them back for. But he was just so damned tired. He let his head slip down so that his cheek rested against the softness of Bridget's breast under her black sweater.

She looked at him with a half smile. "Close yer eyes, darlin.'"

Mick smiled up at her then sat half upright again as two of the roadies, fans and hangers-on that were making up the impromptu hootenanny, song-swap party came through the circle carrying an old tin washtub filled with ice and cans of beer.

"Hey, man," Mick called as they passed, "you think we could bum a couple of those beers?"

"Can you sing for them?"

"Sure thing." Mick started to get up and grabbed for Bridget's hand.

"Mick, no!" Bridget whispered, holding him down. "We're supposed to be hidin'. That's why we're sittin' back here. So we can see the stage, who comes and goes. But they can't see us." She added under her breath, "I hope."

"That's right. Blend, baby, blend."

Bridget pulled his head back down to her sweater.

Someone on the other side of the fire took the guitar and sang about the color of his true love's hair.

"Now we've got a Donovan wannabe," Mick yawned as he settled back again. "Doesn't anyone write their own stuff anymore?"

The big guy holding the other handle of the tin washtub laughed and pulled two cans of Carling Black Label, tossing them to Mick. "Yeah, I know a few guys who do. I'll bring them over later."

Mick sat up again and Bridget sighed. "Oh, fer heaven's sake, Mick, will ya sit still then?"

"Sure thing," he said, unbuttoning the top pocket of his denim jacket. "Just as soon as I wash the dust off my tonsils."

He pulled a rusty can opener from among the many items stuffed into his jacket pocket and opened the cans, passing one to Bridget.

"To music," he smiled, touching his to hers.

"To music," she answered.

And to justice! Mick added silently.

Mick took a long pull of the beer and stared at the wavering image of the back of the festival stage through the fire. He lay down and rested his head in Bridget's lap, yawning.

"Close yer eyes, darlin', and rest a bit."

He raised his head and shook it, trying to drive the sleep from his rapidly fogging brain. "I gotta watch the stage. I know Cataldo's here. I can feel it. That same feeling I used to get in the bush when 'Charlie' was on the move."

He yawned again. The beer was weighing him down like a ton of lead. He couldn't keep his eyes open. Bridget stroked his hair. His eyes closed and he mumbled, "Just gonna catch a few Zs. You keep watch. Wake me… if you see anything and…" He was asleep.

Bridget watched her lover and best friend drift off and thought, *I hope I can do that, Mickey.*

Her mind replayed the traumatic events of the past twenty-four hours. For the hundredth time she fingered her neck and traced the raw red wound that was eating away at her soul. It wasn't just that they had kidnapped, terrorized and scared her. It was that now she had put the life of the most important person in her world at risk as well. She kept hearing his words as they pulled up in front of Sparrow's; "I'm gonna kill the ones that hurt you." Michael Prescott McCarthy did not make a threat lightly. He meant it. He would kill them, or die trying. And that scared her more than anything that Cataldo and the Shadow Man could do to her.

Besides, she had a score to settle. Others had seen the petite Irish girl as an easy target for their own twisted desires and had tried to assault her body and her spirit. And she had dealt with them—in her own way.

County Cork, Ireland | Ballykill police station
March 20, 1958

"Listen, darlin'," the police corporal said, "you might as well go on home. Colin and your Da are gonna be in there for quite some time to come."

The twelve-year-old girl in the green and gray plaid school uniform stared at the floor. She'd been sitting on the hard station house bench for almost three hours, ever since she'd come home from school and found her mother crying and praying in front of the chipped plaster statue of the Virgin Mary. Her father and brother had been taken in after a car bombing up in Kildare and had been held in solitary with no food, drink, or light, for more than ten hours. She'd come with a basket of food.

"Darlin'?"

Bridget looked up. The big, beefy corporal was standing in front of her.

"You're breaking me heart, darlin'," he smiled, "sittin' there all by yer poor self all these lonely hours. And just to give your Da and brother a bite to eat."

He pulled his black belt up over his protruding stomach and smiled down at her again. "Would you really like to see 'em get them goodies you've got in your sack there?"

"Yes," she whispered.

He winked at her, put a huge meaty paw down and wrapped it around her small hand. "Well, then, you just come with me, lass, and let's see if maybe I can't figure out a way that you can do it."

She soon found out the 'way' the corporal had in mind, and only her quick wits and the quicker movements of her small, lithe body had saved her from the payment that the corporal was fantasizing about.

She walked home, shivering in the cold rain. Her wool cardigan sweater and the top three buttons of her white school blouse had been left in the corporal's sweaty, grasping hands.

Two days later, her father and Colin had been released, but she'd never said a word about the corporal. If she did, the corporal would have been dead by nightfall.

But Bridget Ann Connolly was the daughter of an IRA major.

She'd handle it herself, in her own way.

ON THAT SAME NIGHT one year later, a cold, damp mist shrouded The Four Foxes Pub, where the corporal went drinking every night. She'd have close to three hours before the corporal staggered out, plopped his bulk on his bicycle, and pedaled unsteadily home. She'd watched him do it for weeks now.

At the end of High Street, the road made a sharp turn to the left. Twice she'd seen him stamp backwards on the bicycle's coaster brakes and narrowly avoid crashing into the stone wall where the road curved.

Only a drunkard's luck had saved him. Tonight, she was going to give luck a shove in the other direction.

She waited outside the pub. At five minutes to ten, the muffled call of, "Closing time, gents, all out," came to her through the window. The corporal staggered out, belched, and climbed groggily onto his bike. Weaving back and forth, he started shakily down High Street. Despite the slick wet paving stones, the corporal let the bike pick up speed as it went down the hill. When he reached the sharp turn and the stone wall, he stamped down hard on the brakes.

The bicycle careened and smashed into the wall.

She waited until everyone had gone to bed that night before she tiptoed out to the shed and put back her father's needle-nose pliers. It had taken close to three hours in the cold, dripping mist to remove the connecting pins from four links of chain on the corporal's bicycle.

Bridget Ann Connolly handled her own problems, in her own way.

Yes, she thought. The scales needed to be balanced. Not revenge, she told herself. Justice.

She stared across the fire, still looking across the Atlantic Ocean to a decade past. Suddenly she was jerked back to Newport, 1968.

It was *them*.

They were walking down the back stairs from the stage. Mickey was right, they had followed them!

One of them reached out and grabbed a kid with a guitar by the shoulder. The kid pointed toward the left side of the field where a sprawling makeshift city of tents, vans and VW Beetles spread out over the scraggly grass.

They started toward it.

Bridget put her hand on Mick's shoulder to shake him awake then stopped. If she woke him, he'd go after Cataldo with the .38. There'd be a shootout for sure. Mick would either kill or be killed. Innocent people could be hurt, even killed. She couldn't let any of that happen.

She would decoy herself, let Cataldo and his thugs see her and lead them away from the Rounders' tent and, most importantly, from Mick. He thought he was in great shape but he'd never seen her run flat out. Because when she did, there wasn't a lad on either side of the Atlantic who could keep up with her, including him. She kissed him on the forehead and got up.

She hesitated for a moment then reached into the top pocket of Mick's denim jacket and pulled out his Buck knife. She lowered his head to the grass and moved away from the fire toward Cataldo and his men. As she thrust the knife into her skirt pocket, she heard the echoes of five hundred years of Connollys in her head. *You've got a score to settle and you are a Connolly. You settle your own problems—in your own way.*

A MORTAR SHELL burst overhead, and a voice cried, "Look out, Sarge, up on the ridge. They've broken through, rolling up the right flank!" Another mortar shell burst, this one closer. Mick felt the hot metal fragments drift down onto his upturned face. They burned. He was on his feet screaming, brushing the burning fragments away. "Return fire. Return fire, God damn you!"

A hand fell on his shoulder and he grabbed it.

"Hey, man, sorry," a frightened looking guy with long, dirty yellow hair said, shaking off Mick's grip. "Some of the ash from my joint fell on your face. Sorry, man, like, sorry."

Mick looked around. The fire. A bunch of people singing, drinking beer, passing joints. Newport, 1968. Not 'Nam, 1966.

Would it ever stop?

"Hey, babe," he said, shaking his head. "I was having another one of those dreams about being back in 'Nam and I—"

He turned. Bridget was gone.

Chapter 32

Newport | Rhode Island | Lower Thames Street
July 30, 1968 | 9:03 p.m.

"Damn!" A voice from the driver's side of the '67 Firebird 400 exploded. "We're never gonna get up there. These Rhode Island jerks don't know how to friggin' drive."

The slow Kentucky drawl answered from the passenger side, "If ya don't mind my sayin' so, I think you-all are kinda crazy up here. Hell, the way you-all drive would make my moonshine runnin' Uncle Virgil look like Granny Peabody on her way to the church social."

Kevin McCarthy shook his head and said in his Southie nasal rasp, "Man, I don't know what the hell you just said, but you friggin' knock me out, the way you say it."

Kevin swerved the Firebird off the narrow, grid-locked road to the festival. "Screw it! I'm making my own parking place right here!" He pulled up ten feet onto the green, manicured front lawn of a large, hopefully deserted, brick and clapboard summer cottage. He shut off the rumbling engine and stuffed the keys deep into his jeans.

"C'mon, Daniel Boone," he called over his shoulder to his slower walking comrade as he started for the bright lights of the festival entrance. "Let's go hear some music, and maybe kick some ass."

Festival grounds | 9:35 p.m.

Bronwyn Prescott looked at Laney Hewitt through the flickering shadows of the firelight.

"You never told me Buzzen could play."

"Yeah," she called back. "He's pretty good, isn't he?"

Buzzen strummed his guitar harder and sang, *"well I'll do anything in this god-almighty world if you'll just let me follow you down,"* finishing with a flourish and handing off the guitar to the next amateur artist at the impromptu hootenanny around the backstage bonfire.

"Do you sing or play, Brom?" Laney asked.

"No," Bronwyn said, shaking her head, "but my brother Mick does."

She stared across the fire. The flames made the fire-lit figure on the other side of the bonfire waver, but speaking of her own unpredictable, fun-loving and totally wild-ass brother, she could have sworn it was Mick. He got up unsteadily and moved toward the edge of the firelight. Something was standing there.

A motorcycle.

He rummaged in the bike's saddlebags. Something glinted for half a second in the rays of the firelight before he turned and walked off toward the back of the stage.

Bronwyn Prescott-McCarthy now had no doubt who he was. And though she'd seen the object for only a split second, she likewise had no illusions as to what it was. Her mother might be a Boston Brahmin blue blood, but her father was an Irish cop from Southie, and she had seen that particular object many times before: a .38 caliber Police Special snub-nosed revolver. There was only one place Mick could have gotten it—from their father. And that meant that Michael McCarthy Senior must have felt pretty strongly that he'd need it. She looked around the dark campfire-dotted field. Something was out there. Something nasty. She stared into the not so friendly darkness. A bit of a rhyme she'd found one rainy afternoon in a musty book in the Brattle street mansion's attic came into her head: "By the pricking of my thumbs, something wicked this way comes."

MICK RAN THROUGH the crowds and chaos of the backstage festival lot. He was pretty sure where Danny, Cody and Sparrow would be, but would Bridge be there, too? More importantly, why had she gone? They'd agreed to stake out the back of the stage to see if Cataldo was around, and not go to the band's tent until they were sure of where the East Providence crew were. She wouldn't leave without telling him why or where. Not by her own choice, anyway.

Mick tried to shift his sleep-fogged brain into high gear while trying at the same time to quiet that nagging little voice in the back of his head that kept telling him that something was wrong. Very wrong.

He ran faster.

THEIR VOICES SOUNDED as harsh and callous as the gravel-voiced men who had worked in the slaughter-yard that Bridget used to pass on her way to visit her uncle up in Cork City. Slipping between the tents and vans that dotted the field, she edged closer to the evil bastards who had kidnapped and tortured her and Marcy.

Fat Cataldo spoke. "Listen up, Sammy. While we hunt down that banjo-playing hick, you go back to the car and take care of that hippie broad in the trunk. We've beat all we're gonna get out of her."

"Kill her, Mr. C?"

"No, kiss her and give her a bunch of flowers for her hair. Friggin' asshole!"

"You got it, Mr. C. I'll just crack the trunk and put one right in the back of her head."

"No, moron! You want to have us driving around with blood dripping from the trunk for the rest of the night?" He shook his head in disgust and then explained as if to a four-year-old. "You take her out of the trunk. Then you pop her, bleed her out and wrap her up in the tarps next to the spare. Then you put her back in the trunk. You got it Sammy?"

"You bet, Mr. C."

"Good. And Sammy?"

"Yeah, Mr. C?"

"Don't fuck it up, or you'll be joining that chick in the trunk for a one-way trip to the harbor."

Bridget stood frozen in the moonlight. Marcy!

Cataldo and the rest turned and walked off, leaving Sammy to 'take care of' Marcy.

Had she made a mistake? Should she run and get Mick and warn their friends that Cataldo was coming for them? But if she did that, Marcy would be dead by the time she got back.

She had no choice. Her friends might be in danger but unless she stopped it, Marcy was going to be dead.

She slipped around and followed Sammy, the skinny thug in the black suit. He looked like an evil exclamation point outlined against the light leaking out from the back of the stage. She kept pace twenty feet behind him, following him toward a clump of scrawny trees.

She shivered. How was she going to take care of him? She'd have to rely on surprise. She had the knife, but he had a gun. She'd creep up behind him and—

Someone shouted behind her. She looked over her shoulder. Her foot connected with something hard and she went down, sprawling face first into the coarse grass. Pain shot through her knee. *Was it sprained, fractured?* It didn't matter. Sprained, fractured or broken, she had to move. Now!

She gritted her teeth and pushed herself upright. At her feet was a scrap of two-by-four lumber, three feet long. She picked it up, clasping it firmly in one hand, and ran after Sammy.

He stopped behind a black silhouette in the dark; the hell-car of her waking nightmares. Sammy fumbled in his pocket. Something jingled—car keys—a key was inserted into a lock, there was a metallic scrape then a *pop*. The lid of the Bonneville's trunk rose slowly, like a black bat's wing.

She edged closer.

He leaned over, laughing in that ugly nasal voice, muffled by the trunk lid. He reached in and pulled at something. "All out, sunshine, end of the line." He pulled again, and a form rolled over the edge of the trunk lip onto the ground. "Watch that first step, baby, it's a killer!" He laughed and repeated, "Yep, a real killer."

Bridget crept closer, crouching. Sammy hummed tunelessly as he took a long, dark cylinder from his pocket and screwed it into the barrel of his gun.

The moon slipped from behind a cloud, and Bridget caught a glimpse of Marcy's bruised and battered face. And in that same moon-glimpse moment, she saw another face, one that had been seared into her memory like the angry red scar beneath her turtleneck. That skinny pockmarked face, the one who had laughed while he held her and that other scarred-knuckle hand had reached out of the shadows with the glowing cigarette.

Bridget's hand clenched around the cold, hard knife in her pocket. She had crept to within a dozen feet behind him.

"So, afraid it's tough luck, baby-doll, 'cuz Mr. C. says we don't need you anymore. See, him and the guys spotted that other little broad, your friend from last night, and she's gonna lead him right to that hillbilly asshole. So it's lights-out for you, buttercup."

At the sound of the automatic's slide being drawn back Marcy's blackened, swollen eyes opened wider and Sammy chuckled, "Give my regards to St. Peter, kid." He held the gun barrel to her head. His finger squeezed on the trigger.

Thwack!

Bridget slammed the narrow side of the two-by-four into the side of his head, just below his right temple. He fell face forward into the dusty brown grass.

Marcy shook her head and tried to open her eyes wider. She said what sounded like Bridget's name from under the gag that filled her mouth.

Bridget rolled Sammy over with the piece of wood. He was breathing. Good.

She dropped the two-by-four and picked up Sammy's gun then went to Marcy. She helped her to her feet, hugged her then peeled the tape from her bruised, swollen face and pulled the gag out of her mouth.

"Oh, Bridget, thank God!" Marcy sobbed quietly. "Another second and he would have—"

"Hush," Bridget said. The blade flashed in her hand, and the ropes holding Marcy fell away.

Bridget hugged her once more. "Do ya see that campfire glowin' over by the far end of the stage? You go on and head toward it. You'll find Mick there, sleeping by the fire. Tell him that Cataldo and his lot are heading for Cody and our friends."

Marcy took two steps then turned and looked.

"Aren't you coming?"

There was silence for a moment. Then a cold voice that had become one with the night answered, "I'll be along. I've got some unfinished business to take care of."

Marcy backed away and walked as quickly as she could toward the distant firelight.

Bridget watched her retreating. She fingered the smooth, sharp blade, and she remembered.

A COLD DAMP WIND rattled the casement of the rectory library window in the gray stone wing of St. Thomas's school. The girls had been allowed to use the rectory library, but only when one of the sisters was there, and then only in the front section, near the desk where the teachers sat. And never, never under any circumstances, were they allowed to go into the dusty stacks at the rear of the library. That was reserved for Father Donovan or the Brothers from the seminary.

But Bridget had always been curious about the ancient, cracked leather volumes in the dusty back aisles. So, one cold, gray afternoon, she had sneaked back to the "forbidden" part of the library. She read chilling accounts in an ancient book written by monks in the time of Saint Brendan, that told how, long ago, Celtic women had taken revenge on men who wronged them. There had been things, slow things, involving a knife, a very sharp knife.

Her eyes grew wide with horror as she read what those women had done to those men.

Then Sister Margaret had come upon the tiny twelve-year-old sitting cross-legged in a dusty corner of the library, the forbidden tome open on her skinny lap.

"Miss Connolly!"

Bridget jumped up, spilling the book off her lap and scraping her knee painfully on the floor's rough stone tiles. But the pain of the scraped knee had been nothing compared to—

"Hold out both of your hands, you wicked, disobedient girl!"

A decade later, she still felt the smarting pain and humiliation.

Like so many other lessons learned under painful circumstances, this one was burned into her memory.

Right alongside what the bastard lying unconscious at her feet had helped do to her.

She pulled out the Buck knife and pulled the blade open. It clicked softly as it locked into place.

She lightly brushed her thumb along the blade.

Like the bronze knives of her ancient Celtic ancestors, it was razor sharp.

She bent down.

The field in back of the festival stage | 10:07 p.m.

"Hey, man, watch where you're going!"

Mick grabbed hold of a warped wooden pole holding up a tattered tent flap. He looked down at the talking, lumpy mound that he had tripped over, and the image resolved itself into a pair of semi-nude bodies lying on top of an Army surplus sleeping bag.

A guy with wire rimmed glasses and long, kinky hair looked up accusingly and said, "I mean, like, me and my old lady are, like, just grooving to the sounds and trying to mellow out and get it on."

Mick ran a rough hand over his face, trying to wipe away sleep and confusion as he tuned out the zoned-out "flower children."

"Jesus," he muttered, "go back to your dope, you burned out freak." He ran his hand through his hair. *Where the hell was Bridget?*

She must have spotted Cataldo and gone to warn Cody. That was it, that made sense, she... But how could she warn them? She didn't know where the Rounders' tent was.

Then where the hell was she? Why had she left him? Damn!

He started running again. There was only one place he could go. He had to do what they'd come here for, warn his friends and pray that Bridget would find her way to the Rounders' campsite before Cataldo found her.

JOSEPH—JOEY, aka Mr. C.—Cataldo, didn't like to hurry. He always said, "If God wanted me to move fast he would have given me friggin' wheels."

He headed toward the performers' tents. He was gonna mop this mess up and move on to what the whole damn business boiled down to: payday. He smiled in the darkness as he and his crew shuffled doggedly through the dusty grass. Crap, he was ruining a good pair of hand-made loafers imported from the old country. Then he smiled again. His own special 'Joey' Cataldo smile. The smile that had been the last thing a lot of people had ever seen. Yeah, he was gonna buy a new pair of loafers tomorrow. No, make that two pairs. 'Cause tonight was not just payday, it was gonna be *double* payday.

Chapter 33

Route 195 | Rhode Island | 10:17 p.m.

The blue 1959 Buick Electra shuddered as a foot shod with thick-soled size eleven black shoes pumped down hard on the brakes. The worn shocks responded sluggishly as the heavy old car wheeled onto the exit ramp toward Route 138 and the southern Rhode Island coast, going way too fast for the car's years and condition.

"Come on, baby," a voice roughened by too many years of whiskey and cigarettes rumbled to the car like it was an old friend, "you can do it."

The tired eyes stared through the windshield at the yellow line on the road leading south.

"Just get me there, baby. Just get me there in time."

Festival field | 10:19 p.m.

Mick heard voices inlaid with a twang as deep as the moss-green hollows of the Kentucky mountains that had nourished them. He slowed and almost stumbled as he staggered into the full glare of kerosene and battery-powered lanterns hanging outside the same sagging tents that he remembered from two nights ago.

He stood just outside the sulfur-yellow glow of a hissing kerosene lantern hanging from the tent pole. A worn piece of canvas was strung between a campfire and an old rust-brown Econoline Van.

He blinked his tired eyes, willing them to see something that wasn't there. Bridget.

"Hey, son, what the hell are you doing, sneaking around out there in the dark? Come on in here so we can get a look at you-all."

Mick shuffled into the light, looking desperately from face to face. Cody, Sparrow, Cousin Danny. He'd been right about that, at least. But where was Bridge?

"Hey, Cuz, what's up, man? You look whipped. Jeez, sit down and have a beer."

Danny moved up next to Mick and put an arm around his shoulders. "Hell, I thought we were the ones who were supposed to be ducking and hiding. Damn, you look like shit, man. What the hell happened? Where's Bridge?"

Danny guided Mick down into a rickety aluminum lawn chair. Mick closed his eyes and pressed the heels of both palms into his tired eyes. "Aw, crap! I don't know where the hell she is."

He let his hands fall into his lap, but kept his eyes closed.

"Hey, I know this old boy!" A voice boomed out from behind him. A heavy, bear-like hand fell on his shoulder, and Mick slowly opened his eyes.

Dale, the big mandolin player's grinning, hairy face bent down toward Mick's.

"Hell, son, you look like forty miles of bad road. Here, take a couple pulls off of this." He pushed a pint bottle with a hand-lettered label scraped half off into Mick's hand. It was almost clear, with a milky, yellow tinge.

"Drink up, son," Dale drawled.

Mick put the bottle to his lips and got a whiff of its contents. His nose hair contracted, and his eyes smarted, so he closed them again and took a long, shuddering pull. "God damn!" He coughed as liquid fire poured down his throat. "What the hell is that?"

"That, old son," the bearded giant laughed, "is genuine 200 Proof

Harlan County white lightnin.'"

"Hey, Mick," Cody drawled as he squatted down in front of Mick, "I just want to thank you-all for gittin' me away from that fat greaseball and his monkeys."

Mick gave a half-smile. "You can thank Cousin Danny here. He found out where you were and made it all happen."

"Damn straight!" Cody grinned up at Danny. "You know, he sure does talk funny, but we're thinkin' of making him an honorary good ol' boy anyway."

"No problem, man," Danny answered from behind Cody, "just as long as I don't gotta start saying 'you-all.' Hell," he finished, shaking his head, "I'd never get out of Callaghan's alive on a Saturday night."

"Okay, okay," Mick said, shaking his head. "I'm glad you guys got here all right, and that you're all okay, but you're not out of the bush yet. Cataldo's here and it's not because he's a music lover. He's looking for you, Cody, and he is not in a good mood. We gotta stay here and be ready for him."

"Yup, good plan, Cuz," Danny said, picking up one of the heavy metal tent stakes and stuffing it into the back pocket of his jeans.

"Just one question, Mick said to Cody, getting to his feet. "Why the hell did Cataldo kidnap you in the first place? What does he want with you?"

"Good question," a thick voice rumbled out of the darkness. "Why don't you tell 'em, Banjo Boy?"

Mick turned around.

Cataldo.

MARCY STUMBLED into the soft light of the campfire and sank to her knees. Was it over? Was it really finally over? She struggled back to her feet and slowly circled the fire. The guitars were being put back into battered cases decorated with stickers and paper flowers. Everyone was crashing.

Marcy looked into face after yawning face. Some of them squinted back at her through drugged, pinprick eyeballs. Others motioned her to come closer, but she kept on moving.

Still no Mick.

She was about to go back to Bridget when she saw a face that looked familiar. In a flicker of firelight, for an instant, it looked like Mick.

"Bronwyn," Marcy said, her swollen lips still having trouble forming words.

Just as Bronwyn looked up, Marcy's knees gave way, and she sank down in front of Mick's sister.

"Oh my God! Marcy, what happened to you?"

"Oh, Bronwyn," she mumbled through swollen lips. "Where's Mick? Bridget told me I'd find him here. She said he'd take care of me. Make everything all right again."

She was on the verge of tears. Bronwyn squeezed Marcy's shoulders as she swayed forward.

"Mick isn't here. I don't know where he went."

"I… I've got to find him. Tell him that Cataldo… Bridget said tell Mick… tell him to go warn…"

Bronwyn pointed across the fire. "It's okay, Marcy, here comes Bridget. She'll know where Mick is, she'll…"

Bridget stepped into the dim light. An ember popped and flared. Bridget looked like she was a million miles away. When she saw Marcy and Bronwyn, her expression changed, as if a mask had slipped into place. The mask smiled at them but somehow she wasn't the Bridget they knew.

She came around the edge of the fire toward them.

Marcy and Bronwyn exchanged quick glances. Had Bronwyn seen what Bridget stuffed into the pocket of her denim skirt?

Something cold and hard and metallic.

Festival grounds | 10:20 p.m.

"Whoa, hold up a sec, Daniel Boone," Kevin McCarthy called as his eyes fastened on the crowd drifting out of the festival gate. "Look over there."

"What-all am I supposed to be lookin' for?" Kevin's tall, lanky companion drawled.

"There. Damn, I lost her. No, that little chick passing through the gate. Cute, black hair, black turtleneck. See her? She's walking between another chick with long brown hair and the chick with—Shit! That's my cousin! Hey, Brom! Bronwyn!"

But none of the girls stopped or turned back, and a few seconds later, they were swallowed up in the exiting crowd.

"Damn!" Kevin swore, punching his right fist into his left palm.

"You wanna go after them?" his friend asked.

Kevin answered, "It's just my cousin's girlfriend and sister, but he's not with 'em. That probably means he's still here. And if I know Mick, it also probably means that he told them to take off because he's got something nasty to do."

The ex-corporal looked down at the tough, wiry kid from South Boston, and flashed a deceptively gentle smile. "And that's where we come in, right?"

"You got it, Davy Crockett. C'mon, let's move."

Festival parking lot | 10:21 p.m.

Bronwyn winced and closed her eyes at the sight of Marcy's bruised face as she and Bridget helped the thin, willowy brunette toward the festival parking lot.

"I never should have left him," Bridget said, looking back into the festival grounds. "But he was so tired and I was afraid of what he'd do and what might happen to him if he caught up with Cataldo. I thought that he and everyone else would be all right if I could lead those thugs away."

She grabbed Bronwyn's arm and said with a desperation directed more at herself then at Mick's sister, "You've got to understand. It was the only way I could think of to protect him, to save his life!"

Marcy spoke through her cracked, blood-caked lips as if she hadn't heard. "Last night, after what they tried to do to you, they took me somewhere—I'm not sure where, it must have been Providence. They kept hitting me, over and over and over. They wanted to know what I'd told you at the White Rabbit. It seemed like it went on for hours."

Tears stung the corners of Bridget's eyes. She forgot about her doubts. There was a score to be settled, for her, the battered girl in front of her, and who knew how many others.

"I'm sorry, Marcy." She whispered and muttered to herself, "and that's one more thing they'll be answerin' for."

"At times when they stopped, when they thought I'd passed out, they talked. The fat, cruel one, the one they called Mr. C., asked the one in the shadows if he had their payment, and he said he'd have it tomorrow night. That's tonight. I know where he lives. And I know that he—and all the rest of them—will be there tonight."

Bridget grabbed Marcy, her pity momentarily forgotten. "You're sure? You really know who he is?"

Her head moved once in a painful up and down movement.

"I think we've all known all along, Valerie, my Sister, Janet, PJ—and me. About the real truth of his… his 'relationship' with Blair." Her hands passed over her battered face. "But we were all too scared to say anything to you and Mick."

"Not even to the police?"

Marcy shook her head. "Especially not them. PJ said we couldn't trust them because they were 'the man.' Who knows," she whispered almost to herself, "he may have been right."

"Have you told anyone else what you know?" Bridget asked.

"No."

"Good."

Bronwyn stopped in mid-stride. "Why is that good?"

"Because then Mickey won't know where we've gone."

"Are you crazy? If we're going where I'm afraid you want to go, we're going to need my brother and ten more like him."

Bridget shook her head. "That's exactly why I don't want him to know."

She turned around and took both of Bronwyn's shoulders in her small but strong hands. " I know he's your brother and I know how much you love him. I've got five myself and as bloody irritating as they can be, I still do love 'em. But the way I feel about Mick is different. I don't want—no, I wouldn't want to live any more if anything happened to him, and if he knows were we've gone, it will."

Bridget paused and looked at Bronwyn as though suddenly realizing her presence. "Look, Bronwyn, this isn't your fight. It's mine and five hundred years of Connollys whispering in my ear. Go back to the lights and the music and try and forget about this."

Bronwyn sighed and turned away. Before she'd gone five feet, she stopped and looked back at Bridget, then at Marcy. She shifted from foot to foot.

"I won't pretend that I don't want to go back and forget all about this, but—well, I may have been raised a Prescott, but there's a whole lotta' McCarthy underneath." She swallowed loudly. "I'm in."

Bridget squeezed her hand. "It's all right girl, you've got friends with you now." Her hand went to her throat. "Besides, I've got a score to settle with him. A very deep and personal score."

"So do I." Marcy said.

"How are we going to get there?" Bronwyn asked.

Marcy's lips finally moved into something approaching a smile. "If we're in luck, my sister is here at the festival tonight."

Bridget snorted and said, "And why, by all the saints in heaven, would that be lucky?"

"Because," Marcy said, reaching into the pocket of her torn and soiled paisley dress, "I know where she parks whenever she comes down here. And I've still got the spare set of keys to her MGB."

"Where does he live, then?" Bridget asked, a hard line of cold purpose compressing her lips.

"1324 Bellevue Avenue."

Festival grounds | 10:22 a.m.

Cataldo and his punks had Mick, Cody, Sparrow and the Rounders covered with their big, blue-steel automatics. Everyone stood frozen in the kerosene lantern's flickering light, like some waiting-to-be-directed bit players in a bad silent movie.

Mick took comfort in the sharp, cold bulk of his father's well-oiled .38 police special in the waistband of his jeans, its metallic frame pressing against his stomach.

Cataldo stared at Cody, and his sneer deepened, creasing his pudgy cheeks. "Listen up, you banjo-plucking hick, you got two choices. One, you play it smart, take my deal, and take the rap for the Vanderwall broad's murder."

He paused.

"Number two," he continued, slowly raising his .380 automatic, "you take one in the back of the head, right here and now."

Mick stared at Cataldo's bulky frame, outlined against the sputtering lantern's flame. So, this was what it was all about, finding a fall guy for Blair Vanderwall's murder. But what was that to Cataldo, and why should the East Providence mob care? Hell, the only thing they cared about was carving out new turf for new rackets. But in the end, it all boiled down to one thing and one thing only. Money.

Mick remembered what Big Mike had always told him about narrowing down the motive for a murder or almost any other crime, for that matter. If it wasn't passion it was money.

"I'm through screwing around, kid," Cataldo said. He nodded to Paulie and Vinnie, who moved to either side of him, covering the group in front of the open flap of the tent.

"I'm gonna count to three," Cataldo continued, "and if I don't hear a big fat 'yeah, boss' from you, Banjo Boy, Paulie and Vinnie are gonna start popping off your freak friends, one by one."

"One…"

Cody looked at his second cousin and the friends he'd sung and played and grown up with.

"Two…"

He looked at Mick and Danny and Sparrow, who had risked their own skins to come after him and then shelter him. Then he looked back at Cataldo, and the two sneering punks on either side of him. Cataldo shook his head and said, "Okay, Banjo Boy, then go to hell," and pulled the slide back on the gleaming steel .380 automatic, chambering a round.

"Three…"

"Yeah, boss," Cody muttered, before the last syllable died away.

"What was that, cracker?"

"I said, yeah boss. Hell, yeah, whatever y'all want," Cody finished dejectedly.

"Smart choice, kid," Cataldo grunted. "And just to make sure you don't change your mind, Paulie, bring his two little pals along." He pointed his chin toward Danny and Sparrow.

"Vinnie, you stay here and make sure the rest of these hillbillies stay put." He motioned the gun toward Cody, Sparrow, and Danny, who moved slowly toward Cataldo's car at the back of the field.

"Keep 'em quiet for ten minutes," Cataldo said to Vinnie, "then meet us up at *his* house." In a voice barely above a whisper he added, "But before you go, I want you to take care of something that's been pissing me off for the past two days. Whack that smartass kid, Mickey."

10:25 a.m.

Mick looked up at Vinnie. A thin line of perspiration glistened on his upper lip, and his eyes darted back and forth from Mick to his watch.

Yeah, he was going to kill him.

Mick jumped as a loud *crack* broke the silence. The fire flared up with a shower of sparks as Dale tossed a handful of sticks on it. He looked over at Mick.

"I don't know about you, son, but me and Darrell and ol' Charlie there are gettin' kinda tired of watchin' that skinny little greaseball starin' back at us. So, whatcha say we all jest move on over there and take his little peashooter away?"

"Shut up, you friggin' hick!" Vinnie snarled.

Dale threw more sticks into the fire and shambled over next to Mick. He pulled the pint bottle of milky white lightnin' to his lips and murmured as he drank, "There's only one a' him and four of us. Whatcha say? Give us the word and we'll go fer him."

"Uh uh. Thanks, but chill out."

He wiped his mouth with the back of his hand and whispered to Dale, "Back away, slowly."

Mick let his right hand drop. His fingers brushed across the butt of the .38 in the waistband of his jeans. Vinnie saw the move and raised his 9 mm. Mick's hand slipped under his T-shirt, fastened around the butt of the .38 and pulled. The hammer of the revolver caught in the belt loop of his jeans.

He stared into the muzzle of Vinnie's 9 mm automatic.

"So long, asshole," Vinnie sneered.

Something flashed with a sharp *snap*. Vinnie screamed, his gun dropped from his hand. A familiar voice with a South Boston accent said, "Damn! This thing works great!"

Mick grinned as his other bad-boy cousin from Southie stepped into the firelight.

"Hey, Kevin, I don't know how or why you're here, but I'm damn glad to see you. Good freaking timing, man."

"That's me, Mick, friggin' cavalry to the rescue," Kevin replied with a wink.

He bent down and picked up the 9 mm then unwound something

from Vinnie's wrist.

"Damn, where'd you get the nun-chucks, Kevin? Shit, I haven't seen those since 'Nam."

"I guess that'd be me, Sarge."

Mick looked up.

"Smitty!"

Chapter 34

1324 Bellevue Avenue | 10:33 p.m.

Marcy pulled her sister's MGB up to the driveway entrance and turned off the motor. The three girls climbed out of the tiny sports car. For a moment they stood under an enormous elm tree and stared up at the imposing house, a gray granite first floor, topped by lighter gray painted clapboard, offset with white trim around the two upper floors. An arching front entrance, flanked by four white wooden pillars, framed two white doors bracketed by gray-blue stained glass side windows.

It was meant to look beautiful. It just looked cold.

"Let's go," Bridget said, and they approached the house.

"Are you sure we should be doing this?" Bronwyn whispered to Bridget. "Like, what are we going to do if we find this guy? I mean, he's already hurt you and Marcy, and who knows what else he might do? We'd be helpless, just sitting ducks!"

Bridget stopped and looked back at Bronwyn, and the younger girl recoiled from what she saw smoldering in Bridget's eyes.

Bronwyn and Marcy's eyes widened as Bridget calmly drew the gun she'd taken from Sammy, and the Buck knife she'd taken from Mick, out of her skirt pockets. She smiled and ran her finger along the cool steel barrel then opened the long blade with a *snick*. With the gun in one hand and the knife in the other she looked straight into Bronwyn's eyes.

"No, Bronwyn. We're not helpless. Now come on."

She crouched and sprinted across the lawn to the front doors, the others following.

"Bridget, I don't know about this," Bronwyn whispered. Murmurs of conversation drifted through the living room window.

"What don't you know?" Bridget asked without bothering to look up. She slowly worked the Buck knife blade into the tiny space between the upper and lower half of the hall window next to the doors.

"Well," Bronwyn continued, "this is breaking and entering, isn't it?"

Bridget stopped working at the window's corroded catch and pulled the blade out from between the two window halves.

Bronwyn looked into Bridget's eyes and swallowed slowly. Bridget took a deep breath and answered calmly, "Yes, Bronwyn, it could be considered that, or you could look on it that we were just too bleedin' considerate to disturb the folks inside while we go about finding the thief who stole something from Marcy and me."

"Stole? Stole what?"

"What?" Bridget gave a laugh and turned back to the window's catch. "The worst thing a thief could steal. Some part of yourself."

She froze. "Shush—someone's coming."

Footsteps clattered down the hallway.

Bridget pulled the two girls toward her and whispered, "We'll never get in here now. We'll have to find another way in where we won't be seen. Come on, we'll look around back."

As she led the others around the side of the house she stopped in her tracks.

"What in the name of God is that?"

A replica of a Japanese teahouse sat at the edge of the cliff at the far end of the back lawn.

"That's the teahouse," Marcy said. She paused and drew a breath. "Do you remember the story I told you about Blair and the young art student? That's where he painted her, where... it happened. If *he* is here, he won't be far from that painting."

Bridget nodded. "Then I think we'd better have a look. Come on."

Festival grounds | 10:35 p.m.

Mick smiled as he looked back at the lopsided grin of his former corporal and the best friend he'd ever had. Without thinking, he reached out and grabbed Smitty's lean, tanned arm in the old 'Nam brotherhood salute.

"How's it hanging, man?" They pumped two rough-knuckled fists together.

"Can't complain, Sarge," Smitty grinned back, adding, "and who the hell would give a rat's behind if ah did, anyway?"

"Just me, Smitty. Me and the other 'old ghosts.'"

"Yeah, ah hear ya, Sarge," the ex-corporal form Kentucky added.

"But what the hell are you doing here? And even more importantly, how the frig did two of my favorite 'bad pennies' wind up together in Newport just in time to save my sorry butt?"

"Hey, Cuz," Kevin answered, folding the nun-chucks and stuffing them into his back pocket, "when Danny found out from your old man where you were and high-tailed it down here to get in on the action, you really didn't think that you wicked-pissa' bunch of smart-asses were gonna leave old Kevy cooling his heels and drinkin' all by his lonesome up at Callaghan's, now did ja?"

Mick knew that nothing his brace of wild-ass Southie cousins did should surprise him by now. Kevin smiled his perpetually insolent grin, as if daring the world to stop him from doing whatever outrageous escapade he was cooking up underneath that curly thatch of bright red hair.

"What's up, Cuz, did I just grow another head or somethin'?"

"Naw, Kevy, I was just thinking you look ugly enough to be the brother of someone else I know who's down here getting into trouble with me."

"Nice mouth, kid, and after I just gone and saved yer ass!"

"Yeah, you're right, Kevy," Mick said, wrapping his arm around his cousin's shoulders. "Thanks, man, both of you. But hey, finish answering my question. How did Smitty wind up here with you?"

"Go ahead, Davy Crocket," Kevin winked in Smitty's direction. "You tell 'em."

Harland Beaufort Smith ran a work-roughened hand through his long sandy hair and said, "You remember that old 'witchy woman' I used to tell you about sometimes when we were on late night picket duty that first year in 'Nam?"

"Granny something?" Mick answered.

"Granny Harper," Smitty said. "Now, Ah know you Yankee-boys—"

"Hey, watch it, Daniel Boone," Kevin broke in, "we're all Red Sox fans here!"

"Sorry, fren.' No offense. Well, anyhow, I know you-all don't believe in the stuff we do back in the hills, and hell, most of the time, I don't either, but sometimes, well, I've seen that old lady know things she couldn't possibly know, but she does. Anyways, I was frettin' something awful after I called you and told you about the mess that old Cody had got hisself into, and one morning, I was jest hangin' around the courthouse steps down in Parkersville. Jest pacin' back and forth, I suppose, when old Granny Harper comes up to me and says 'You be Will Smith's boy, don't you?' Well, it never does no good to get a witchy woman mad at you, so I jest says, 'Yes, ma'am.'

"Then she looks me up one side and down the other and says, 'You gots to git yerself up nawth, right quick. You got kin in danger. But you got a friend who's in worser danger still. Him and you has been through some danger times together, but he's walking hisself into the biggest passel of danger I ever see'd. So, you better get to him right quick, boy, if'n you want him and yer kin to keep seeing the sun come up.'"

Smitty shrugged his shoulders. "She knows things, Mick. Ah don't know how, but she knows things."

He paused then went on. "So I threw some stuff in my old duffle bag, jumped on a big ol' jet in Louisville, and, well, here I am."

"And getting hooked up with Kev?"

"Well, when I landed, I looked up yer pa's name in the phone book and told him my story. Next thing I know'd, this funny-talkin' red-haired devil here pulls up in front of the Logan Airport terminal in this mean-looking black car with a big chromed air scoop that looked like good enough to be a moonshine runner back home."

"Hey, if there's money, booze and fast cars involved, then I'm your boy," Kevin quipped.

"Well, however it happened, I'm damn glad it did," Mick said.

"Sarge. Mick," Smitty said, laying a hand on his shoulder. "There was one other thing that Granny Harper said to me jest before she walked away." Smitty shook his head with a puzzled expression. "She said, 'Harland Beaufort Smith, you mind the shadows, ya hear? You and all those who be friend and kin to you. There's death thar in the shadows.'"

Smitty kept shaking his head. "What d'ya think she meant by that, Sarge?"

Mick froze. "Oh, my frigging word!"

SMITTY LEANED BACK in the rickety old folding aluminum chair and poked at the embers of the fire with the toe of his work boot.

"Hey Sarge—Mick—damn it man, leave off a that pacin' will ya? Shee-it, you're gonna git me as riled up as you if'n ya' don't knock it off."

Mick walked over to the fire and kicked two of the half empty Budweiser cans into the smoldering embers. The spilling beer sizzled and sent up a cloud of smoke and sparks.

He rounded on Smitty with clenched fists. "Knock it off? I'll frigging knock it off when that punk tells me where Cataldo took Danny and if they know where… if they've got Bridget, and if they …" Mick stood in front of Smitty, his breathing ragged, fists clenched.

A long, low moan came in from the darkness outside.

"Sounds like yer cousin is making some right fine progress with that possum-faced little city boy," Dale smiled.

"Ah-h-hhh, you mother-fuc—!"

Smack!

Mick started toward the sound.

Smitty grabbed his shoulder. "Mick, he's doing what's gotta be done."

Mick wrenched out of his grasp. "God damn it Smitty, I wouldn't put up with torturing prisoners in 'Nam and I'm not gonna frigging start now! Kevin!" he yelled into the darkness, "Untie him and bring him here."

"Whatta' gonna do, Sarge?"

Mick pealed off his denim jacket and threw it on the ground. He stood in front of the fire, breathing hard through his nostrils and quivering with adrenalin. "We're gonna go at it. Just that punk and me, until he tells me what I wanna know. He may beat my brains out or I may beat him to death, but I won't stand here and see anyone tortured. Not even a piece of human crap like him."

Mick balled his hands into fists and growled "Kevin!" into the darkness.

"Hey, Sarge," Smitty said with a smirk, "I think you can stand down. It looks like old Vinnie there is ready to start singin' like a Kentucky warbler."

Kevin pushed the East Providence tough guy into the firelight.

"Hey, Cuz, siddown and take a chill, man. Mr. Slick here just had a change of heart. Haven't you, Slick?"

Vinnie looked up from his swollen right hand at Kevin, naked hatred showing on his face until Kevin took a step toward him. Raw fear replaced the look of hatred.

"I've got two questions for you," Mick said, "and if you don't want to spend some more time in the dark with Kevin, here, you better have answers."

Vinnie nodded.

"Where's Bridget, and where's Cataldo?"

"I dunno about the broad, honest I don't."

"All right, then. Kevin, why don't you take Vinnie back out for—"

Vinnie moaned. "Look, I'll give you whatever you want. I ain't holdin' back. You gotta believe me. I don't know where she is."

"And Cataldo?"

"Some rich guy's house. Vanderwall, up on Bellevue Avenue."

"Vanderwall," Mick said. "I knew it. But why?"

"All I know's that we was supposed to take your pal Cody there and he was gonna confess to the cops and everyone that he killed that Blair broad. I don't know nothin' more."

THEY HEADED for Bellevue Avenue, Mick on the BSA and Kevin and Smitty following close behind in Kevin's Firebird 400.

Think, Mick, think! Where would Bridget have gone? Why had she left him alone at the field? Had she gone down that crap-filled road to revenge after all? How many times had she tried to talk Mick out of taking that no-win track? But after what they'd done to her...

He should have killed them. All of them. Starting with that fat bastard Cataldo.

It was the Shadow Man she was after. That was where she was going. Cataldo, Sammy, Paulie and the whole East Providence sleazeball crew, they were all connected to the Shadow Man, working for him, and they needed Cody to take the fall for killing Blair Vanderwall.

Did that mean the Shadow Man killed Blair? He was obviously a murdering psychopath, but why Blair Vanderwall? A jilted boyfriend? A frustrated lover? Or was Blair just another random victim on his list? No, there had to be a connection. If only he could see it! But Christ, he was so damn tired.

Pop always said look for the motive. Cataldo was obviously in it for the money. So the Vanderwalls were protecting someone in, or closely connected with, the family. That someone had to be the psychopathic Shadow Man. But who was—?

"Hey Cuz, what's the problem?"

"Huh?"

Mick looked around. They'd been stopped at the intersection of Bellevue and Elm Street for several minutes.

"Yeah, sorry. What was the street number again that you got from that Vinnie punk?"

Kevin snorted, "Vinnie. The big tough East Providence bad boy." He shook his head. "They sure ain't makin' hoods like they used to back in Southie when we were kids. Why, I remember once Keegan and Johnny Donavan boosted a truckload of scotch outside of their turf. Them two took a beatin' for three days from a couple of the Westies and they still wouldn't give it up." He sighed with fond nostalgia. "Christ, this little punk gets a couple of teeth knocked out, a few fingers broke and starts spillin' his guts like a little girl. Why all I did was…"

"Kev. Kevy!"

"Huh?"

"The address, Kevin. The street number. What was it?"

"Oh yeah, sorry, must be gettin' old, kid. You know that reminds me of that old fart who hangs around Callaghan's, his brain is so booze-soaked he can't even remember—"

"Kevin!"

"Oops, right. Ah, 1324 Bellevue Avenue. And the guy's name who lives there is …"

"Yeah, Kev, I know. Vanderwall. Jonathan Vanderwall."

Mick looked up and down the street. The houses were set so far back from the street that they couldn't see the numbers. They'd have to pick one direction or the other and hope it was the right one. They were running out of time.

He looked back at his cousin's head hanging out the window of the Firebird idling next to him.

"Hey, Smitty, back in 'Nam, when we were out on recon and didn't know where the hell we were going, do you remember what we did when we came to a fork in the trail?"

Ex-corporal Smith smiled to his former sergeant and said, "Hell, Mick, we'd just toss us a coin. Heads we went right, tails it was left."

Mick pulled a quarter out of his pocket and flicked it high into the air. The silver of the coin gave off tiny winks, like a miniature strobe light, as it spun in the dim glow of the streetlight.

With a small wavering *clank* it settled onto the pavement.

Mick leaned down over the BSA's handlebars. He straightened up and revved the bike's twin cylinders into life again.

As he stamped down onto the foot shift and let the clutch out with his left hand, he called back over his shoulder, "Right!"

Chapter 35

1324 Bellevue Avenue | 10:47 p.m.

Jonathan Vanderwall sat in the den with the lights off. He liked to sit with the lights off most of the time now. Light gave him a headache. It was much more pleasant to sit in the dark. Really, much more pleasant. Especially in this room, so filled with memories. Most of them good, some not so good. But still, this was where he liked to be. Where he could think, and remember. Only the good. Only the good. Mustn't let any of those bad thoughts intrude. After all, wasn't it bad thoughts that caused things like momentary lapses in generations of good breeding and even better judgment. Bad thoughts that brought chaos and complications into his ordered home. Bad thoughts led to bad deeds that could lead to disgrace, dishonor and… prison.

No! Thoughts like that could also lead to madness. It was all over now, so he was only going to think good thoughts. Only the good. Only the…

"Is that you? Are you in here, dear? Are you all right?"

The tremulous voice hung in the air at the double-door threshold between the library and the cavernous hallway. On the other side of that hallway was the enormous French Empire living room, and—people.

"Please, dear," the vaguely irritating and softly pleading voice continued, "our guests are beginning to wonder where you are."

He sighed, putting down the large crystal glass of single malt Scotch he'd been nursing. He put it down on the cork coaster resting on the cherry-wood desk and stood up. Pausing at the library's double doors, he turned back to look at the painting that hung over the mantelpiece. A low moan escaped his throat. He shook his head once and turned away, closing the library doors with a click of finality.

1324 Bellevue Avenue | The teahouse | 10:55 p.m.

"Is that… is that *him?*" Bronwyn asked. Her hands shook and her voice too.

Bridget stared through the louvered door panel at the figure seated in the center of the teahouse.

She had never seen his face clearly, but somehow she knew that the man slumped in the black lacquered chair in the center of the room was *him*. Her hand went to her throat, now covered by the black turtleneck, thanks to him. She reached into her skirt pocket and clutched the handle of the gun.

Marcy shuddered, drew in a breath and breathed out heavily, "It's *him.*"

"Bridget, please," Bronwyn whispered, "let's go. Find help. Call the police or something. Or we could go back to the festival and find Mick. He'd know what to do."

Bridget bit the inside of her lip. She knew that was what she should do, but she'd made a vow. To herself and to all of those uncounted generations of Connollys behind her who had fought hopeless fights against overwhelming odds. She couldn't turn tail and run back to Mick.

As soon as Mick discovered the identity of the Shadow Man, he'd be coming after him too. And, she thought, almost guiltily, herself as well. No, she had to take care of *him* first, with the help of her two friends. She clenched the gun in her pocket.

But maybe Bronwyn was right about one thing. Maybe she should send her and Marcy to alert the police, despite Marcy's misgivings, and bring them here. She would stay and watch the Shadow Man, stop him if he tried to leave. That way it wouldn't be just revenge, it would truly be justice.

The beginnings of a smile softened the corners of Bridget's mouth. "You may have a point, luv. Maybe we are bitin' off more than we can chew. I tell ya' what, you and Marcy go into town to the police station and tell them that…"

Muted footsteps sounded on the wooden boards inside the teahouse. They froze. The footsteps approached the door then stopped.

The three girls held one collective breath. Bridget set her jaw. Her hand grew moist clutching the gun.

For a full minute that seemed just short of forever, they crouched on the teahouse steps, the only sound the pounding of the surf in tempo with the pounding of their hearts.

Finally Bridget said, "Well, I'll be bothered if I'm going ta sit on these bleedin' steps all night." Standing up, she looked inside through the shutter louvers. The room was empty.

How could that be?

Bronwyn breathed a sigh of relief. "Let's go, please!"

But Bridget was already turning the door handle. A gust of sea wind caught the door and flung it wide open. Bridget, Bronwyn and Marcy stood frozen, staring into the empty place. Bridget stepped inside, followed by the others. Warily they crept around the sparsely furnished room.

In front of the fireplace they stopped.

"Mother of Jesus," Bridget said, gazing up at the portrait of twelve-year-old Blair Vanderwall in her sailor suit on the yacht. "Who'd a thought a pretty girl like that would cause such destruction around her?"

Marcy slumped onto the red and gold chaise and rested her bruised cheek against the cool silk cushion.

"Where did he go?" Bronwyn asked, looking around her.

Bridget came from a gray, mist-haunted village on the southwest coast of County Cork, where belief in spirits, myths and strange happenings abounded. However, belief that a flesh and blood man could up and vanish from a one-room structure with no other exits was not among the myths she gave credence to.

"There has to be another exit," Bridget said. She walked around the perimeter of the room and looked at every window, then she grabbed Bronwyn's hand, all thoughts of sending her and Marcy to get the police forgotten in the excitement of the impending chase. She dragged her to the center of the room, looked from side to side then took Bronwyn by the shoulder and pulled her into a position at dead center of the teahouse, as near as she could estimate.

"Stand there," Bridget ordered, and held out her right hand. "Take my hand and stretch your arms out as far as you can." Bronwyn wrinkled her brow and followed Bridget's instructions.

"All right, then," she said, taking Bronwyn's hand. "Every time I pull, you take one step toward the outside wall of the room and then stop. Got it?"

Bronwyn nodded uncertainly.

"Now," Bridget said.

Bronwyn took one step outward and stopped. Bridget kept hold of her right hand, but leaned outward, making a 360 degree circle around Bronwyn, stamping her left foot at every step.

"What are you doing?" Bronwyn asked.

"Shush, I'm tryin' to listen, girl."

The bizarre dance continued for one, two, three, four, five outwardly spiraling circles.

"Hush." Bridget stopped. "There, did you hear it?"

Bronwyn shook her head.

Bridget stamped her left foot again.

This time Bronwyn did hear it. A hollow sound.

Marcy lifted her pale cheek off the silk cushion.

Yes, a hollow sound.

"Bronwyn, Marcy, help me roll back this carpet," Bridget said, falling to her knees and tugging at the fringed edge of a sixteen-foot octagonal Oriental rug.

They rolled back a six-foot section of the carpet. Bridget lay flat on the floor, closing one eye and squinting along the almost invisible seam of a mortised cut in the floorboards. She slid her fingers along the seam between the two boards and felt along its length until… Yes! She inserted the fingernail of her pinky finger and slowly pulled out a thin silk cord running the length of the floorboard. Its almost invisible path ended at a small wooden pulley set flush into the floorboard and curved cunningly to look like a knothole. She tugged on the cord. The corner of the rug moved. That's how he did it!

Now, all she had to do was find…

"It should be," she mumbled, "right about here!" She pressed her thumb down into a small dimpled depression in the wood. There was a click, and a four-foot section of the floor dropped away revealing a narrow spiral staircase cut into the stone.

"Yes!" Bridget hissed. "C'mon!"

Bridget, her heart racing, led the two girls down.

"Bridget, I need to stop for a minute." Marcy said when they'd gone a hundred feet or so through the tunnel at the bottom of the stairs. She leaned against the slimy fieldstone and granite of the tunnel wall, her face almost as gray as the stones.

Bridget had been counting the number of steps they'd taken and multiplying by her stride of two and a half feet but she'd lost count after thirty-one when Marcy dropped behind.

Marcy said again, "I need to sit down... just rest for a minute."

Bridget took her hand. It was cold and clammy.

"You look all done in, girl. Why don't you wait here while Bronwyn and I go see where—?"

"No!" Marcy almost shouted. "No," she said again, her eyes darting back and forth around the tunnel. "I'm better now. I just needed to catch my breath. Come on," she tried to smile, "let's go."

Bridget looked back at her skeptically but nodded and continued on down the tunnel. The floor sloped downward and they encountered first small, then increasingly larger, puddles of water. Bronwyn's nose wrinkled at the smell of damp mold, stale air and something else.

"What is that awful smell?"

Bridget sniffed. She'd smelled it before too. In the crypt underneath the monks' chapel next to her old school. All of the girls had been afraid to go down there and had never gotten past the old iron-studded door at the top of the stairs. But the smell had been the same. Cloying, musty and terrifying. And it was getting stronger.

They rounded a corner and Bronwyn put her hand to her mouth, gasping, "I think I'm gonna be sick!"

Marcy caught one quick glance of what was reflected in the dim light before Bridget stepped in front of her. Marcy shook so badly she sank to the wet stone floor.

"Okay, Marcy, that's it, you've done enough. Either go back to the teahouse, or wait for us back up under the light."

Marcy looked up with panic. "Don't leave me here alone. I'm okay now. I can keep up." But as she tried to stand, her knees buckled and Bridget shook her head.

"No, you can't," Bridget sighed. She called to Bronwyn.

"C'mon, luv. We need to get Marcy out of here. We're going to have to get her somewhere safe and warm." She helped Marcy up and Bronwyn ran to her side.

"Gladly," Bronwyn said, looking over her shoulder at what she'd seen. "I can't get out of here fast enough."

They each put an arm around Marcy and retraced their steps.

Bronwyn said "I think it's better this way. Once we get out of here, we'll go for help, okay Bridget?"

"No," answered a voice from behind them. "I think you'll be staying here. For a long, long time."

Chapter 36

1324 Bellevue Avenue | 11:03 p.m.

"Stop!" Mick yelled as Kevin's '67 Firebird pulled up alongside him.

"Why?" Kevin shouted over the liquid growl of the Firebird's glass-pak-filled twin mufflers.

"Because…" Mick yelled back, shook his head, reached through the driver's side window, and clicked off the ignition key. "Because," he repeated in a conversational tone, "we're here."

Mick pointed to the large house surrounded by shrubs and set far back across the wide street.

Kevin grabbed for the keys, but his hand slowed and stopped as he looked up at the imposing pile of gray clapboard. Three stories of windows stared back onto Bellevue Avenue like sullen, accusing eyes.

"Damn," was all he said.

"Smitty," Mick murmured as the trio worked their way around to the east side of the house, "remember the drill when we had to check out what 'Charlie' was doing in the bush?"

Mick's former corporal stopped and stared at the strange sight that greeted them from the expanse of manicured lawn sloping down and ending abruptly with a sheer granite cliff that dropped off into the sea. A full-scale replica of a Japanese teahouse stuck smack in the middle of one of the greenest lawns in Newport.

"Hell, yeah, I remember. You go first. Zigzag right. Cover me while I work my way up left. Then ol' Kevy here, he goes up the middle and draws Charlie's attention, or whoever's in there. Then we come in from either side. And Sarge, I mean, Mick?" Smitty looked over at his friend, who was staring at the teahouse.

"What, Smitty?" Mick answered, never taking his eyes off the structure.

"What the hell do you suppose is in there?"

Mick stared at the delicate teahouse, and the hairs on the back of his neck quivered. The secret erotic painting that Marcy had told them about, the painting of the nude, twelve-year-old Blair Vanderwall, commissioned for the pleasure of her own father, had been made in that teahouse and might have cost the artist his life. The evil behind that painting had led to Blair's death, he was sure of it. But how, and why? Mick shuddered. What other sick, twisted things had taken place there, and what would he find there now? Whatever was there, he had to see for himself.

Silence stretched away toward the cliffs, and dropped off until it was lost in the pounding surf below.

Mick looked at Smitty. "In there just might be the one with all the answers."

"Mick," Kevin called from a dozen feet away. He was pressed against the wall, looking through a set of French doors into the mansion. "I think you better have a look at this."

1324 Bellevue Avenue | 11.15 p.m.

"Benjamin?"

Ben Cortland's heavy eyelids flew open.

"I'm sorry if I woke you, Benjamin," Felicity Prescott said, "but it's late, and Valerie hasn't called, which must mean that Bronwyn hasn't come home, and I, well, I'm getting worried, Benjamin. Very, very worried."

"Yes, Ben," his wife, and Felicity's old school roommate, said from the wingback chair on the other side of the room. "It's getting quite late. I think we should be going."

"Yes, of course, you're right. Certainly, dear." *And thank God!* he thought. They'd been sitting there for the past two hours, making inane small talk with the Vanderwalls, trying to find a polite way to leave two grieving parents who probably didn't want to be left alone with each other and their memories.

And just what kind of memories were they? Benjamin Cortland was getting an increasingly uneasy feeling that he didn't want to know.

"JONATHAN, DEAR," Margaret Vanderwall called to the man who sat in the gold Queen Anne chair, staring at the closed door to the library across the hallway. His eyes drifted slowly back to the living room. "Jonathan," the polite, vaguely annoying voice droned on, like an endless tape loop of stilted phrases and mindless manners. "Our guests are leaving, dear," she continued.

"Ummm? Oh, yes, of course," he answered. "Here, I'll walk you out."

He stopped between sitting and standing.

The library door was opening.

For a moment, his heart stopped, his breath caught in his throat. Something—someone—was outlined in light against the blackness of the open library door. Two dark-suited figures emerged into the cavernous hallway lit by an enormous antique brass chandelier.

"Pardon the interruption, folks," the fat man with the purple silk shirt, wide flowered tie, and piggy little eyes chuckled.

"Who are you?" Benjamin Cortland burst out.

The fat man in the dark sharkskin suit looked at him like a coyote contemplating a nice, plump, and not-too-bright pigeon. His grin was somewhere between a sneer and a snarl. "We're from the newspaper. That real big newspaper up in East Providence. You know the one I'm talking about, right, Mr. Vanderwall?"

Jonathan Vanderwall felt sick.

"Yeah," he continued, "you remember all them newspapers you owe us for, don'cha, Mr. Vanderwall?"

Jonathan Vanderwall remained silent.

"And not only did we deliver all them dirty, muddy old newspapers to all them people you wanted them to go to…" he smiled a shark-toothed smile to match his suit, "but we brought ya an extra added surprise. A nice, dumb little newsboy who's agreed to take all of them nasty, cruddy old papers, and pack the whole big mess up off a' your doorstep and deliver 'em to the Newport County Courthouse."

Jonathan Vanderwall stared at the floor and gave a small nod of his head.

The fat man stopped grinning. "And now, Mr. Vanderwall," he said in a flat, cold voice, "it's collection time."

MICK TURNED to Kevin and Smitty crouching next to him in the dirt outside the French doors. "Keep Cataldo in your sights," he said and backed away.

"And where the frig are you gonna' be?" Kevin asked indignantly. "I'm not one of your freakin' tin soldiers, fer Christ's sake!"

Mick drew a breath and tried to be patient.

"I'm going to see what's out there in that teahouse."

"Okay, okay, that's fine General Mick," Kevin scoffed, "but what the hell are me and old Daniel Boone supposed to do if these guys decide they don't want us following them. Throw acorns at 'em?"

Mick sighed, "Where's that sweet little .32 you used to carry?"

"Ah-h, I leant it to a… friend"

"What was her name, and did she have a jealous boyfriend after her?"

"Husband." Kevin mumbled.

'Well if it comes down to that, you're pretty good with those nun chucks."

Kevin shook his head. "Against a .380 auto or a 9 mil? Whatdya' think I am, friggin' Superman?"

"Kev," Mick said, "we don't have much choice. By the time we found a phone and called the Newport PD, Cataldo could be long gone and it would be our word against the most powerful man in Newport. Assuming that they'd even come."

"Yeah, okay, I suppose me and Davy Crocket here can take 'em if it comes to that, right champ?"

Smitty smiled his lazy smile and nodded. Then his look turned serious and he said, "Mick, are you sure you don't want me to come with you? Cover yer back. Ya' know, like when we was trackin' Charlie in the bush."

Mick paused. "Thanks anyway, man, but Cataldo and Paulie are both packing, so Kevy's gonna need all the help he can get."

"Hey, I resent that!"

"And Kevy—listen to me good. Just tail them. Do not let them see you. Keep well back."

"Crap, do I look like a friggin' moron?"

Mick looked across the lawn to the Japanese teahouse sitting on the seaside cliff like a dark seagull-vulture. He knew deep down inside that something was waiting in there, and it was going to be evil.

He sprinted across the lawn and peered through the louvers in the teahouse door. The room was empty. He stepped inside. His eyes quickly scanned the room. His breath caught in his throat as he saw the glint of gold in a framed picture over the fireplace. But this was a portrait of an impishly smiling Blair in a summer sailor suit, standing on the foredeck of the family yacht, her hands on her hips, head tossed back, white-blond hair swept from her face by the wind. She radiated an iridescent, innocent-erotic sexuality. No wonder the nineteen-year-old artist had been smitten.

He touched the chaise, the one where Blair had posed for that other, secret painting. Where was it now? Had it been destroyed too, as Blair had been?

His eyes restlessly searched each corner. The smell of the sea was in the room, a trace of some long-ago incense and something else, very, very faint, but more recent. Faint but so familiar. It almost smelled like…

His eyes dropped to the floor behind the chaise. A section of the oriental rug had been folded back on itself. He ran to it and looked down. His heart hammered as he gazed down into the dark stairway and tunnel.

Then that scent again, just there beneath the sea air, so tantalizingly familiar. Perfume. *Tigress* perfume, given last Christmas to—

Oh, God, no.

Bridget!

1324 Bellevue Avenue | 11:38 p.m.

Jonathan Vanderwall snapped the fireproof steel lockbox shut and shook his head with a snort of disgust.

"That's the final payment," he said, getting up from the desk and wiping his hands on his white cashmere sports jacket, as if to rid them of some invisible stain. "There's the balance, fifteen thousand dollars, which, added to the ten thousand that I gave you as a retainer," his tongue twisted around the word, as if tasting something bad, "adds up to the agreed upon total of twenty-five thousand. Thus completing our business."

Cataldo continued to look at the tall, self-styled patrician with his lifeless shark eyes set into their piggy little sockets. He dragged a practiced thumb across the five bundles of hundred-dollar bills, riffling them with a lifelong expertise that could tell if a stack was even one bill short. Satisfied, he stuffed the packets into the inside pockets of his suit jacket.

Jonathan Vanderwall opened the double doors of the library and looked back at Cataldo. He swung his head in the direction of the main door to the house. Cataldo didn't move.

"Good night, Mr. Cataldo. I said our business is concluded."

Cataldo finished stuffing the last package of bills into his suit jacket and his hand emerged holding something else. His polished steel .380 automatic. "No, Mr. Vanderwall," he grinned, his eyes glittering in the light from the hallway's brass chandelier, "we still have one more little piece of business to take care of."

"What are you talking about? We had a—"

"A deal?" Cataldo smirked.

"Yes, a deal. I paid you twenty-five thousand dollars to secure that banjo player. Where is he? You've taken my money, you—"

"Shut up, Mr. Vanderwall." The East Providence hood almost spat the name. "You're gonna get what you paid for plus a whole lot more. Oh, yeah," he sneered, "you're gonna get an unexpected little 'bonus.' You see, Mr. V., I've always been a hustler. And whenever I seen my opportunities," he reached a stubby hand into the air and squeezed, "I took 'em. So, I've been working for you, and took your money and you're gonna get what you paid for. But I also been working for someone else. And just like you, he's gonna get what he paid for. And you know what that is, Mr. V.? Do you know what he wants?"

Jonathan Vanderwall felt faint. He knew who *he* was, and he was despairingly sure that he likewise knew what *he* wanted.

Never taking the gun off Vanderwall's midsection, Cataldo walked across the tiled hallway and pushed open the doors to the living room. He waved the gun at the people inside and said in a loud voice, "What he wants, Mr. V., is to see you. Right now, downstairs, and I think he'd like it if your friends came along, too."

Cataldo turned to Paulie. "Give us a few minutes, so as him and Mr. V. here can 'catch up on old times', and then bring the rest of them along."

Paulie nodded.

Cataldo swung the heavy automatic back toward Jonathan Vanderwall and nudged him toward the back of the entrance hall where he opened a massive brass and iron strapped door. A musty smell drifted up from the stairwell. Cataldo shoved the gun into Vanderwall's back and chuckled, "After you, Mr. V. He's waiting."

BRONWYN LOOKED at Bridget and made a muffled mewing sound around the gag taped over her mouth. Bronwyn's eyes seemed to strain out of their sockets then she squeezed them shut tight. She didn't want to, she couldn't, just couldn't, look any more. She hung her head and let the tears drip through her eyelids. When she opened them again, Marcy had fainted. Lucky Marcy. This final straw had broken what was left of her shaky courage. Marcy had checked out of this nightmare hotel, and might not ever be coming back, Bronwyn thought almost hysterically. She had to get out of here. She had to get free.

She struggled with the coarse strands of thick black fishing line that bound her wrists, but the more she twisted and strained, the tighter they became. She sucked breath through her nostrils in great ragged gasps. She was hyperventilating. She would pass out, or go insane, or both.

And the whole time, he kept talking. To *her*!

Oh my God!

Bronwyn's eyes rolled back in her head. Her senses were shutting down. And then someone kicked her ankle. She looked up and into Bridget's eyes. They were fierce. Bridget locked her eyes on Bronwyn's and shook her head. Bronwyn could see Bridget's lips moving under the tape of her gag. They were saying something. Something like, *Don't! Don't! Don't let him scare you. Fight it!*

Bronwyn finally drew in a deep, gasping breath and nodded her head.

SHE WAS PULLING it together. Good girl! And bloody good thing Bronwyn didn't know how close Bridget was to losing it herself. Oh, God, she despaired, it was all her fault. She'd led them into this. Her pain, her rage, her need to take control of her life again and—she hung her head as she realized—her thirst for revenge. Why hadn't she listened to Mick?

"Leave that kind of crap to me, babe."

She turned away so that Bronwyn wouldn't see the tear leaking out of the corner of her eye. "Oh, Mickey," she mumbled into the gag, "where are you, darlin'? We need you. I need you."

If only she could reach Mick's knife in her pocket.

She heard laughter.

"Look, dear heart," the voice mocked, "I don't think they're enjoying our company." He stared at Bridget from out of the shadows with his insane eyes, and whispered to the blond head next to his own.

"I think they're just jealous because you're the prettiest girl in the room."

He looked at Bridget again and smiled his mad smile.

He wants me to break, Bridget thought. She sucked in a breath, set her jaw, and put the steel of a daughter of the IRA back in her eyes.

Not bloody likely!

MICK SLITHERED from shadow to shadow along the slimy stone walls of the tunnel. His boots made squishing sounds in the shallow puddles dotting the crumbling passageway. Water dripped constantly from tiny chinks in the ceiling's mortar and seemed to ooze through the old stone walls as well. The right shoulder of his denim jacket was soaked through to his skin.

Electric lights with old-fashioned bulbs and fixtures looked at least a century old and gave off a few feeble watts of illumination. Medieval sconces with guttering torches would complete the spooky scene: a dank, dripping tunnel lit by flickering torches.

Hell, all we need now is a couple of skeletons hanging along the wall.

Mick rounded a curve in the tunnel wall and stopped short.

Oh, shit.

"Be careful what you wish for, boy-o," Mick heard Big Mike laugh from the echoes of his childhood memories.

Stuffed into a shallow alcove that had been bricked all the way up to a grinning face, was a partially mummified, decomposing corpse.

"WHERE ARE YOU taking us?" Benjamin Cortland demanded

It was not a good idea, the demanding part.

Paulie turned around, looked at Benjamin, and smiled.

That was also not good, Paulie smiling. Because when Paulie smiled, people got hurt. Especially people like Benjamin Cortland. As a matter of fact, that was one of the things that Paulie liked most about his job, hurting people like Benjamin Cortland. So now, he started to enjoy himself by smashing the heavy barrel of his 9 mm Sturm Ruger automatic into an astonished Benjamin Cortland's stomach.

Still grinning, Paulie bent down and whispered into the ear of the silver-haired man who lay gasping on the living room carpet, "Shut the fuck up."

Paulie straightened up and looked at the three women fluttering their hands and making little sounds of distress. He leaned toward them and said, "Anyone else have any questions?"

One of the women shrieked, "My husband" and dropped to her knees, cradling his head as he struggled to draw a breath.

"Let's go," Paulie said, waving the gun in the direction of the hallway.

"He can't move!" Benjamin Cortland's wife said angrily. "You've knocked the breath right out of him."

"Aw, too bad," Paulie smirked. "That's tough, 'cause if he's not on his feet by the time I open those doors to the hallway, I'm gonna put one in his kneecap."

"Oh, no, please." The woman made ineffectual little movements with her hands while trying desperately to help her husband up.

Paulie crossed over to the double doors and put his hand on the doorknob. He turned back toward the Cortlands, making a great show of sighting down the barrel of his automatic.

"Benjamin, please! Get up, dear. You really must!"

Benjamin struggled to his feet and stood with one arm braced on his wife's shoulders.

"Okay," Paulie grinned, "if everyone is ready, and there's no more questions," he sneered at Benjamin, "then let's all go downstairs and see what Mr. Cataldo and his little buddy have got cooked up."

He threw the heavy double doors open and grinned even wider. Two startled figures stood frozen with their hands on the handle of the door that led to the basement.

"Well, well," he chuckled, "whadda we got here? Two more little pigeons to add to our party."

Paulie grinned as the red-haired guy turned to the tall lanky one and said,

"Aw, crap!"

THE CORPSE had been a nasty surprise, but Mick had a feeling it was only the start of the nasty surprises.

Around the next corner the tunnel opened into a gigantic wine cellar.

His stomach rose when his eyes confirmed what he didn't want to admit but had already known down deep in his gut.

Marcy and Bronwyn. And Bridget. They weren't safely back at the festival, singing 'Kumbaya' and passing around a joint. They were tied to filthy, moldy chairs, gagged with duct tape.

Marcy looked unconscious. His sister's eyes bulged like a scared child. But pain stabbed his heart to see Bridget this way. Damn them! God damn them all! How much more did this tough and tender little girl from County Cork have to take! She'd been drugged, kidnapped, tortured and scarred. And now this! Tears glistened at the corners of her eyes as she worked against the strands of black fishing line and thick hemp ropes that held her to the chair.

He fingered the steel frame of the .38 and cautiously inched his way into the cellar. He froze then slowly stepped back into the tunnel behind a massive brick pillar when a familiar fat man emerged from the stairway across the room. "Well, look at this, boys and girls, our host has got the makings of a nice little party going here."

Another voice, hidden in the darkness at the other end of the table, said, "Cataldo, finally. Did you bring him?"

Cataldo laughed. "Don't I always keep my bargains, kid?"

The voice answered with a strange chuckle of its own. "Yes. When you're being well paid."

"You got that right. And here's what you paid for."

The double-crossed Jonathan Vanderwall stumbled into the room and looked around him like a fox surrounded by hounds.

"I don't know whatcha want him for, kid, and I could care less. All I want to know is, where's my money?"

"On the end of the table," the voice answered. "Just in front of the girls."

"Whatcha doin', settin' yerself up for a little 'nookie' party?" Cataldo smirked.

There was no reply, then a sound between a laugh and a cry.

"I don't need them. I've already got the most beautiful girl in the room."

Cataldo stepped forward, looked at the open briefcase filled with cash, snapped it shut and backed away. He nodded at Bridget.

"If you decide to get it on with this little spitfire, just remember, no hickeys. You already gave her one last night."

BRIDGET STRAINED against her bonds, every nerve fiber screaming to let her sink her fingernails into that fat, mocking face. The movement attracted the attention of the figure sitting in the half light at the head of the table. He stopped stroking the blond head of the girl by his side, slowly got up and moved down the table until he stood next to Bridget.

She stopped struggling and looked up into the bottomless eyes. It was like looking into a deep black well.

Fear chipped away at her rage. The memories of the night before came rushing back. Her stomach constricted as he reached out one of his scarred muscular hands and stroked her cheek, just above the gauze covered wound underneath her black turtleneck.

"You're right, Cataldo. I did give her something to remember me by last night, but where is it? It should be right here." His finger traced a line down her cheek. "It should be right here, but it's not." He took Bridget's heart shaped face between his massive thumb and forefinger and looked into her frightened eyes.

"Didn't you appreciate my gift? Whether you realize or not, it really was a gift, you know. It would have saved you from becoming a soulless, heartless bitch, whose only purpose was to seduce men with those perfect eyes and lips and—face." The steel-like fingers pressed into her jaw.

"But you rejected my gift. You've kept that beautiful face which can only cause you, and everyone around you, pain and tears and regret." His voice was getting louder.

"Where is your mark, little girl? I know I struck your skin. I heard you scream. I smelled burnt flesh. Where is it?"

Bridget pushed back into the moldering chair but his fingers rolled down her face, gripped the collar of the black turtleneck and pulled.

There was a sound of tearing fabric and a satisfied, "Ah, there."

Tears rolled down her cheeks and he caressed them with his

fingertips. He put one tear-wet finger between his lips and licked it.

"Do you know what it tastes like, little girl?"

Bridget bit her lip beneath the gag to keep from crying but it was no use.

"I'm afraid that it still tastes like… beauty." His eyes burned. "I thought I had saved you and everyone who would look at that beautiful face and be poisoned, imprisoned and emasculated. But somehow you avoided my healing brand. I failed. I apologize."

Bridget writhed and tried to pull away from his hands. He smiled. "But I promise you, I won't fail again."

He took a gold engraved cigarette lighter out of his pocket.

"Shall we complete what we started?"

Bridget's nostrils flared as she tried to scream underneath her gag.

"Oh, forgive me." He reached down and ripped the taped gag from her mouth. "You'll want to scream, won't you?"

He flicked the wheel over the lighter's flint and a bright blue flame sprang from its tip. He grabbed Bridget's jaw in a vise-like grip.

"It was such a pretty face, wasn't it? But now it's going to be better. So much better for all concerned."

He moved the lighter to her face. Bridget gritted her teeth as the uncontrollable tears ran down her cheeks. *Don't cry. Don't scream. You are a Connolly girl!* she screamed in her mind. *Remember the beatings your father's taken, your grandfather. You are a Connolly, damn you. Don't cry!* But the tears didn't listen; they kept dripping onto the stone floor.

He looked at her with something that far back in his dim past might have been a feeling close to compassion. He bent down and kissed her cheek. "That was the last kiss that this beautiful face will ever receive."

He pushed the red-hot lighter toward Bridget's milk-white cheek.

She screamed.

And the dusty mahogany tabletop exploded into splinters in front of the Shadow Man.

"Get away from her or I'll blow your fucking head off, you son of a bitch!"

Mick stepped into the wine cellar holding his .38.

The Shadow Man stood motionless next to Bridget, his face still obscured in the wavering shadows that had now permeated his soul so completely.

"Drop the lighter!"

He looked at Mick contemptuously and closed his giant fist around the lighter, extinguishing the flame with the flesh of his sizzling, uncaring hand.

"Okay, McCarthy, now it's your turn. Drop it."

Mick spun and pointed the .38 at Cataldo's fat gut while the East Providence mob boss aimed his pearl-handled .380 automatic right between Mick's eyes.

"Back away Cataldo. I can blow your head off from here."

"Not if I blow yours off first, smart ass." A voice called from the stairs.

Another figure emerged from the stairway, pushing four frightened fifty-somethings in front of him.

Paulie pushed a stumbling, ashen-faced Benjamin Cortland and the three long-ago boarding school roommates ahead of him into the wine cellar, keeping his 9 mm Sturm Ruger aimed at Mick. With one eye on Mick, Paulie looked out of the corner of the other and called up the stairs, "C'mon boys, don't be shy. Join the party."

Mick's glance darted from Cataldo to Paulie, who had his mother, Margaret Vanderwall, and the Cortlands covered. He motioned for whoever was on the stairs to hurry. Mick had a sinking feeling he knew who it would be, confirmed seconds later when Kevin's contrite face emerged from the stairwell, followed closely by Smitty's.

"Kevin, Smitty," Mick called without taking his eyes off Cataldo. "He can't cover me and you two at the same time. When you see me move, go for him!"

"Sorry, Mick." Smitty's voice was a dejected drawl.

"What the hell do you mean?" Mick snapped.

"What I mean is, there's a bunch of guys in blue uniforms standing right behind us, and one of 'em's got this big old .38 pistol pointed right at my head."

Unfrigging-believable! Kevin and Smitty walked into the room with their arms over their heads. But the next to emerge from the stairwell, the Newport Police Department's desk sergeant and two other uniformed patrolmen, pushed the situation over the edge into a whole different category of weird.

They fanned out, the desk sergeant nodding slightly to Cataldo, who nodded back then laughed at Mick.

The three guardians of law and order from the Newport Police Department stood next to Cataldo, their guns trained on Kevin, Smitty and Mick.

Chapter 37

Newport | Rhode Island | Newport Police Department

11: 47 p.m.

'Big Mike' McCarthy pulled the massive old Buick into the slanted parking space in front of the Newport Police station. He got out of the car and tried to stretch the crinks and pains out of his fifty-five-year-old back.

He looked at the red brick front of the station house. If Tommy O'Donnell was on tonight then he had a good chance of getting the information he needed. If not…?

He walked inside.

"Yeah?" the uniformed patrolman sitting behind the desk said without looking up.

"I'm looking for O'Donnell."

"Nah, he's not here."

"Where is he?"

"Who the hell are you?" The patrolman finally looked up.

The big man in front of the desk pulled out his wallet and flipped it open. The patrolman glanced at it, snorted and said, "And I'm supposed to be impressed?"

Time to trot out the big guns. "Look, I got a friend up in Boston by the name of…"

"Detective … or should I say 'former Detective' McCarthy?"

Mike turned around toward the well-dressed, silver-haired man sitting behind him. He sized up the smiling, shark-faced man quickly.

"And just what brings you out to a small-time station house at this hour of the friggin' night, Parmenter?"

"Probably the same thing as you. Business. Should I call you Detective or just McCarthy?"

"McCarthy. Just like my son. And where is he?" Mike quickly crossed the six feet separating them and stood over the immaculately clad lawyer.

"I'm sorry," Parmenter said with a smile, "I'm sure I don't know—"

"Cut the crap, Parmenter. I know you're the shyster working for that sleezeball, Cataldo. Yeah, I read the files on your brilliant defense of that cockroach and his slimy crew." Mike looked him up and down with contempt. "Don't you think you've just about worn out that fifth amendment by now?" He snorted. "But I guess it pays better than chasing ambulances, huh?"

The lawyer's smile said that sticks, stones and perhaps a well swung aluminum baseball bat might break his bones, but insults like "sleezeball" and "Ambulance Chaser" could be well assuaged by the healthy monthly retainer Cataldo kept him on. He stretched out his hand to Mike.

"Edmond Parmenter, at your service."

Mike batted his hand down. "Mike McCarthy, pissed off parent. Where is he? And Bridget."

"Okay, McCarthy, turn around. Slowly. You're going downstairs to cool off for what's left of the night."

Mike turned around. Slowly. And what he saw didn't frighten him. It didn't even faze him. It just made him smile.

"Fahey. Johnny Fahey. Who the hell gave you a badge and a gun? Why, last time I saw you, you were sweepin' out Station B on Boylston Street."

Jonathan Fahey started to sweat. "Hey listen, Mike, you may have been hot stuff up in Boston, but down here you're just…"

Johnny never got a chance to finish the sentence. Mike covered the distance to him in two quick strides, pulled the gun out of his hand and slammed him unceremoniously into the dapper lawyer Parmenter.

"Next time, Johnny, stick to cleaning floors."

The big man leaned his face across the desk and whispered a name into the ear of the patrolman who had just experienced an attitude adjustment.

"I thought he was retired," he answered warily.

"He is," the big man answered back, "but he can still make your life a living hell if you don't open your big mouth a little wider and tell me where the hell O'Donnell is."

The patrolman stared back for a few moments then dropped his gaze and muttered sullenly, "Him and two of the other uniforms said they had some 'loose ends' to wrap up on a case."

"What case? Where? With who?"

"The Vanderwall case. The rich girl who got murdered this week. That's where they are right now, up at the house on Bellevue Avenue. Number 1324. Jonathan Vanderwall."

1324 Bellevue Avenue | 11:48 p.m.

"Drop it, kid."

The desk sergeant's revolver, aimed at Mick's chest, didn't waver. He wouldn't miss.

Mick gritted his teeth. There were too many of them, he was outgunned four to one. If only he could put a slug into Cataldo's ugly face. But that wouldn't help Kevin or Smitty or his Mom or sister. Or Bridget.

He let the gun drop to the floor. The patrolman standing next to him scooped up Mick's gun and pushed it into his black service belt.

"Lie down and put your hands behind your head," the sergeant said, and looking over at Kevin and Smitty, added, "you too."

They joined Mick on the floor, and Kevin muttered, "Hey, are we having fun yet?"

"Shut up," the desk sergeant said in a weary voice. He turned to Cataldo. "Okay, let's get this over with. I want to get the hell out of here and go take a long, hot shower."

"Jeez, O'Donnell," Cataldo said, shaking his head, "you wanna be careful with the remarks. You might hurt me and Paulie's feelings."

"Can it, you fat, greasy punk. Give us our cut and let's finish this."

Cataldo shrugged and opened the briefcase. He counted out two stacks of bills and then a third, larger stack, and pushed them across the water-stained old table.

The three cops picked up their stacks, and the desk sergeant turned back to Cataldo.

"We're leaving."

"Hold on," Cataldo rasped, grabbing the sergeant's arm. "That wasn't the deal. The deal was you help us clean up these… loose ends."

The sergeant stared back at Cataldo. "Get your frigging hands off of me, you greasy piece of slime. I said I'd look the other way, and that's it. Period! I don't want to know what you're going to do here, and if I ever do, then I might have to come looking for you. I only let it get this far because this family has poisoned this town for way too long!"

"I resent that, Sergeant." The strange sounding voice at the dark end of the table penetrated the room. "You know nothing about our family except that which we choose to let you know."

"I know enough," answered the sergeant, "and what I know about your father turns my stomach!"

"It turns mine too, sergeant," answered the choked whisper.

The figure stood up and moved towards the lighted end of the table. From his prone position on the floor, Mick raised his head and looked up.

The figure stepped into the light.

Mick stared. That face. On the pier in back of the White Rabbit. And yes, the three people leaving the cemetery. Mick looked up at his mother and her two old friends and saw that the pale blond standing next to his mother, now shaking her head in disbelief, was the woman in the black pillbox hat and veil. The older man from the cemetery stood before the table, his sallow complexion turning chalky white And the third familiar face, the younger man, was the murderous Shadow Man who had haunted Mick and Bridget's waking and sleeping nightmares. He looked almost normal, ordinary. About five feet ten inches, slight build, with hands that looked too big for his body frame and were covered with scabs. He was young, no older than Mick. His face was thin, almost ascetic, and as he approached the end of the table, that face contorted into a mask of hate.

"Get him up, Cataldo," he snarled.

Cataldo reached down and pulled the gray-haired, shaking figure slumped on the floor to his feet.

Jack Vanderwall, The Shadow Man, leaned forward and looked into eyes that mirrored his own.

"I've looked forward to this for a long, long time," the young man said in a voice filled with a lifetime of hate, "father."

JONATHAN VANDERWALL slumped, holding on to the edge of the table, his shoulders shaking.

"Why, Jack, why? I did all of this—hired this scum—to protect you. To keep you from going to—"

"Jail, father? And would that have been worse than the Pinewood School, where you stuck me when I was fourteen because I—Do you remember why you took me out of this house and put me in that expensive hell hole?"

"It was an exclusive boarding school for troubled young people."

"It was a fucking loony bin!" Jack Vanderwall spat back.

"Do you remember why, father?" he asked again

Jonathan Vanderwall whispered, "Because you murdered, Jack."

Jack reached forward with his thin scar-covered hands and pulled the older man toward him.

"It was," he hissed, "because I saw you that night in the library. You remember that night. It was just after that art student had completed the third painting. Before you locked it away in the teahouse where it would be viewed by only you, you asked Blair to come into the library to see it with you. Beautiful little Bair with her long blond hair and blue, blue eyes. She came to see the painting. You remember that painting, don't you? You should. You told the artist how to paint it. You gave Blair that robe to wear. The Japanese silk robe. Only she didn't wear it, she let it fall open—and then took it off. Look, do you see?" He pointed to the wall at the head of the table. "I did. I watched the whole thing through the teahouse window. The whole disgusting thing! But I made him pay. Oh yes, how he pleaded for his rancid little life at the end. Just the way you will. Was it worth it? Take a last look and tell me!"

He reached up to the dripping water stained bricks and pulled a huge canvas in a guilt frame off the rough wall. The guilt had begun to tarnish around the edges, but the riveting image in the center of the portrait was still visible. Blair. Beautiful, stunning, innocently knowing and erotically precocious Blair stared out from the mottled frame with ancient eyes that could bind a soul to her, and had.

Jack hissed into the older man's face, "You unimaginable bastard. That night, after the Regatta Club dinner, I saw you sitting in that big leather chair of yours. *She* was sitting in your lap and you were kissing her. She had taken her blouse off and you put your hands all over her. Touching her. Kissing her!" His voice rose to a scream.

"Your own daughter, my sister, Blair!"

Jonathan Vanderwall moaned again and shook his head.

His son grabbed the front of his shirt and pulled him toward the dark end of the table. His other hand reached out and slammed into a light switch. As the harsh light of the bare bulb illuminated the room, he screamed,

"Look! Now she's with the one she was meant to be with. Me!"

He pushed his father's face to within inches of the waxen, golden haired figure in the chair. "And she will be, forever."

Vacant-eyed Jonathan Vanderwal slumped to the floor, whimpering and moaning as he rocked himself back and forth.

Jack Vanderwall turned toward Cataldo.

Cataldo stared, speechless with the rest of them, at the work of the very best undertaker that money could buy: the almost lifelike form, the corpse of Blair Prentiss Vanderwall.

"Did you bring it all?" Jack asked Cataldo.

"Huh?" Cataldo continued to stare, his mouth hanging open.

"Did you bring it all, you moron?"

For once, Cataldo didn't even respond to an insult. "Yeah," he whispered. "Yeah, you sick, sick fuck."

"Watch your mouth, Cataldo, if you want the other briefcase."

Cataldo looked toward the other end of the table, where a second briefcase was being pushed toward him.

"Did you put it in all of the wine bins?"

"Yeah," Cataldo answered, still shaking his head.

"That's good," Jack the Shadow Man said quietly. He turned to the corpse that almost seemed to retain something of Blair's love of devilry. "I know how much you like to have admirers and former lovers around, so I hope you appreciate how much trouble I've gone to, to fill this party room with all those people who 'couldn't live without you.'"

He chuckled, reached over, and flipped another switch. The other side of the table was thrown into the harsh light. Seated facing Blair across the table, were Janet, the pudgy red-haired girl they'd met at Father's; Suzy Cantrell, the White Rabbit waitress, and poor 'can't-get-a-break' PJ, Marcy's skinny, hippie boyfriend.

Cataldo looked at Jack contemptuously as he picked up both briefcases and backed away from the table.

"What the hell are you going to do with all that crap anyway?"

Jack smiled and whispered into Blair's hair, "It's the party favor. The noisemaker."

Sergeant O'Donnell turned to Cataldo and said, "What did you get for this maniac?"

"Four hundred pounds of army C-4 explosive."

The Newport desk sergeant stared at Cataldo.

"You gave this friggin' psychopath four hundred pounds of C-4?"

"He paid for it," Cataldo snarled, and added, "and that's all you need to know, O'Donnell."

A mottled red flush crept up the back of Sgt. O'Donnell's neck and settled around the collar of his blue uniform.

"Don't push me too far, Cataldo, or I might take this wad of bills and shove them down your throat, one by one."

He turned to the two uniformed patrolmen. "I'm not gonna let him blow up half this town. Ed, Charlie, find the detonators on this stuff and disarm it."

Ed, a skinny Barney Fife look-alike, took a half dozen reluctant steps into the nearest wine vault and stopped. He called back over his shoulder, "Sarge, I think you better come back here."

O'Donnell edged sideways and moved his head around the corner of the vault.

"Son of a bitch!" he exploded. He turned back to Cataldo and shouted, "That's my sister you've got tied up in there, you guinea bastard!"

Cataldo shrugged. "I needed the banjo player for the deal, and I took your spacey sister and her boyfriend to make sure he behaved himself."

"Well, that tears it, Cataldo. Our part of your 'deal' is off. Ed, untie 'em. We're outta here."

"Yeah, I guess you are at that," Cataldo said softly, cocking the .380. "But no matter. Did you really think I was gonna let you walk out of here with all that dough?"

The cop nearest the stairwell unbuttoned his holster and reached for his gun. Cataldo's eyes flickered toward Paulie. Paulie nodded and shot Charlie right in the center of his forehead. As the cop slumped forward, Ed ran out of the wine vault, followed by Danny, Cody and Sparrow. Paulie swiveled his 9 mm and shot Ed in the chest. He folded up like a wet piece of paper and lay gasping for breath on the cold stone floor.

O'Donnell bent down and pulled off his tie, wrapping it into a ball and trying to stanch the flow of blood that the skinny old cop was pumping onto the stone floor.

"Ed. Eddie. Jesus, man, I'm sorry I got you into this."

The blood gurgled in Eddie's throat. He tried to speak and his eyes rolled up toward the ceiling.

"Leave him," Cataldo said in a flat, cold voice. "He's dead."

Cataldo motioned with his gun. "Now, push that cash over here, and keep your hands where I can see them, or I might have to put a few more holes in your sister's empty head."

"Tommy," Sparrow asked, "what's going on? How could you be involved with that killer? You're supposed to be the law!"

"Sorry, Sis," O'Donnell mumbled. "I had ten years to go for my pension, and I was trying to help you out with the rent and pay for Mom's nursing home bills, and, well, when this slime bag showed up Wednesday afternoon and offered me twenty grand just to release the musician kid to him and his lawyer, it seemed too good to pass up."

"Did they tell you what they wanted him for?" Sparrow asked.

Her brother shrugged his shoulders.

Cody stepped from behind Sparrow. "They wanted me to take the rap for killing Blair while I was drunk. They said they'd get me a short sentence and give me a whole pile of money when I got out." He looked at Cataldo bitterly. "That was a big crock too, wasn't it, Mr. C?"

Cataldo grinned. "Life's tough, ain't it, kid?"

He turned back to the group. "Now, everybody, down on the floor."

Paulie pushed the Cortlands, Felicity, and Margaret Vanderwall into the center of the room, where they joined the others lying in a semicircle on the stone tiles.

"You're all going to stick around to enjoy the party that our young friend has planned."

Cataldo looked over at the amused face of the young man sitting in the flickering candlelight at the end of the table.

"How you want 'em, kid?" Cataldo called, "alive or dead?"

"Alive," he whispered. "For now."

"They're all yours," Cataldo said, picking up one of the briefcases. He motioned to Paulie to take the other one. "But before I go, I got one piece of unfinished business to take care of."

He looked at Paulie, and then over at Mick's prone form on the floor.

"Paulie, be a good kid, do the job I told that asshole Vinnie to do."

Paulie grinned and said, "Sure thing. Be a pleasure, Mr. C."

He leveled the 9 mm at Mick as Mick tried to scramble to his knees.

"Get away from him, ya dirty spalpeen!" Bridget yelled, wielding a wickedly gleaming little .25 caliber Beretta in one hand and Mick's Buck knife in the other.

Cataldo laughed. "Where did you get that? Is it even loaded? Or are you gonna stab me with your penknife?"

"It should be loaded," Bridget smiled back. "I took it off your own thug after I laid him out with a two-by-four back at the festival."

"Okay, missy, so go ahead and shoot me, if you can."

The smile evaporated from Bridget's face and was replaced by a look of raw hatred.

"Yes," she hissed from between clenched teeth. "And then I'm gonna make sure that *he*," her eyes darted to the head of the table, "is never going to kill, or hurt anyone again." Her fingers touched the black fabric of the turtleneck sweater around her throat.

"All right then, you dumb bitch," Cataldo snarled, "go ahead and shoot!"

"Drop it!" Paulie yelled from the stairwell, cocking the big 9 mm.

She shook her head. Her fingers tightened on the trigger. Her heart raced, her hands trembled.

The lord knows if ever men needed killin', it's this filthy lot.

She looked around the room at all of the people there. Friends, Mick's family, Mick. He was crouched on the floor like a tiger waiting to spring. If she didn't shoot, he'd be dead before he got half way to Paulie and Cataldo. Her finger tightened again, then stopped.

"That's why little girls shouldn't play with guns, sweetie," Cataldo mocked. "They never heard of safety catches." His smile turned back into a snarl as he picked up one of the briefcases and said, "Let's get the hell outta here, Paulie. Shoot her. And her boyfriend, too."

Paulie raised his gun, and the back of his head exploded. He collapsed backwards into the stairwell. It looked as if he was moving again, but the illusion was shattered when a size eleven foot, shod in thick-soled black shoes appeared in the stairwell and nudged Paulie's lifeless body down the last few steps.

MICK LOOKED UP at the big, scarred, broken-nosed face.

"Pop!"

Big Mike McCarthy stepped into the room.

Cataldo pointed his .380 at Mick. "One more step, McCarthy, and I'll plug your kid."

Mike shot him in the kneecap.

He walked over to where the fat East Providence mob boss lay writhing in his own blood and said, "That was always your problem, Cataldo. Your mouth moved faster than your gun."

He turned back to his son. "Mickey, get his gun and untie your sister and that other girl."

"Hello, Michael," a voice spoke from behind him.

Mike's eyebrows shot up. "Felicity?"

"Once again, you've come to my rescue, dear," his former wife answered with the wry little smile he used to love so much. "What are you doing here?"

Mike looked at her and nodded his head. "Ah, you mean 'here,' as in 'places that I don't belong?'"

"No, Michael, I mean as in, here to rescue everyone, and me, again."

Mike rubbed his chin and pointed down at Cataldo. "This big shot ran his mouth once too often in my direction about people I care about, so I did a little digging, and what I found out made me decide to take a ride down here to see what was up."

Bridget untied Marcy and Bronwyn. Mick's sister ran over and put her arms around her father. "Daddy," she said, holding him. "We were so scared! You have no idea what he is, what he's done!"

She pointed her shaking finger toward the silent, still figures seated around the long table.

"All those people, they're—"

"Yes," interrupted a hollow voice from the head of the table, "they're here for my sister's party. Perhaps you'd all like to join us."

Marcy looked up at Mick and his father and whispered in a shaking voice, "What about *him?*" She pointed to the end of the table.

Mick looked at the bruises on Marcy's face, at his frightened sister, and at the torn black turtleneck that partially covered the neck of the woman he loved. He took two steps, bent down and scooped up Paulie's fallen 9 mm. He whirled around, pointed the gun straight down the table, and drew a bead on the young man with the strange eyes that glittered in the flicker of a massive, silver candelabrum.

"Mick!" his father said sharply.

"I'm gonna do the world a favor, Pop."

"Mickey, no, please!" Bridget ran to him and put her arms around him, forcing his gun hand down. "He's not worth it, darlin'," she whispered.

Mick pushed her away.

"No, but you are." He raised the gun again.

The hollow voice echoed off the dank brick walls once more. "I suggest you listen to her."

There was a motion from the far end of the table, but before Mick could react, Shadow Man Jack's hands came up from under the table, holding a pair of dueling pistols.

"A legacy from my grandfather Randolph's collection. He taught me how to load and shoot them, and I've replaced the solid lead balls with buckshot, so it will take out half of the room. Besides, you don't have any time to waste, those of you who are planning to leave."

"What are you babbling about?" Mick snarled.

"Do you really think I'm going to let them lock me up in some insane asylum, like 'dear old Dad' here wanted to do? No, Blair and I and all of her 'admirers,' especially 'dear old Dad,' are staying here."

"What's he talking about, Mickey?" Big Mike asked.

"He's got the whole place stuffed with C-4. I worked with that crap in 'Nam, Pop. He's got enough of it down here to lift the roof off the friggin' house."

Mike looked around then snapped out, "Mickey, Kevin, Danny, get into the vaults and pull out everything that looks like a detonator."

"You're too late," the young man said. "You'd never find them all in time. You see, while you were busy shooting Cataldo, I tripped the detonators. I believe they're on a ten-minute timer. Isn't that what you said, Mr. Cataldo?"

Cataldo, holding his bloody knee, gasped out, "Yeah. Shit, let's get the hell out of here before this whole place goes up!"

"You're not going anywhere, Cataldo," Big Mike said and herded everyone else upstairs.

Sgt. O'Donnell spoke up for the first time. "Mike, shouldn't we bring him?"

Mike looked back. "That's up to you, Tommy. But remember, if you do, he can rat out your part in this any time he wants, and he'll always have that to hold over you."

Sgt. O'Donnell looked back at the big veteran of Boston's tough Station B. He looked from Cataldo, writhing on the floor, to his sister, watching him, to the dead cop.

"No. I screwed up, Mike. But maybe it's not too late to make it right. Get 'im outta here. I've had explosives training, and I did two years with the bomb squad in Providence. I'm gonna disarm the C-4 and bring in Cataldo and this sicko. For what it's worth, he and his father live in Newport, and they're my responsibility."

Mike paused by the stairwell leading from the wine vault as Mick and Bridget disappeared up the stairs. He looked back at the Newport desk sergeant.

"Okay, Tommy, if that's the way you want it."

O'Donnell nodded his head.

Mike held his eyes for a moment more and then disappeared up the stairs.

"Take care of my sister," Tommy O'Donnell called to the empty stairs.

Chapter 38

1324 Bellevue Avenue | Front lawn | 12:08 a.m.

The group that huddled, exhausted, on the front lawn of number 1324 Bellevue Avenue looked like they'd been "rode hard and put away wet," as Cody Ewing would have said, and taking one look at the tattered remnants of some of Newport's "best families," he turned to Sparrow, Danny and Mick and said exactly that.

Mick slumped and lay on his back in the cool, dew-wet grass of the Vanderwall front lawn, looking up at the stars. "Damn, what a night!" he mumbled. For that matter, what a strange, whacked-out couple of days. Thank God it was over

He looked up and saw Sparrow coming toward him with a worried look and closed his eyes again.

"Mick," Sparrow said, kneeling beside him. "Did my brother come out?"

Mick looked back to the open double doors of the mansion and shook his head.

Sparrow stared at the open doorway and chewed the knuckle of her left hand for a moment before murmuring to herself, as much as to Mick, "He wants to bring in Cataldo and the Vanderwalls." She turned to Mick. "He wants to do the right thing, finally."

She looked at the front door again. "How much time does he have?"

Mick looked at his watch. Six or seven minutes left on the C-4 detonators. Eight, tops, even allowing for some corroded army surplus detonator caps. Not enough time.

He looked over at the sweet, aging flower child. Christ! He had to help her. He pushed himself to his knees then to his feet. Pulling off his damp denim jacket, he handed it to Sparrow.

"Just make sure that the front door stays open, 'cause when we come through it, we're gonna be coming fast." *That is, if we come out at all.*

As he trotted to the front door, a hand grabbed him from behind. "Hey, hold up, Cuz. I heard what Sparrow said, and I'm coming, too. And so are Kevin and Smitty and Cody and—"

"This is a job for one man, Danny," Mick called back, never breaking his stride.

"Bullshit, man, I'm coming to watch your back, just like a bar fight in Southie."

Mick reached the open door and paused for half a second. Bridget was with Sparrow, looking in his direction. She moved toward the doorway.

Mick grabbed Danny by the shoulders. "Listen, Danny, make sure Bridge doesn't follow me back down there."

Danny looked back across the lawn. Bridget broke into a full run.

"Keep her here, man, I'm counting on you."

Mick disappeared into the spiral staircase, his boots echoing faintly as he descended toward the cellar.

ON THE EDGE of the milling crowd on the wide front lawn, Marcy watched Bridget run toward the mansion's front doors. She stopped for half a second, said something to Danny, then turned and ran toward the teahouse. Danny ran after her, but she was gone, leaving Danny standing in the middle of the lawn.

Now, it was Marcy's turn.

She had to repay Bridget and Mick for what they'd done for her, and that meant following them back into that damp, horrible cellar.

Maybe I can borrow a little bit of Bridget's Celtic courage and take it back down those stairs.

She followed Bridget to the trapdoor in the teahouse and looked down the dark spiral staircase. She put her left foot on the first tread and froze. "C'mon, Marcy," she said to herself. "Are you gonna let some refugee from a prep school nuthouse scare you?"

A little voice in the back of her head screamed, *yes!*

But she thought of her new friend, the five-foot, two-inch, Irish warrior-princess down there, and her true inner voice shouted,

Not bloody likely!

THE NEWPORT POLICE Department's Sgt. Tommy O'Donnell would have kicked himself if he had time enough to move his feet. The first rule of the first day at the police academy had been to treat every gun—*every* gun—as if it were loaded, and lethal, even two-hundred-year-old dueling pistols.

He finished tying a tourniquet around Cataldo's leg, and was straightening up to read Vanderwall Senior and Junior their rights and cuff them, when…

"I want you to reach down slowly and pull that revolver out of your holster using only your thumb and forefinger. Do you understand me?"

Tommy O'Donnell stared into the muzzle of the enormous pistol, held by the worst homicidal maniac Newport had seen since the turn of the century. Damn! Why hadn't he disarmed the bastard! Still, there just might be one slim chance. He looked at the pistol in the flickering light of the candelabra and tried to focus on the ancient flintlock. He was no expert, but he did know that the standard old flintlock method of firing required bringing the mechanism to half cock for loading and then full cock to fire. It looked as though the pistol was still at half cock. He should have at least an even chance of drawing his service revolver and firing before the last of the depraved Vanderwall line could cock and fire. It was worth—and he almost laughed out loud at the ironic phrase that leapt into his brain—a shot. He took it.

There was an ear-splitting explosion.

He looked down at the dripping mess of hamburger that the casual shot from Jack Vanderwall's pistol had made of his right arm.

"What's the matter sergeant," Jack Vanderwall said cheerfully as he walked over to Tommy and kicked his dropped revolver away, "did you really think I'd go off half-cocked?" He laughed and pushed O'Donnell into one of the mold-covered chairs then wound a loop of thick hemp rope around him.

Damn! He didn't know which mess hurt worse—his arm or the mess he'd made of everything else. He was helpless, bleeding, while the psychopath, his permanently checked out father, and the dead guests, waited for four hundred pounds of army surplus C-4 to blow them all into Newport harbor.

FROM THE STAIRCASE, Mick heard the muffled "crump" of an explosion. Christ! The C-4! He flattened himself against the cold brick wall and waited for the scorching rush of flame. It didn't come. He took a deep breath and continued down the stairs.

If there'd been time he would have gone down through the teahouse tunnel and taken Jack from behind. Now his only chance, a slim one at best, was to draw his fire and come in with his .38 and Paulie's 9 mm blazing.

He stopped four steps from the bottom and pulled off his worn cowboy boots. He took one more deep breath, threw both boots down the stairs and pulled the guns out of his waistband. Tucking his left shoulder under his chin, he rolled into the room, both guns firing as fast as he could pull the triggers.

The smoke was blinding. Mick pumped two rounds from each gun into the ceiling hoping that would keep Jack the Shadow Man's head down while he got his bearings.

He came to rest in a crouching position and peered through the smoke. He tasted sulfur and saltpeter. Jack must have fired one of his black powder pistols.

As if reading his thoughts, Jack called from the head of the table. "These old horse pistols do a wonderful job of discouraging heroics." He paused and added mockingly, "Don't they, Mr. O'Donnell?"

"Fuck you," the sergeant mumbled.

Jack laughed softly. "No, sergeant, I'm afraid you're the one who's 'fucked.' You'll be staying here with me." He raised his voice and called to Mick, "And so will you, McCarthy, if you don't get out of here in, oh, what would you say, Mr. Cataldo?" He looked at the sweating figure lying on the floor, clutching his bloody knee. "In about five minutes?"

"You sick bastard," Cataldo moaned. He tried to get up, but his leg collapsed under him.

Mick edged around the back wall, working his way to the other side of the room. He heard an antique pistol being cocked.

"Last chance, McCarthy," Jack called softly.

"Mick, beat it," Sgt. O'Donnell rasped through gritted teeth. "Get the hell out."

Mick stood up and fired off two more rounds from each gun toward Jack's outline, which wavered in the dissipating smoke.

A blast of orange-yellow flame erupted from the head of the table, and the bricks splintered as dozens of buckshot pellets hit the wall to his left. He straightened from his crouch and walked toward the table.

"It's okay, sergeant—Tommy," he called through the sulfur smoke. "He only had two pistols. He got you with one and missed me with the other. That was his last shot."

Mick walked to the dim outline of Tommy O'Donnell's chair and bent down to untie the knots.

"Mick, no!" O'Donnell hissed. "He—"

Another pistol cocked. Mick looked up as a long, very deadly looking barrel emerged out of the smoke.

Jonathan Randolph Vanderwall Jr. walked toward him, pointing the muzzle directly at Mick's chest.

"I might have forgotten to mention, McCarthy," he smiled. "Besides teaching me how to fire these pistols, my grandfather also taught me how to reload them. Quickly."

"OKAY, KID" the blue-uniformed patrolman called as he walked up to Danny, "what's your name, and what the hell is going on here?"

"He's with me."

The patrolman turned around toward the sound of the gravel voice.

"And who the hell are you?"

"I'm the guy who told that little weasel Fahey to put out a call and get as many Black & White units as possible up here pronto—and you're late," Mike said, lighting a crumpled Lucky Strike cigarette and drawing the raw smoke deep into his lungs.

"Well, we're here now and the question still stands, who are you?" the patrolman asked, his hand dropping to his nightstick.

Mike reached into his back pocket and flipped open his wallet.

"Yeah? So?"

"So, if you want a biography, you can ask Tommy O'Donnell," Mike grunted. He looked around and then looked at his nephew. "Where is O'Donnell? And for that matter, where the hell is Mick?"

Danny shifted his weight from foot to foot as he began. "Well, Uncle Mike, you see, Sparrow, ah, that's this girl—I mean Tommy's—I mean the cop—it's his sister, and she was worried, 'cause he, you know, the cop, he stayed behind, I guess to bring those other guys in. You know the crazy guy, his old man and the hood. So, his sister was worried, 'cause he hasn't come out. So she asked Mick to please go back in there and help him."

Mike snapped his head around and stared at the open door. He turned back to his nephew and glared. "You let him go back in there alone?"

"Uncle Mike, I tried to go with him. I wanted to! He told me I had to stay here. To take care of Bridget, and to make sure that she didn't—"

"And where is Bridget, who you're supposed to be takin' care of?"

Danny looked at his shoes.

"She outran me."

Chapter 39

The cellars below 1324 Bellevue Avenue | 12:14 a.m.

Mick looked into the long muzzle of the pistol as it slowly rose through the gunsmoke to meet his eyes. Jack stepped out of the smoke and pushed the pistol barrel another foot toward Mick's face. Mick backed up. His back brushed against one of the pillars supporting the vaulted ceiling. He glanced down for an instant and saw thin wires, attached to detonating caps, embedded in mustard colored blocks of C-4 explosive.

"Sweet Jesus," Mick murmured, his back pressed against the cold brick.

He looked into the pistol's muzzle and at Jack's mad, grinning face behind it. *You don't have a whole lot of time, Mick.*

A footstep came from somewhere behind Jack. Jack swiveled his head.

It's now or never. Mick sprang forward, grabbed the barrel of the pistol and twisted it away from his face with all his strength.

Red-orange flame erupted in a gush, followed by a deafening concussion. Blinding smoke filled the cellar again.

The pistol barrel burned his hand. Jack pulled and twisted it. Mick braced his feet, struggled, but Jack wrenched it away from him.

The hot barrel smashed into the side of his head and Jack was on him, pushing Mick's head into the cold, stone floor. Jack's hands squeezed his throat.

Two years of Army training and combat experience taught him how to grab Jack's hands with an overhand twisting motion and pull them from his neck but they didn't budge, only got tighter. Christ, the guy had hands like steel bands. Mick was woozy from the blow to his head. Blood dripped into his right eye, partially blinding him. His throat was being slowly crushed. Hard to—draw—a—breath.

"You're dying, McCarthy," Jack whispered. "And as you die, you're asking yourself, how can a pampered little rich boy from Newport have such incredibly strong hands? I'll tell you," Jack hissed. His lips drew back from his teeth. "The doctor gave me handgrips, for therapy. Whenever I felt myself losing control, I should squeeze the handgrips and work through my aggression constructively."

He laughed. "I think you've guessed what that 'therapy' really accomplished."

Mick pulled on Jack's thumb. Jack didn't even notice. "So, every time she loved me and then humiliated me, every time she teased and mocked me," a small drop of spittle leaked out of the corner of his mouth, "every time I saw her go off with some other boy, or man, or woman! Every time—then I'd squeeze those damn handgrips. I squeezed them until my hands were black and blue, and then kept squeezing them. I'd pretend that it was the throat of whoever she was with, and—" his insane eyes stared into Mick's —"and *hers*."

Jack moaned. His fingers spasmed inward. Mick's windpipe was collapsing.

"Good night, McCarthy," Jack rasped, spittle spraying from his lips.

The black walls of Mick's tunnel vision contracted and faded away. Was he dead? No. He drew one shuddering breath.

Something flashed in a silver streak over Jack's head. He reached one huge scarred hand behind him and caught the object as it descended a second time and with a powerful twist of his hand turned it away.

"Leave him alone," Bridget shrieked, wielding a large silver candlestick, "you damn psychopath. You bloody monster!"

Jack stood up and pulled the candlestick toward him, Bridget holding on with a death grip. He pulled her toward him and backhanded her, spinning her around and sending her crashing into a brick pillar.

Mick tried to push himself to his knees. "Bridge," was all he could choke out before Jack turned back to him and kicked him in the stomach.

"Question," his voice rose. "Should I kill you right now, or just wait a few minutes until we all join—"

"Jack!" an imperious, throaty voice, a voice used to getting its own way, snapped out.

Jack stopped as if he'd been hit with a sledgehammer. He turned toward the dark end of the table.

The voice continued, now laced with sarcasm and contempt. "Nice party you've put together here, loser!"

Jack stood frozen, one word escaping from his trembling, white lips.

"*Blair.*"

He stared at the motionless form in the wavering candlelight. It wasn't supposed to talk. It was dead.

Mick shook his head. His brain must be foggy from lack of oxygen, but one thing was sure; either Blair's corpse had acquired the power of speech, or Mick had crossed the lunatic line with Jack. Because although a psychotic schizophrenic Jack Vanderwall might be, Mick had heard the voice, too.

A shiver traced icy fingers down his spine.

He'd never met Blair, or heard her voice, and the voice he'd just heard sounded strangely familiar. But that cool, mocking voice was keeping the one who should know it best, the one responsible for silencing it, paralyzed in the center of the room.

The spell was broken for Mick when he heard a small moan in a voice he did know and love coming from across the room. He crawled painfully to where Bridget lay slumped against the pillar. He pulled himself to his knees and lifted her chin.

"C'mon, babe," he whispered as she came to. "Can you walk?"

Bridget's left ankle buckled under her. She shook her head.

"Okay," Mick whispered, "I'm gonna carry you, fireman style, 'cause we've got to move fast. Ready?"

"What about Sgt. O'Donnell—Tommy?"

Damn! That was why he'd come down here in the first place!

There wasn't time. He had to get Bridget out. But what was he going to tell Sparrow? Damn!

He pulled off his battered old Timex watch and pushed it into Bridget's hands.

"Listen, mark the time now. Start crawling to the stairs, and in exactly one minute, call me, no matter what I'm doing. One minute. Got it?"

Bridget nodded.

"And when I come, I'm gonna be at a dead run. And I'm gonna reach down and pull you over my right shoulder, and you're gonna keep your head down and hold on tight! Okay?"

"Okay."

Mick crept toward the solitary figure frozen in the center of the room. He picked up the silver candlestick that Bridget had used. If only he wouldn't turn around for the next three seconds, the next two, just one more, and—

Jack turned and looked into Mick's eyes.

"She can't be talking," he said.

Mick froze.

Jack's eyes narrowed as they registered Mick. "And you're not supposed to be walking."

He reached for the other pistol stuck into his belt, pirate-fashion. Mick shifted his balance to the balls of his feet and felt the weight of the sweat-slippery candlestick in his right hand.

Jack pulled the pistol from his belt.

"Jack!"

He turned around.

The voice had turned pouty. "I thought you had planned a party for me, Jack?"

"I did, I have, I—"

"You call this a party, Jack? Where are all the cute guys? The guys who want to dance with me? Close, Jack," Blair's dead voice whispered seductively. "They always want to dance with me very, very close."

"Shut up!" Jack screamed. "You're not supposed to be talking. You're supposed to be listening. You're supposed to be—"

"Dead, Jack?"

"Yes! Bitch! You're supposed to be dead!!"

"That's right, Jack," she hissed, "just like everyone else at this party. Dead. Including you."

From the still, blond figure seated at the dark end of the table came a cruel, mocking laugh. "You pathetic loser!"

Jack screamed and aimed the pistol.

"Do you want to see dead, you evil bitch? I'll show you dead. Die! Die again!"

The pistol belched flame, and the blond head exploded with dried blood and formaldehyde.

Jack's scream became one long, continuous moan.

Mick ran to the half-conscious sergeant, untied him and pulled him toward the stairs, shouting, "For Christ's sake, O'Donnell, move it. Move it!"

At the stairs Mick bent down to Bridget. Jack turned, pointing the automatic and Mick's revolver at the three of them.

"No one leaves this party," he rasped. "No one. Not ever."

"Mickey," Bridge choked out, "the time! We're past the one minute mark."

A GHOST ROSE UP behind Jack, the ghost of the man who had, ten years earlier, given up on being a man and a father.

"Jack," Jonathan Vanderwall Sr. sobbed out to his only son. "I'm so sorry. Sorry for what I did, what I let happen. For what happened to you, and for what I let your sister become. I'm sorry, Jack."

The deathly man put his arms around his mad son and hugged him.

And he didn't let go.

He looked up at the group on the stairs and whispered, "Run. Run, run, run!"

Mick paused for a heartbeat, threw Bridget over his right shoulder and headed for the stairs.

A pale figure with long brown hair darted from the shadows behind the ruined corpse of Blair Vanderwall. She ran past Jack, and he screamed, but his father held him locked in his doomsday embrace and kept whispering, "I'm sorry. So sorry."

The brown-haired girl reached the stairs in two strides. Mick and Bridget said in unison, "Marcy!"

Tommy O'Donnell pushed Marcy in front of him, and they all ran, stumbling up the stairs.

The little voice in Mick's head kept repeating over and over, in time to the banging of his heart against his ribcage, "Out of time, out of time, out of…"

Carrying Bridget, Mick staggered into the hallway and crossed the threshold of the house at 1324 Bellevue Avenue just as the world exploded at his back.

HE HEARD SIRENS and voices. Someone was lifting him up.

"Mick, are you okay?"

The world came back into focus. Pop?

"Yeah, Pop," Mick mumbled as he staggered slightly, trying to regain his equilibrium.

"Mickey?"

"Bridge."

He sank back to his knees and put his arms around her.

A second and then a third explosion rocked the front lawn. The roof erupted in a shower of flame and sparks, followed by a strange cracking sound.

"Mickey," Bridget whispered, awe-struck, "it's like that story I read in freshman English."

"Edgar Allen Poe," Mick answered, never taking his eyes off the flaming, shuddering house.

"Yes," Bridget breathed as the remaining chunks of the house, lawn, gazebo and gray stone tunnels crumbled and fell into the cold sea below.

"The Fall of the House of Usher."

Chapter 40

Crosby Landing beach | Brewster, Massachusetts | Cape Cod
August 1, 1968 | 10:37 a.m.

Bridget rested her head on Mick's shoulder and sighed, "It's so beautiful here."

"Yeah," Mick smiled, "especially when there's no one shooting at you."

She gave him the barest of nods and an expression that clearly said she didn't want to think about shooting, thugs, mind-altering drugs, or psychopathic madmen on a beautiful August morning on Cape Cod Bay.

She looked down toward the other end of the beach, away from the blankets and umbrellas of the families who were arriving, busily setting up folding chairs and arranging beach bags as they staked their one-day claim to seaside paradise.

They were both very quiet for a long while. They sat close to one another and watched the waves race across the bay, while seagulls hovered on the morning breeze, hunting for the shimmering schools of baby cod making telltale streaks of silver in the warm water.

"What's that town up there?" Bridget asked, pointing.

Mick shaded his eyes with his hand. "I think it's Orleans."

"It looks pretty. Can we go up there? Maybe we could find a room and stay there for a day or two. It looks so nice and quiet and peaceful. A little village by the sea. Like home," she said. "I think I'd like that."

"Sorry, Bridge," he said, shaking his head. "Pop said I gotta be back in Rhode Island this afternoon for the depositions and all that crap."

Bridget sighed and nodded her head.

"I promise we'll come back and stay there, soon. Maybe in a week or two. We'll make it a real vacation."

Bridget smiled. "And remember, McCarthy, vacation means no cases. Just you and me and a big basket of fish and chips."

"And fried clams," Mick grinned back.

"All right, then, so there's to be no crime solving after this bit is all said and done."

They sat and watched the eternal, uncaring, but always changing ocean wash the waves in and out. Mick leaned back on the sand dune and propped himself up on one elbow while he watched Bridget make small patterned designs out of seashells and seaweed. He knew the movements and the look on her face. She wanted to say something, needed to say it.

She reached into the pocket of her skirt.

"Here's something that I 'borrowed' from you," she said, handing him the Buck knife.

"I've been meaning to ask you. I saw that you had it last night, in the cellar. Why did you take it?"

She picked up a thin, weathered stick of driftwood and traced small intricate circles in the sand. "At first, when I left you by the fire…" She glanced up for a moment before looking back down and adding, in a voice so soft that Mick almost couldn't hear it over the hiss of the waves, "and I'm sorry, I shouldn't have done that. It was wrong to leave you there with no word, and go off looking for, I don't know, justice."

"And you were going to find it at the point of a knife?"

Bridget shrugged her shoulders then shook her head. "I'm not sure what I was thinking. Justice, revenge, not being a victim anymore? I don't know."

"And the knife?" Mick asked.

"I guess I thought I might be needin' something for protection. But when I followed that Sammy, and saw what he'd done to Marcy, and remembered what he'd helped the Shadow Man do to me, I…" She drew in a shuddering breath and then spat out, "I wanted to kill him! Slowly. The way I'd read about in those books in the abbey, when I was a girl back in County Cork." She looked at her hand as if she could still see the welt Sister Margaret had given her, then went back to her sand doodles. "After I'd laid him out with that two-by-four, I thought about what I'd read, what me ancestors had done in ancient times to men who'd hurt them and theirs. And here I was, the daughter of an IRA major, and there was that creature lying on the ground, who had it comin' to him. But despite all that, I couldn't bring myself to do it. I guess that's why I'll never know if I really could have pulled that trigger on Cataldo down in the cellars." She shook her head. "Some daughter of the IRA, huh?"

"No," Mick answered. "Some woman."

Two young kids who looked liked brother and sister chased each other through the glistening puddles left by the outgoing tide.

"Seems like a million miles away from cellars, psychopaths and mobsters. I wonder how a man like Jonathon Vanderwall ever got mixed up with scum like Cataldo and his thugs."

"Business," Mick said. "Vanderwall senior already had a connection with the New York mob for importing expensive foreign cars. It seems it showed a much better bottom line when the Bonnano crime family added a few dozen 'select models' to his inventory every month. At wholesale prices that were a 'steal.'" Mick winked. "Vanderwall was desperate when Jack finally lost it and killed Blair. All the shit in his own past suddenly came back to haunt him and he must've seen himself losing it all. So he did the only thing he could. He had his 'business associates' call in Cataldo to hide the mess."

Bridget shook her head. "So in the end, all of Blair's power and domination over everyone only got her murdered."

"Yes. Murdered by the one that she'd first practiced her manipulation skills on."

Mick lay back on the warm sand and clasped his hands behind his head. He watched snow-white seagulls making lazy circles against a cobalt blue sky.

Finally, he propped himself up on one elbow, turned towards Bridget and said, "You know, I think we were both wrong about Marcy Trainor, about her being just another spoiled little Newport rich girl."

Bridget smiled and nodded her head. "I think you're right, luv. Do you know what she said to me as they were lifting her into the ambulance last night?"

Mick shook his head.

"She said, 'Thanks for being my friend,' and then she said that she learned something from me."

"How to be cute, and sexy, and tough as nails, all at the same time?" Mick grinned.

"No," Bridget said, lightly punching him in the shoulder.

"She told me she'd learned that she didn't have to be a victim. That she could stand up for herself. And that the next time Jackie laid a finger on her, she was going to find herself flat on her pretty little butt." Bridget paused. "And you know something else? She taught me something, too. When she said that, I realized that the worst scars that the Shadow Man had given me were in my own mind. And I wasn't going to let him win by being another one of his victims."

She shook her head, drew a deep breath and said slowly, "Not bloody likely."

Then she turned to Mick and, one by one, began to unbutton the buttons of her brown, fringed leather jacket. She raised herself up on her knees in front of him and let the warm, yellow morning sunlight wash over her face and soft, white throat.

The black turtleneck was gone.

Mick smiled at her as he reached up and pulled her down to him.

"Welcome back, babe," he whispered as he proceeded to cover that soft, white, and to him, always beautiful, neck with kiss after kiss after kiss.

About the author

Ric Wasley thrived on music in the sixties and performed as a folksinger and in several rock bands all over New England. He met the likes of Bob Dylan and Joan Baez.

In a recent interview Ric said, "I started keeping a kind of journal of my own 'adventures on the road' traveling around on my motorcycle, playing as a single folk act, and later in a VW Mini-bus touring with my rock band. Equally fortunate, I kept these journals which many years later became much of the source material and inspiration for the adventures of Mick and Bridget, my two main characters of the "McCarthy Family" detectives featured in Shadow of Innocence. "The sixties was just so cool," Ric added. "The largest segment of America's population, myself included, grew up in the sixties. It remains the most influential decade of social and cultural change in the past 200 years."

Ric has been writing for over 30 years. He has been published in several literary magazines in L.A. and San Francisco while living in California. He currently lives outside of Boston with his wife and three children, works for a major media company and retains his love of music and writing.

Kunati Spring 2007 titles

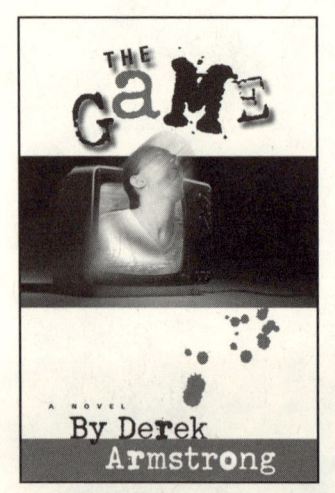

KÜNATI
Provocative. Bold. Controversial.

The Game
A thriller by Derek Armstrong

Reality television becomes too real when a killer stalks the cast on America's number one live-broadcast reality show.
■ "A series to watch ... Armstrong injects the trope with new vigor." *Booklist*

US$ 24.95 | Pages 352, cloth hardcover
ISBN 978-1-60164-001-7 | EAN: 9781601640017
LCCN 2006930183

bang BANG
A novel by Lynn Hoffman

In Lynn Hoffman's wickedly funny *bang-BANG*, a waitress crime victim takes on America's obsession with guns and transforms herself in the process. Read along as Paula becomes national hero and villain, enforcer and outlaw, lover and leader. Don't miss Paula Sherman's one-woman quest to change America.
■ "Brilliant"
STARRED REVIEW, *Booklist*

US$ 19.95
Pages 176, cloth hardcover
ISBN 978-1-60164-000-0
EAN 9781601640000
LCCN 2006930182

Whale Song
A novel by Cheryl Kaye Tardif

Whale Song is a haunting tale of change and choice. Cheryl Kaye Tardif's beloved novel—a "wonderful novel that will make a wonderful movie" according to *Writer's Digest*—asks the difficult question, which is the higher morality, love or law?
■ "Crowd-pleasing ... a big hit." *Booklist*

US$ 12.95
Pages 208, UNA trade paper
ISBN 978-1-60164-007-9
EAN 9781601640079
LCCN 2006930188

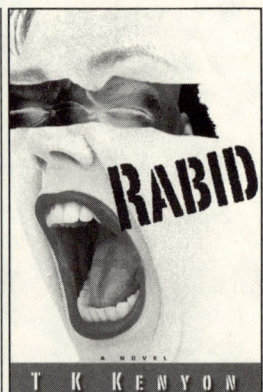

Rabid
A novel by T K Kenyon

A sexy, savvy, darkly funny tale of ambition, scandal, forbidden love and murder. Nothing is sacred. The graduate student, her professor, his wife, her priest: four brilliantly realized characters spin out of control in a world where science and religion are in constant conflict.
■ "Kenyon is definitely a keeper." STARRED REVIEW, *Booklist*

US$ 26.95
Pages 480, cloth hardcover
ISBN 978-1-60164-002-4
EAN 9781601640024
LCCN 2006930189

Kunati Spring 2007 titles

The Secret Ever Keeps
A novel by Art Tirrell

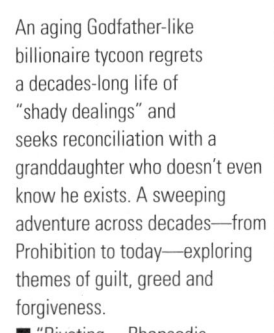

An aging Godfather-like billionaire tycoon regrets a decades-long life of "shady dealings" and seeks reconciliation with a granddaughter who doesn't even know he exists. A sweeping adventure across decades—from Prohibition to today—exploring themes of guilt, greed and forgiveness.
■ "Riveting ... Rhapsodic ... Accomplished." *ForeWord*
US$ 24.95
Pages 352, cloth hardcover
ISBN 978-1-60164-004-8
EAN 9781601640048
LCCN 2006930185

Toonamint of Champions
A wickedly allegorical comedy by Todd Sentell

Todd Sentell pulls out all the stops in his hilarious spoof of the manners and mores of America's most prestigious golf club. A cast of unforgettable characters, speaking a language only a true son of the south could pull off, reveal that behind the gates of fancy private golf clubs lurk some mighty influential freaks.
■ "Bubbly imagination and wacky humor." *ForeWord*
US$ 19.95
Pages 192, cloth hardcover
ISBN 978-1-60164-005-5
EAN 9781601640055
LCCN 2006930186

Mothering Mother
A daughter's humorous and heartbreaking memoir.
Carol D. O'Dell

Mothering Mother is an authentic, "in-the-room" view of a daughter's struggle to care for a dying parent. It will touch you and never leave you.
■ "Beautiful!, told with humor... and much love." *Booklist*
■ "I not only loved it, I lived it. I laughed, I smiled and shuddered reading this book." Judith H. Wright, author of over 20 books.
US$ 19.95
Pages 208, cloth hardcover
ISBN 978-1-60164-003-1
EAN 9781601640031
LCCN 2006930184

KÜNATI

www.kunati.com

Available at your favorite bookseller